# SUGAR CREEK

KAREN DAUGHERTY

PORCH CONFESSIONS PUBLISHING

*Cover Design by Bianca Bordianu | www.bbordianudesign.com*

Special thanks to Steven Douglas for background image.

*For Mom*

# CONTENTS

# PROLOGUE

I ALWAYS TRUSTED people more than I should and believed a person's word mattered. So, when I met Wyatt Simpson, and he promised he wouldn't get me into trouble, I believed him. Why wouldn't I? He was the hottest 12-year-old I'd seen all summer at Sugar Creek, plus he was nice to me. However, on the last day he was there, things fell apart.

After Wyatt made me a white clover necklace, we walked down to the small creeks that crisscrossed through my grandparents' backyard. The Missouri rains had filled the creek beds, and my grandparents had strict rules about the water. The current was swift behind their house, and the embankment was high; they worried I'd fall in. But Wyatt Simpson held my hand and told me not to worry about the fast current. He said he'd protect me.

I wasn't worried. I grew up in the water, and the swift current didn't scare me, but I pretended to be so that he would hold my hand tighter.

"I have a surprise for you," he said.

"What is it?"

Wyatt walked me down the creek where he'd stowed an abandoned canoe. "Get in," he insisted.

"We can't. I'll get in trouble."

"No, you won't. I promise. And if you do, I'll take the blame. Come on. Please?"

I hesitated. It was hard for me to say no, and I didn't want to disappoint Wyatt, but my grandparents had trusted me to follow their rules. I was stuck somewhere between doing the right thing and trusting Wyatt's word, and his adorable side-smile and bottle-green eyes weren't helping. He pleaded one more time before I caved and jumped in the canoe with him. Moments later, the fast-moving water slammed us against two rocks, tipped the canoe over, and stranded us in the water. Wyatt panicked and started to scream as I dragged him downstream, where the water was shallow. He was fine, but people came running. A few minutes passed before my grandpa showed up.

"Leah!" He shouted.

"Grandpa, I wasn't—" I started.

"Are you okay?"

"Yes."

A crowd had gathered around Wyatt, who was whimpering and being dramatic. As he sat on the rocks, his mom stood up and gave me a dirty look.

"Mom, she made me go with her. I was just trying to help," Wyatt whined.

"You could've killed him," she hissed.

I glared at Wyatt as Grandpa stepped in front of me.

"Grandpa, that's not true. I didn't—"

"Leah, stop. Let's go."

Grandpa led me away, but his face said it all. Panicked eyes, sharp mouth, his thinned-out hairline peeked through under his St. Louis Cardinal hat as he adjusted it a few times before he slammed the screen door shut.

"Listen to me, Cricket," he began as he put a towel around my wet body. "What have I told you about the water?"

"That it's not always safe," I mumbled.

"That's right. It's not always safe. The water is up, and the current is swift. It may seem fine, but you can't see the undertow, and that's what's dangerous. You got lucky today."

"I know how to swim, Grandpa."

"The water is unpredictable, Leah. You never should've been in that canoe alone."

"He's the one who made me go. I didn't want to."

"But you did. You made that choice, and you can't blame that on someone else."

"Give the kid a break, Pops," my Uncle Jack joked, walking through the kitchen. "She's just havin' fun."

"Well, that fun is going to get her hurt or worse. I know someone else who acted like consequences didn't matter," Grandpa said as he shot Uncle Jack a stern look.

"And I turned out fine."

Uncle Jack fake punched Grandpa in the stomach and laughed as he flinched. In return, Grandpa balled both his fits up and told Uncle Jack he'd "whoop his ass," but instead, Uncle Jack wrapped him in a bear hug. Grandpa smiled wide, his dentures perfect in line, and fought to get out of Uncle Jack's embrace.

"You can't protect me from everything, Grandpa," I insisted as the two of them took playful jabs at each other.

"Well, I can damn sure try."

"I agree with Leah," Uncle Jack said as he sat down beside me. "She's gotta learn how to swim on her own. Let her dance too close to the edge, so she knows what life is about. If my favorite niece is anything like me, she'll land on her feet."

"She's exactly like you, and that's the problem," Grandpa grumbled as he set a green coffee cup of cinnamon hot chocolate in front of me. "Drink," he ordered and kissed my forehead. He walked out of the kitchen, mumbling about an apple and a tree before he yelled back, "And I don't want you hanging around that boy anymore."

My face flushed as Uncle Jack stared at me wide-eyed.

"He lied to his mom and told her I made him do it, but I didn't, Uncle Jack. I swear."

"I know you didn't, Cricket, but people lie. It's part of who they are, and you better learn that now."

"But he was nice."

"People can be nice and still be liars. It's the ones who do it on purpose and *aren't* sorry—those are the ones you have to watch out for. That's why you have me," he said, giving me a wink. "But, listen, kiddo—the old man's right. You do gotta be careful out there. Those edges are rough, and that undertow is no joke. You can't just jump into a canoe with the first boy you see. Some—no, most—can't swim with you, which is why the more familiar you are with knowing that, the better equipped you'll be when you fall into them."

"Boys are stupid."

"You think that now, but one day a young man will come along, and he'll swim beside you and you won't have to save him. When that day comes, I'll be ready with my shotgun."

I smiled and took a drink glancing down at the white clover necklace on the table. "Will you show me the undertow Grandpa's talking about?"

He smiled and sat back in the chair. "Of course. But you gotta promise to keep it between you and me."

"Keep what between you and me?" My cousin Kate asked as her sister, Allison, followed behind her. Kate was eight years older than Allison and me and acted like an unofficial, annoying babysitter most of the time.

"I told Leah I'd show her around this place, so you kids don't get lost and break something or worse."

"Daddy wouldn't like that, and Granddad already told us not to, Leah," Allison said.

"Your daddy and I ran this place like crazy growing up. Ask him. He's not going to care."

"Allison, you wanna come?"

"No. Kate and I are helping Nana cook. Just don't get us in trouble again, Leah."

"A little trouble is good for the soul. It's what keeps the fire lit," Uncle Jack proclaimed. "Finish your drink, Leah, and then we'll go."

The hot chocolate was delicious. Still wet from the water, it coated my throat like medicine, instantly warming me up. It never occurred to me that cinnamon could feel anything other than curative.

# 1

Now, though, twenty years later, that same taste of cinnamon has me dry heaving in the back of an Uber.

"The fireball was a bad idea," I mumble to my boyfriend, Nash, as the mid-October air hits my face.

"One shot was probably fine, but six? It was too much, babe," he chuckles.

"Fun night?" Our driver asks.

"She had a little too much to drink. Her uncle just passed away. The funeral was yesterday," Nash explains.

"Oh, I'm sorry," the driver murmurs.

The car grows silent as I lean my head against Nash.

"He was a great man."

"He was."

"Like a dad to me."

"I know, babe."

"He never should've been on that motorcycle."

"It was a heart attack, babe. The wreck wouldn't have mattered."

"But still, he could've gotten to a hospital sooner."

"I know."

"Did he really leave me Sugar Creek?"

"He did," Nash answers.

"He told me I was his favorite. I miss him so much. But I'm never going to be able to do what he did. I made heart-shaped bullet points in my college business class and couldn't manage my group projects. Some business owner, huh?" I ask the Uber driver. He glances at me through the rear-view mirror and laughs.

"Relax, babe. You're drunk and emotional. You'll have plenty of time to figure it out. Seems more like a burden than a gift anyway," Nash groans.

"It's not a burden."

"Yeah, we'll see."

Uncle Jack's funeral had been a disaster. My cousins were furious about his Will and the fact he'd only left them $50,000 when they thought they deserved more. But with Kate and Allison's spoiled lives—it wasn't shocking they made the entire thing about themselves. As the whole family erupted in a screaming match, I tried to remind them that we just lost our beloved uncle and no amount of money or property could ever replace him. They didn't care—but instead, were furious that their measly fifty grand didn't compare to the inheritance I'd received. It was true and the responsibility of taking over Sugar Creek freaked me out—so I accidentally got drunk. Partly because Kate and Allison were unbearable humans, partly because my responsibility skills were horrendous and mostly because the absence of Uncle Jack left my heart torn in two.

Stumbling into our loft apartment, I open the fridge to get water while Nash steps out to the balcony. As I take a few sips, I try to recall the times I've been responsible, hoping the list will lift my spirits. Drinking—no. Cooking—no. Showing up on time—no. My job—sort of. Making our bed

—yes. One and a half times. If I was a reviewable place on Yelp, one and a half stars didn't seem like an adequate number to brag about, and as I join Nash on the balcony, I wonder if my girlfriend skills add to my star credit.

"The city is so beautiful at night," he says as we admire the orange and white lights that adorn the downtown skyscraper.

"Am I a five-star girlfriend?"

"What?"

"Like if you were ranking me, am I five stars?"

"I think you're drunk."

"Nash."

He rubs his hand down my back and cups my butt as he squeezes it. "This is five stars," he laughs.

"Really, Nash? I mean, of all the things I do in this relationship, you only like that?"

"I'm kidding, babe. Of course, you're five stars."

He leans down, kisses me, and smiles, "But are we deducting stars when you leave hair in the drain and dishes in the sink?"

"Babe!"

Nash laughs hard and wraps me in a hug. "I'm just messing with you, Leah."

Nash's humor was one of the things I fell in love with first. His light-hearted approach in life and ability to turn any situation into a joke drew me in with ease. Three years ago, he had told me he loved me for the first time. We had only been together for a month, and while the timing was fast, I had never met someone who matched me on every level. We had the same hobbies, loved the same foods, and listened to the same music. It was like the stars aligned and made the male version of me but delivered it in the form of Nash. He was messy, but so was I, and we navigated those messy parts together. Two months after Nash told me he loved me, we moved in together, and that next Christmas, in front of our tree, he asked me to spend the rest of my life with him. There wasn't a ring, but there was a promise and commitment to each other that surpassed jewelry. We both believed in the power of giving your word to someone, and that word between us meant everything.

I breathe in the fresh air as Nash pulls me in tighter. He kisses my neck as the lights sparkle in front of us. "Let's go in," he whispers, slipping his hands under my sweater. My body melts against his touch. I wrap my hands around his waist and pull him close as he strokes my back.

Once inside, Nash pulls my sweater over my head, revealing my lacy, purple bra. It was his favorite and the one I wore for special occasions. His eyes widen, and his boyish smile spreads across his face as he kisses down my neck. I giggle and run my hands through his wavy hair.

On the wall behind him hangs the quarterback award he received in college. The picture was taken in the last seconds of the Louisville-West Virginia game. Nash had told the story so many times I had it memorized. The Mountaineers were ranked number three, but a late drive in the fourth quarter pushed the Cardinals to victory, propelling them into the Orange Bowl.

In the picture, the all-white uniform fits snug on his body, as the shot captures him dropping back into the pocket.

Still embraced, I recall Nash's anger when I suggested moving his award to hang up our unofficial engagement pictures. The argument lasted a few days, but ultimately, at his suggestion, we had our picture—the one where he was kissing my hand—turned into a magnet and placed it on our fridge. It was a *feeble* compromise, and I made him promise our wedding pictures would be different. Some arguments aren't worth the stress, and as I breathe in his Calvin Klein aftershave, his poster-sized award glows against the light.

"I love you," I whisper, running my cold hands underneath his black Polo sweater. He flinches as they move up and down his back.

"Love you, too."

His lips are on mine in an instant. Slow and soft at first, and as the kiss deepens, his hands tangle in my hair. We make our way into the bedroom when his phone buzzes in his pocket.

"Who is it?" I ask, kicking off my heels.

"It doesn't matter," he breathes. Nash unhooks my bra as his lips travel down past my collarbone. I unzip his pants, ready for our night to begin, but as my hands make their way down—Nash isn't *ready*. I know I'm more drunk than he is, and we've struggled with his 'readiness' before. I'm trying not to take it personally, but it's frustrating.

As his pants fall to the floor, his phone slips out of his pocket and lands at my feet. The screen lights up with a text from Mika Templeton. *The* Mika Templeton. Nash's coworker he slept with six months ago.

"Stop," I order, pushing him away.

Nash picks up his phone and rolls his eyes as the screen shows Mika's name. "Come on, Leah. It's nothing."

"Don't bullshit me. That nasty whore texting you at midnight is not nothing."

"Nasty whore?" He laughs. "Don't be dramatic, Leah. I was drunk. We've been through this. I don't even know the girl. Why are you acting so crazy?"

"Read it," I demand.

"What?" His eyes follow me to the other side of the bed as I flip on a small lamp.

"Read the text to me."

"I'm not reading it, Leah."

Nash pulls up his pants, walks out of the room, and shoves the phone back in his pocket.

After his affair, we went to three therapy sessions before he declared them useless. I'd wanted a male therapist, but Nash insisted on a female one. But when our first therapist mentioned her wife, Nash wouldn't return until we found someone else.

"You told me you would never talk to her again. You promised it was over."

"We work together. We have to talk sometimes. You know that. And it is over. She's not the one in this picture, is she?" He yells as he grabs the magnet off the fridge and throws it on the counter.

"If it's nothing, then read the text."

"You never stop, do you? He runs his hand through his hair and then slams it on the counter. "You know what? Fine. If it'll get you to shut up, then fine, Leah, I'll read it." Nash pulls the phone out of his pocket, and as he unlocks it, my heart pounds in my ears. I don't want to know what the text says, but I can't stop myself from demanding the truth. Midnight text messages only serve one purpose. I'm not stupid, and the trigger makes me want to throat punch him.

"It says *hey*. But you're right, Leah. Let's make a huge deal out of nothing like you always do." He grabs a beer from the fridge, pops the top, and takes a long swig. His cockiness infuriates me.

"*Hey*, still doesn't sound work-related," I stammer. Nash's anger soars, and I consider our counseling sessions. *Trust is a partnership*; our therapist's words run through my head.

Nash and I have made some progress in therapy, but cheating is the worst kind of betrayal. The kind that makes me lose my mind late at night over a one-word text.

"You're not going to let me win, are you? She literally sent me three letters. How are we going to commit to each other if you keep acting so crazy? I gave you my word, Leah, and you know what that means."

I swallow hard and push back the tears. "Win? I didn't realize this was a contest. And I'm not crazy, Nash. Don't say that. Your word should matter."

He makes a noise somewhere between a sigh and a growl. "You have to trust me, Leah. And you need to take fewer shots. Both at me and of alcohol. You get so emotional when you drink."

"Oh, it's my fault, right? I do tend to overreact when you screw someone else."

"Exactly my point," Nash smirks. "You can never let anything go. You're like a dog with a bone."

"And you're just a dog."

Our therapist had said name-calling was childish, and we should use *I-statements* instead. She'd made a point to explain that no one could make us feel a certain way, but Mika's text does. It infuriates me and makes me *feel* like I want to kill both of them, but I'm sure how to convey that *I-statement* appropriately without landing in jail, so I play it safe. "Oh wait," I correct. "When you cheat on me and then stay in contact with said girl, I feel like you're a dog."

"Okay, Leah. Well, how about this. I'm not going to Dallas this weekend. This dog will stay here."

My stomach drops. "What?"

"I mean, these are your friends, not mine. And after tonight, I think you need some time to consider if this is what you really want."

"They're not my friends, Nash. Allison and Kate are my cousins. And you know this is what I want. How dare you even question that."

"All I know is that I made a mistake once, and every time I turn around, you're accusing me of something else. You don't trust me, and we both know it. Call it what it is."

"Which is what?"

"I don't know. But I'm not going to Dallas."

"Don't, Nash. We've been planning this for months. You can't back out. Allison paid for our plane tickets."

"I've made my decision. It's been a long night, and it was fun until you accused me of shit again. But, we're going to bed. It's late, and I have work."

"I work, too, Nash!"

"Please, Leah. Don't compare the two. Babysitting isn't work. We're going to bed."

Nash has belittled my job as a principal in the past, and his new promotion as a sales executive at one of Louisville's top tech companies hasn't helped. Instead, it has given him a sense of entitlement that his new job somehow means more than mine—and when he gets angry—he strikes low.

"*We?*" I emphasize. "No, not *we*. I am going to bed. And you can sleep out there," I inform and point to the living room.

Our apartment-sized couch is too small for Nash's long body, and the suede fabric makes him break out, but I don't care. I told Nash months before that I didn't want to go to Dallas alone. Allison and Kate had planned a family weekend to celebrate Allison's engagement and a christening for Kate's daughter, Caroline. My pretentious cousins have always been hard to handle, but I always managed our family gatherings by relying on Uncle Jack. With his passing, Nash knows how important this trip is to me—and more than that, I need his support.

Laying in bed, I try to force myself to sleep, but the anger and frustration push tears down my face.

Behind closed doors, all couples fought. Nash and I aren't any different, but the betrayal of cheating has forced us into unknown territory. We'd broken up after his affair with Mika, but a month later, Nash begged me to try again. I agreed as long as we went to therapy and Nash gave his word that things would be different—and they have been, until Mika's text.

The next few days are awful. Nash leaves before I get up for work and comes home after I go to bed. We haven't spoken since our fight, and I am still too angry to be rational. But, by the end of the week, I've had enough.

I set my alarm for 5AM to make coffee and talk to Nash before he leaves for work. He loves the straight black roast I special order for him, but neither of us ever gets up on time to make it.

As I stumble into the kitchen, the dim light above our stove reveals our fridge magnet, the hands of two people in love. We've been through a lot in three years, and with a hot cup of coffee, I am determined to make things right with Nash or at least allow him to apologize. Wiping the sleep out of my groggy eyes, I walk over to the couch to find a messy pile of blankets. He's gone. I toss the coffee in the sink, walk back to our bedroom, and grab my phone. The shouty caps, curse word-laden text is brutal, but I don't hit send. Angry texts are never effective. They only add more frustration to the existing situation, but there has to be a balance. So I delete the angry words and try a different approach.

*Me: Made coffee this morning. Went to wake you up, but you aren't here. We should talk*

I send the message and lay back down, angry he ruined the morning. As I pull the covers under my chin, I wait. Ten minutes pass. Then twenty—and nothing. No buzz of an incoming message. Silence is the ultimate way to ruin a relationship, and our therapist had told both of us not to shut down communication during a fight—but here we are.

I glance at the time and realize I still have an hour before my alarm. Exhaustion takes over my body as I close my eyes, only to be woken up by a tornado siren ringtone. I was deathly afraid of storms and purposely used the ringtone as my eighth alarm. If the other seven alarms failed, the eighth would get me out of bed quicker than a vampire in sunlight, and when it goes off, I know one thing—it's 8AM, and I'm late.

## 2

As the tornado siren blasts, I run from one room to the next, searching for an outfit and matching shoes like a reckless teenager. Waking up late has to be a version of hell only given to procrastinators. And when it occurs—which in my case is often—every outfit I own goes missing instantly along with my shoes, keys, and phone. Most people have a designated spot for those items and know exactly where they are at all times—I'm not most people, and the last place I remember leaving my keys turns up empty. Frantic, I start digging through random drawers and under the bed—funnily enough, one time, they were under the bed—but not today. I open the catch-all drawer in the kitchen, and there they are next to the scissors. There isn't an explanation, and with little time, I don't search for one. Instead, I grab them and throw in a few last-minute things for the trip to Dallas as a reminder lights up my phone. BIBLE —STORAGE.

*Crap.* The one item I'm supposed to bring to Dallas. Allison mentioned it at Uncle Jack's funeral, and like always —I've left it until the last minute. Annoyed, I jump in the car and speed toward the storage unit, cursing the morning for being such a disappointment, and worse—Nash still hasn't responded.

I pull up to Hazelwood High School as the tardy bell rings. A few kids hustle inside the three-story brick building, which is in desperate need of a makeover. Four white pillars stand at the entrance with chunks of paint missing, and the rusty bike rack—next to the front steps—has come loose from the concrete. In addition, the school lacks functioning air-conditioning and contains a basement lunchroom that rivals most haunted houses. But as bad as the old building is, our students love it—always commenting about the charm it has over newer schools.

"Good morning, Miss McKinney," Estreya, a tenth-grade student, says as she holds the door for me at the top of the stairwell. Her blue backpack is worn and frayed, with a mechanical pencil that peeks out the side pocket.

"Running late this morning?" I ask, a wave of embarrassment coming over my own tardiness.

"Yes, ma'am. I couldn't get my little brother up this morning, and we missed the bus," she grunts and shakes her head in frustration.

"Is your mom still working third shift?"

"Yes, ma'am. She's picking up some doubles, too. Just through the holidays, though," she informs—a reassurance for herself more than me.

"It's a busy time. I'm sure they are grateful for the extra help."

"Yeah," Estreya sighs. She gazes down at the ground and rubs the corner of one eye. Tired eyes are common with teenagers and their bizarre sleeping habits, but Estreya's eyes are a different kind of tired. The kind that forces her to be an adult at fifteen.

Her mechanical pencil starts to protrude out, and I push it back into the bag. "I'm sure it's tough for you especially. I know little brothers can be hard to get up sometimes."

"Sometimes?" She smiles as her straight teeth beam bright white against her brown skin.

Estreya's mom isn't the only single parent who works third shift hours and sometimes doubles. With seventy-five percent of our students on free and reduced lunch, most are just scraping by. Growing up with my own single mother, it's a situation I knew too well and a call to be an educator I couldn't turn away from.

"Okay, always," I say. "Which means you're doing an even better job than you think." Estreya trails behind me as I walk to the office.

"Thank you, Miss McKinney. I'll go get my tardy."

I examine Estreya's tired brown eyes. She doesn't need another tardy; she needs a new backpack and some sleep. With a smile, I say, "No, go to class. Tell Mr. Davis I'll send him an email to excuse you."

"Thanks, Miss! You rock," she gasps, flashing her bright smile again, and turns down a long hallway toward her English class.

I round the corner and wave to the attendance secretaries through the large windows that enclose our office, including Miss Kay, the eldest by a decade of the four ladies.

Miss Kay was an anomaly. From the mystery of her real age to her actual job title, Miss Kay's identity confused us all. She sort of came with the school, and everyone did their best to stay out of her way. She sat in the office and wandered around the school, but we were unaware of her actual duties other than routinely cause chaos and primarily operate at her own awkward frequency. She beams at me through the window, her beehive updo in full effect.

As I head to the side entrance of my office, I'm hoping to sneak in so no one notices my late arrival, but when I open the door, I hear Trista Miller's voice. Trista is the president of our school PTA and the biggest helicopter mom of them all. She complains about everything, and when she can't find an audience at school to listen to her, she takes to social media. She's *that* mom, and as I walk in with a few seconds to spare before a catastrophic disaster, Trista Miller pulls out her phone.

"Good morning, Mrs. Miller," I state as cheerfully as I can.

"Miss McKinney, I was just texting you. We need to talk."

Trista is petite, a size two if I have to guess. She is loud, boisterous, and always smells like patchouli. Her manicured nails are a vibrant shade of red, and her short, blonde bob is perfectly styled like always. There are rumors that she's sleeping with Coach Pike, our baseball coach, and that's why her son, Trevor, who is a terrible athlete, starts every game in right field.

Coach Pike has a thing for large breasts, and Trista is fully equipped with implanted 32DDD's. The rumors don't bother me, but her constant complaints do.

"I'll be with you in a minute. Why don't you have a seat in my office? Feel free to grab some cof—" I start to offer, but the pot is empty.

"It's okay, Leah. I brought my own," Trista announces as she pulls her monogrammed coffee cup from her black designer tote. "Y'all have such a stressful job, and normally the coffee is made when I come in, but being so close to fall break and all, I understand how those things become *unimportant*. Plus, I know this whole interim principal thing is new for you, Leah. You're overwhelmed. We can all tell. Bless your heart. We actually talked about it at the last meetin'. So, no worries about the coffee, hon. I understand," she says as she flips the lid on her steaming coffee and takes a quick sip.

She's impossible, and after my hellacious morning, Trista's snarky comment sends my anxiety into overdrive. Fearing an uncontrolled eye roll, I force a fake smile and thank her for her sincere understanding. Turning sharply, I walk away and knock on my assistant principal's door.

"Julia? I'm coming in."

At her computer, Julia is transfixed on her screen and doesn't even acknowledge my presence. Her staple black boat neck sweater, slicked-back bun, and gold hoop earrings make her resemble a high-end fashion model rather than an assistant principal at a high school, and her attitude matches. TLC's "Waterfalls" plays from her computer speakers, and she's hard at work as she clicks things on her screen.

"Good morning," I say.

"You're late," she snaps.

"I'm aware. My storage unit. I'll tell you about it later."

"Bless your heart."

I laugh. "Stop it. She's so rude. I'll tell you what she can bless. Do you know why she's here? She said they were talking about me, *they* meaning her board member friends. Like I'm doing a terrible job. Is that true? Am I getting fired? Is she lying to me?"

"Whoa," Julia puts up her hand to stop me. "You're saying a lot of things, and it's too early. Sit down. Relax."

"So, you don't think I'm getting fired?"

"I didn't say that."

"Julia."

She laughs. "Trista is messing with you. It's what she does."

"Do you know why she's here?"

"She didn't tell you? It's probably to complain about something we're not doing her way. Seems like a principal problem, though," Julia quips.

"Julia, there aren't *principal* problems. We have shared problems."

"No, girl. You have problems. Like, I don't understand this outfit choice today. Just because it's fall doesn't mean you should wear burnt orange, Leah. It's not really in your color wheel."

"Thanks. I'll make a note of that. I need to get rid of Trista."

"Tell her Coach Pike is in his office by himself all alone, and he's so sad," Julia suggests.

I roll my eyes. "Is he?"

"I don't know, but that cleavage she's showing this morning tells me she's not here just to talk to you."

"So, you did see her," I point out.

"Principal problem."

Behind me, Trista's tacky heels clack against the floor. "Miss McKinney, I know you said to wait, but I just had to peek my head in to say hi to Miss Julia. And oh my goodness, girl, you get more beautiful by the day! You must tell me how you stay so young. You look incredible!" Trista gushes.

"No kids," Julia declares with a thin-lipped smile.

"Oh, isn't that the absolute truth!" Trista laughs. "I ran into your daddy the other day at the chamber meetin'. He is the sweetest man. The way he brags on you. Girl, it's precious! But I bet he is just itchin' for some grandchildren."

"No, he's really not," Julia insists.

"Oh, my goodness, you are so funny! Well, maybe one day," Trista giggles and gives Julia a wink. "While I've got you both here, I brought Trev's extra medication today. The poor thing has terrible dry skin, and when he has to wear his baseball glove, it rubs his hand raw. I already dropped some off with Coach Pike."

"I bet he was so thankful for that. Always thinking ahead, Trista. How is Coach Pike? Are y'all doing some fundraising activities together?" Julia asks.

I almost lose it. I stare at Julia wide-eyed, but she just sits back in her chair, arms crossed, with a menacing smile as Trista describes a BBQ fundraiser Coach Pike wants her to help with. "I mean, y'all, he is just so incredible to those boys and what he does for this school. We are lucky to have him here."

"Well, you of all people should know," Julia says. But Trista doesn't flinch. Instead, she rambles on about a bad cold season and a few more pointless topics before I take Trevor's medication from her. As she leaves, she mentions a rumor on social media that Hazelwood has a student vaping problem.

"I'm just telling y'all that some moms from other schools are starting to talk and send me texts about it. I didn't want it to get back to certain people and, you know, cause problems for you ladies. We love you, and we love Hazelwood."

Trista's remarks and artificial concerns are as fake as her knockoff Louboutins with maroon soles. She doesn't care about the school; she cares about her reputation and how she appears to her private school mom friends.

As a native to Louisville, Trista is also an alum of Hazelwood. In the nineties, the school had been a landmark for public education, sought after by affluent families living close to downtown. But over the years, as the neighborhoods started to change and the city became more diverse, those downtown families began opting for private education —a tuition Trista can't afford. But she won't admit that. Instead, she parades around and acts the part of a social class she doesn't belong to but constantly chases.

"Thanks, Trista. I'll check into it," I respond.

"Thank you both so much. And y'all have a terrific long weekend!"

"You, too," Julia and I say in unison as she walks out.

"She is such a nightmare."

Julia doesn't comment but instead is back on her computer screen.

"What are you doing?"

"Bidding."

"On what?"

"A Louis."

"Vuitton? Like you're online shopping at work?"

"Well, if you must know, I'm bidding on a vintage Louis steamer trunk. They are rare and beautiful, and I want one."

"Steamer trunk?"

"Yes, Leah."

"Like a suitcase?"

"No, like a steamer trunk."

"But it's kind of like a suitcase?"

"No. Here," she grumbles and turns her screen, so I can see.

"Oh," I say.

"Yes. A steamer trunk."

"It's like a cedar chest. You could've just said a cedar chest."

"No, it's not—never mind, Leah," she says as she shakes her head.

"What?"

I am not a Louis Vuitton aficionado, and I don't know many high school principals who can afford the expensive brand, but Julia is different. Her family—the De Loughrey's —have a thriving horse ranch in southern Kentucky. They have raised championship breeds since the early 1900s. They are old money socialites, but she's not an entitled brat despite her prissy moods. She is funny and kind and has a deep love for kids that she won't admit. She also loves Louis Vuitton and owns almost every bag.

"I'm going to make coffee. Do you want some?" I ask, watching her screen refresh, showing YOU ARE THE HIGH BIDDER each time.

"Sure."

A few minutes later, with two cups of coffee in hand, I take a seat on her black leather loveseat as she continues to bid. Julia's office is double the size of mine, with cool gray walls, natural light, and equal parts New York City meets classic Audrey Hepburn. A little spunk, but always classy, just the way Julia likes it. After I was hired, she informed me of her claustrophobia and let me know that taking the bigger office would benefit both of us. But funnily enough, her claustrophobia never bothers her as we eat lunch in my office almost every day. Her fake paranoia is comical, but to her credit, her eye for decor is much better than mine. With funky art deco paintings, black and white stills, white chiffon curtains, and a dazzling teal and red Tiffany lamp, her office is comfortable for students to be expelled. As Julia continues to refresh her screen, I scroll through the newest emails on my phone.

"Did you talk to Dr. Bradley about the job?" Julia inquires.

"Not yet."

"Hmm."

"I know. I need to."

Taking a long sip of coffee, I am delaying the conversation on purpose. I've only been the interim principal since July. Our previous principal, Mrs. Cummins, had left with her husband after his unit had been re-stationed overseas. The abrupt departure left the district scrambling for her replacement, so I took my chances and applied. With almost four months down, I have received proficient reviews from Dr. Bradley, our superintendent. But recently, rumors surfaced that Cammie O'Neal has applied for the job, and I'm worried. As an instructional facilitator in the district, Cammie has almost a decade more experience. She leads professional development courses, has three kids in our schools, and her husband organizes the Donuts with Dads group at their daughter's elementary.

"Leah? Leah?"

"Did you say something?"

Julia shakes her head. "You didn't hear me scream *I win*."

"You win?"

"The Louis. The steamer trunk. What's going on with you today? You seem even more distracted than usual."

"Nash and I aren't speaking."

"Still?"

"Still."

"Because he's a man-child who lies all the time?"

"Stop, Julia."

"But basically, that's it. Truth hurts, sister. You know he's not going to apologize."

I turn my head away, not ready to hear another one of Julia's talks. "We'll get it worked out. We always do."

"Giving in and being his doormat isn't working things out," Julia argues as she makes air quotes around *working things out*.

"I know, Julia. It'll be fine." But as I go to my messages, my coffee text is still unanswered, and Nash and I aren't in a good place. He has done the silent treatment stuff in the past. It's selfish and one of the things our therapist called him out for, and even though he said he'd change and not shut down communication with me, he is back to his old ways. He won't talk to me until he is ready, and he won't care if I sent him fifty texts; he'll ignore all of them. So, I put my phone away, focus on work, and hope my busy day keeps me distracted.

By mid-morning, I have worked my way through most of my emails, and, except for one parent phone call, I have almost finished my AM to-do list. Impressed by my ability to stay productive after my rough morning and the stale coffee, I walk into my office to see Julia in my chair, thumbing through some old pictures from a stack I left on my desk.

"What kind of hillbilly upbringing did you have? I mean, these pictures are sad," she muses.

"Newton is a small town."

"Did you have running water? Is this one of those places where you hand-made your own clothes? There's a Netflix special about that—it weirds me out. Does this village you speak of have internet and cable? Based on these outfits, I'd say not. Except for this kid," she holds up a picture, "at least his tux is from this century," she jokes, pointing to a picture of Damien Harris and me at prom.

Damien was part of a tiny group of minority students we had at Newton High School—a stark contrast to the diverse population at Hazelwood. Newton, Missouri, was the average small town. It was a predominately white community with a church on every corner. Before social media and even after, towns like Newton thrived because everyone was always in each other's business, to begin with. No one needed to update a post because the town reported what happened before the internet could react. It was a blessing and a curse.

Damien and I grew up together in daycare and went to the same elementary school. And in 10th grade, after my mom passed away, Damien was the only one who didn't treat me like a freak. Uncle Jack hired him at Sugar Creek, and we became best friends. He was hilarious—the dry humor kind and a phenomenal artist. When we weren't busy at work, he drew pen tattoos on my arms, their intricate designs detailed and unique. We remained close during our first year in college, but we drifted apart when I moved to Louisville. Uncle Jack told me he'd opened a donut shop in Newton, and I'd see him sometimes when I visited, but life had opened different doors for us, and our friendship had faded into the social media zone.

"That's Damien, and he was my prom date," I say, taking the photo out of Julia's hand.

"Why are these even here?"

"They were in a box in my storage unit. I had to go by there this morning to get our family Bible for Allison. She wants it for the wedding. I was moving a box and Darrell, the guy who works there, helped me. I handed him a box and didn't know the bottom wasn't taped, and both of my vibrators fell out on his feet. It was so embarrassing."

Julia rubs her temples.

"I mean, he completely freaked. Like he started to pick them up, and I yelled at him. I'm going to have to find a new storage building."

"Backup. Your vibrators were where?"

"In my storage unit."

"Because they're broken?"

I laugh. "No."

"Were you using them too much? Like is this a fasting season for you?"

"Stop."

Julia's stare has turned to confusion.

"You can tell me. It happened to a friend of mine, and it became an issue for her, so she had to do intermittent fasting with them. Sixteen hours off, eight hours on. It worked out."

"Stop. No. I put them there."

"So, this was a drunken decision you made one night out of anger, right? Because no sober person locks up their vibrators by choice. I mean, this explains so much. Have you talked to your therapist about this?"

I roll my eyes and sit down across from her. "No, I haven't. Nash wasn't a fan."

"Of course he wasn't. They emasculated him. What a child."

"You're ridiculous."

"Says the one who locked her vibrators in storage prison."

"Well, they're in the dumpster now. He tried to pick them up—with his hands."

"Gross. Like you could never—"

"Right. Never."

"I'll send you a link for some more. You can thank me later. What time do you leave for Dallas?"

I had already missed two texts from Allison earlier that morning. "Two," I answer as I scan over the messages for anything important.

"So, engagement party, and that's it?" Julia asks.

"No, we have a christening, too."

"Like a Catholic christening?"

"Yes."

"But you're not Catholic."

"No, but Kate's husband is. She converted before they got married. It was a whole deal."

"Kate converted, so she could marry her billionaire husband?"

"Real estate developer. He's not a billionaire."

"Same thing. Didn't Kate work at the makeup counter before she met him. I mean, come on."

"Yes, she and Allison both did, but at least Allison put herself through college. I mean, she did get a great job with a marketing firm."

"No. She went to college on her trust fund that your grandpa left her. Isn't it funny that both your cousins found billionaire bachelors just in time to upgrade their Honda Civics to cute Range Rovers?"

"Coincidence?"

"No. And don't get me started with Allison. You never should've accepted her invitation to be a bridesmaid with all her bridezilla demands. Your hair must be a certain length, the overload of Pinterest texts, her ridiculous spray tan demands, and now the family Bible. She does realize that just because she writes her marriage in that thing doesn't mean it will last, right?"

"Julia, she's planned her wedding since we were five years old. She wants it to be perfect."

"Nothing is perfect, Leah. And that doesn't give her an excuse to be an asshole about everything. I'm surprised she even agreed to share the weekend with Kate. That spotlight is going to have a nervous breakdown trying to please both of them."

"That might be the truest thing you've said all day. But I think my grandparents talked to Allison at my uncle's funeral and tried to put some things in perspective for her."

"The only perspective those two have is their own. I'm a little disappointed I won't be there to witness the award for biggest meltdown. My money's on Allison, but I'm not counting Kate out."

"I'll keep you posted."

"What did you pack for this trip?"

"Stuff."

"Like?"

"I'll be fine, Julia. I can pack for myself."

"Debatable," she says, walking over to her office. She reappears a few minutes later and hands me a black knee-length dress and a fancy designer sweater.

"I don't want to know why you have clothes like this in your office."

"Do we want to rehash the plaid disaster of last year, Leah? They made memes of you. That's all I'm saying."

"That holiday party was lame, and my outfit was cute."

"In 1998, it was cute. Or if you were guest-starring in 90210."

"That's rude."

"Take it, put it in your suitcase, and text me when you get to Dallas."

"I will."

"And Leah, wear real lipstick instead of Chapstick. Just because it says 'cherry' doesn't mean it makes your lips red."

"Real lipstick," I smile. "Love ya, Julia. See you when I get back."

"All the things," Julia replies, giving me her best form of please be safe, I hope you have a good time, and I love you.

"All the things."

Boarding the plane, I sit in my favorite spot—a window seat in the middle of the plane. The only benefit to Nash's abrupt cancellation is his seat is empty, and I can spread out.

I am a terrible traveler, and my plane etiquette is even worse. I admire people who manage the whole flight with their shoes on and sitting upright, but that isn't me. I am more of a splayed house cat in a sunny spot on the carpet who needs a blanket, neck pillow, eye mask, and legroom. It's embarrassing, but I have no shame or awareness of personal space rules on flights. I mean, I do. I know they exist—I just don't follow them.

As I stretch my legs into Nash's empty seat, my naked toes barely hang in the aisle. Most passengers are seated, but as the stewardess comes by, she glares at me. My stuff is everywhere, and I understand her frustration, but her judgment is a bit much.

"Ma'am, can I help you?" She asks.

"No, I'm okay."

"It's a forty-five-minute flight."

"I know."

"Can you get your feet out of the aisle so others can pass through?"

She's dramatic. They can pass through; she just doesn't want me to be comfortable. But I smile politely, scoop my feet in, and tuck them under my blanket.

"And your seatbelt needs to be fastened," she says.

I lift the blanket up to show her that I have it buckled, but she has already passed by my seat. The guy across the aisle stares in disbelief as I situate my body a few more times between the two seats. Dressed in a suit and tie, he flicks a newspaper a few times as he tries to figure out if I am drunk or twelve years old. It's a fair point—either could be true—and I am sure others have questions, too, but after too many turbulent flights, I have determined the best way to fly is asleep—no matter how long the flight is. With my eye mask at rest on my forehead, I shove my neck pillow against the window and watch the grounds crew make final checks. As the plane starts to taxi forward, my sleep preparation is complete. The captain makes a few final announcements, and we take off. It's my favorite part of flying. The disappearing act where the lights below vanish, and the plane breaks through the clouds. There's nothing quite like the clarity of 40,000 feet.

## 3

*5 THINGS:*

*Your smile melts me*

*I love falling asleep with you...even though you snore*

*You make me a better person*

*I love you...even on the hard days*

*I don't want to fight*

I send the text to Nash and wait. The morning sun is barely visible behind the hotel curtains, and I need to get up if I am going to make it to the country club on time, but Nash's silence consumes me. It's been over twenty-four hours since the coffee text, and I am getting desperate. My kind words sit unanswered on the screen for fifteen minutes. He has ignored me again. Ghosting has to be one of the lowest forms of human decency. Nash is an expert at it, but I found a way around his silent treatment—the five things text. Whenever we would fight, and his ghosting ways would surface, I'd send him a text telling him the five things I loved most about him. It always worked. He would respond, he'd tell me he loved me too, and he'd apologize —except he hasn't. I grab my phone, ready to throw it against the wall, just as it buzzes in my hand. The text is from Julia.

*Julia: Did you make it?*

Disappointed, I send a quick thumbs-up emoji and go back to Nash's text—nothing. I slump down in the sheets, scream into the blanket, curse Nash's name, and then I do what all angry girlfriends do; I delete stuff. In less than two minutes, I delete the five things text, the coffee text, and the last text Nash sent telling me he loved me. His words are meaningless now that he has ignored the standard time to reply, and I am done reaching out—so they're gone—all of them. I mean, I take screenshots before I delete them; I'm not an idiot. But they are still off my phone, sort of. With a clean slate, I pull myself out of bed, jump in the shower, and vow to return Nash's silence with my own silence.

The Dallas weekend is kicking off with a bridesmaid dress fitting for the girls and a round of golf for the boys, followed by an engagement dinner. A social nightmare I do not want to be a part of. I hate small talk and the shallowness of people as they pretend to care about strangers they'll never meet again. It's weird and uncomfortable and, more than that, a waste of time. Allison insisted the engagement dinner will be small and intimate, just family and a few close friends, but I have my doubts. Nothing she does is small and intimate, and I expect her engagement dinner will not be the exception.

Allison and I were six months apart, and even though we were cousins, we grew up more like sisters. Before my mom died, we had spent every summer barefoot and sunburned, running around our grandparents' property at Sugar Creek. Their five-mile campground was like our private amusement park. But it was also much more than that. Our grandpa taught us how to fish in the creek waters and made sure we understood that life was sometimes about how you baited your hook and less about how many bites you got. Allison and I would lie awake at night and laugh at his weird lectures, but I secretly loved them. They were better than any lesson I learned at school. But all that changed when my mom died my sophomore year. As the shock of her death—from an undetected heart condition— rippled through our family, decisions were made about where I would live. My dad, the youngest McKinney brother, was incarcerated—again. As an addict, his stints in jail were frequent, and his role in my life was absent. Grandpa had made several attempts to help him early on, but he took a step back after my dad's fifth arrest. Uncle Dave—Kate and Allison's dad—lived in Kansas City with my Aunt Kathleen and while they offered to let me live with them, moving to Kansas City and away from my friends in the middle of the school year was not something I wanted to do. So, my grandparents became my legal guardians, but it was Uncle Jack who filled the pages my dad never could.

As the eldest McKinney brother, Uncle Jack was easily the smartest but only managed one semester of college before moving back and taking over the family business. Grandpa disapproved, but Uncle Jack had bigger ideas. He renovated Sugar Creek and turned it from a small camp-ground to an elaborate glamping resort. By the time my mom passed away, Uncle Jack had expanded the five-mile property to ten miles and quadrupled the value in three years.

But life was difficult after my mom passed away, and Uncle Jack was there to pick up the pieces. He put me to work at Sugar Creek and kept my mind busy. He taught me the business, and he was impressed by my natural accounting skills. And on the days when I couldn't get out of bed because the grief and pain were too much, he showed up just to sit with me so I wouldn't be alone. Uncle Jack and I became close, but jealousy began to appear between Allison and me. She stopped coming to Sugar Creek in the summers after my mom died. Or when she did, she'd stay a few days and then make an excuse to leave. Her changed behavior was apparent to everyone, but Allison denied it. And as our senior year arrived and college was being discussed, no one was ready for her sudden change of direction.

Allison had talked about being an Arkansas Razorback since birth. Grandpa was a Razorback, Uncle Dave too, and it was expected that Allison and I would follow in their footsteps. We were supposed to be roommates, but tensions mounted when she changed her mind and chose Baylor instead. Allison needed more money in her trust to pay for out-of-state tuition, so the money was given. But she didn't realize that Uncle Jack had purchased a furnished downtown Fayetteville condo for us to share—a gift he never told the rest of the family. After Allison's decision, Uncle Jack gave me the keys to our rent-free condo. The gift was more than I ever could've imagined, and when Allison found out, she was livid, and we didn't speak for six months. When she did call the summer after our freshman year, the conversation was curt, and it was clear Allison blamed me for the strain on our relationship. She said Uncle Jack showed favoritism and accused me of being jealous of her. After that phone call, we fell out of touch for a couple of years as our lives took off in different directions. We were cordial on holidays, but Allison and I were never the same, which is why her invitation to be a bridesmaid came as a surprise. I'm sure it was a box she needed to check on her customary wedding planner, but we were not close like we used to be, and as I get out of the shower, I'm dreading the pending weekend.

I pull into the country club five minutes late and hurry in. Large mahogany pillars stand in the entryway while the marble floors and tray ceilings guide members down long hallways. The exclusive country club membership is home to Dallas' finest socialites, and the annual dues could buy a lovely, four-bedroom house in Newton.

"Leah!" Allison's high-pitched voice comes from across the room. She is exquisite in a blush maxi dress. Her long, blonde hair is parted in the middle and has enough volume to make every girl in Dallas jealous. Yet, there is a glow about her. She's beautiful, from the pink in her cheeks to the sparkle in her blue eyes, and her engagement makes her radiate more. Thad, her fiancé, stands beside her, his hand interlocked with hers.

"Hey, Allie," I say as I wrap my arms around her petite body. Family feuds are funny. A week ago, Allison and Kate were lashing out about Uncle Jacks's inheritance, yet, today, we act like everything is fine. The fakeness of it all is annoying—but I guess we're both good at acting when we need to. We let go as Thad steps forward, places his hand on my shoulder, and greets me with a kiss on the cheek.

"I'm glad you guys made it. How was your flight? Where's Nash?"

"The flight was good, but Nash couldn't make it."

"What?"

"Something came up at work, and he had to stay in Louisville." I twirl the ring on my index finger and hate the sound of my words.

"Oh. Well, that's unfortunate," she says dryly and types out a text on her phone. Allison and Kate had met Nash the previous Christmas, and their personalities clashed. Nash enjoyed the spotlight, and so did Allison and Kate, but there wasn't enough room on the stage for all three of them. Allison never said it, but she hated him, and his absence doesn't seem to bother her.

"Kate just got here," she smiles. I turn around as my older cousin, and three other girls walk through the door, all dressed like Allison. The maxi dress memo must've missed my inbox.

"Hey, Leah," Kate says as she kisses me on the cheek.

"Good to see you, Kate," I reply. "Where's the baby?"

"Oh, our nanny has her. She would be too much today."

"Amen for nannies, am I right, Kate?" Lily, one of the bridesmaids, laughs. "I mean, I can't even imagine how I'd be able to do it without mine."

"Absolutely. Sylvia is a lifesaver. You know, since Caroline's been born, I've thought so much about how my own mom did it, how she raised us with just our dad. It's crazy," Kate says.

"Oh, I know. I think about that, too. Or even like single moms. Can you imagine? I mean the toll that has to take on them," Lily adds. The other two bridesmaids, Vanessa and Andrea, nod their heads in agreement like robots.

My stomach knots and anger boils down deep as I stare at Kate and Lily. The stigma of single moms was grossly inaccurate. Of all the jobs my mom ever had, being a mother was her favorite, even though she had to raise me on her own. It didn't make her less of a mother, and our lives weren't squandered away by her single mom status. It was the opposite. My mom was full of joy, she loved hard, and she believed there was good in every situation. It may not have been the ideal path, but it didn't take a toll on her. The two of us embraced the gaps in our story, but those gaps gave us courage and made us believe that life was always beautiful. Single motherhood wasn't some desolate toll that Kate and Lily made it out to be.

"I think some people can handle kids and some can't," I say, the words out before I can reign them in.

"What?" Kate snaps.

"I'm just saying, I agree with you. Some need help. Motherhood isn't for the weak."

"No, but you—" Kate starts.

"I know all the baby talk is fun, and I love my sweet niece, but, Kate," Allison whines, "you promised today would be about my engagement."

"Oh honey, it is," Lily says.

"Yes, Allie. Today is *your* day," Kate adds as she shoots me a death glare. "And we are so excited for you. This is exactly why I left Caroline at home. So, she wouldn't take all the attention away from you. See, I did you a favor," Kate says, giving her an awkward side hug.

Allison pulls away, her tight lip smile plastered on her face as the baby talk ceases, but the tension between the three of us is palpable. Determined to remain calm, I focus on the other bridesmaids and hope my attempt at small talk comes across as sincere and not bitchy.

As we drive to the bridal boutique, the clan of maxi dresses talks about the latest Dallas gossip and how perfectly Allison and Thad's pastel wedding colors blend with their springtime wedding.

"So, everyone has a different color and different style of dress," Allison explains.

She rattles off the colors from teal to baby pink to Kate's soft purple and then to mine.

"Leah, yours is canary yellow."

"Yellow?" I ask too loud.

"Yes, and I know how fair you are, but it's so pretty, it

matches perfectly with the other colors, and you're getting a spray tan, so it's going to be fine."

But that's a lie. It's not going to be fine. No fair-skin, Irish girls pull off golden yellow even with a spray tan. She's crazy or blind, or maybe both.

The boutique is small and has an aroma of wedding cake, a scent I'm sure they are pushing through the ventilation system based on the overwhelming odor. A petite sales associate dressed in all black greets us warmly, and I can't help but notice the white tape measure draped around her neck. I panic and regret my decision to shovel hotel pancakes down right before a dress fitting. It was one of Julia's pet peeves. "*Never eat forty-eight hours before trying on any type of formal dresses, bikinis, or skinny jeans,*" I can hear her say. I smile and retrieve my phone from my back pocket as the overhead music plays the instrumental version of a familiar song.

*Me: They are playing Shania Twain at the bridal boutique*
*Julia: Let me guess. From This Moment*
*Me: Yep*
*Julia: Puke*
*Me: Remember when you said your money was on Allison to be a snotty brat?*
*Julia: yes*
*Me: So far...Kate, but it's a close tie*
*Julia: what happened?*
*Me: Kate brought up her nanny. Another girl said she felt so sorry for single moms and how they could possibly raise a baby without a nanny*
*Julia: Did you tell Kate she's going to be a trash mom?*
*Me: LOL! Also...my dress is canary yellow*
*Julia: Stop it*
*Me: Her colors are pastel...for spring*

*Julia: Canary yellow isn't pastel. Is she dumb?*
*Me: Julia...YELLOW. Me, in yellow*
*Julia: That might be worse than the single mom comment*
*Me: I know. I gotta go. We're trying on*

I stow my phone as the sales associate brings out the dresses and try to stay optimistic.

"Here you go, darlin'. Such a pretty color," she says, handing me the dress. Allison beams as I examine it. The color is hideous; like a school bus and a jar of mustard had a baby. I give a fake smile and duck into a dressing room.

As I hold it up, I can already tell that my fair skin and blonde hair are no match for the yellow dress. It's hard to determine where the dress ends and my skin begins. I am two eyeballs washed out in a sea of yellow.

"All right, on the count of three, everyone come out at the same time," Allison shouts from outside the dressing room door. With a heavy sigh, I force a smile and walk out on her count.

"Oh my gosh, I love it!" She exclaims as she stands up and claps her hands together. The five of us stood in a line that closely resembles a bag of tropical Skittles. Blues, pinks, purples, greens, and that god-awful yellow, but Allison is ecstatic.

She pulls on the skirt of my dress and runs her thumb along the fabric, "It's perfect!"

"It is," I reply.

"It's too long, but we'll make arrangements to get it altered. And you *have* to get a tan, but your boobs are amazing. Maybe a little *too* amazing," Allison stares. The sweetheart neckline accentuates my C-cup size, and I'm hopeful my cleavage is impressive enough to distract from the ugly frock. As the sales associate pins the bottom of my dress, Allison asks if it comes in another style, but it doesn't. I can sense from her worried eyes she's upset she gave me the most revealing dress. It serves her right for putting me in the one color I should never wear. I walk back into the dressing room and make a mental note never to choose wedding colors that will make my friends look like garbage and curse the yellow dress as I unzip the side. It falls to the floor like the rotten skin on a clove of garlic.

We make our way back to the interstate as the conversation shifts from dresses to Thad's proposal. Allison retells the story, careful not to leave anything out. What was supposed to be a regular vacation to the Caribbean turned life-changing by the second day. As Allison prepared to meet Thad for dinner, a lantern-lit boardwalk welcomed her arrival to their private beach. Rose petals covered the sand as Thad knelt on one knee and read a letter he'd written her after their first date. Allison's friends are nearly in tears as she divulges parts of the letter.

Julia had laughed when I initially told her about Thad's proposal and commented how corny and cliché beach proposals were. Still, as I listen to Allison describe it, again, there is nothing corny or cliché about it. I rub my naked ring finger and recall the night Nash asked me to spend my life with him. I'd always romanticized that night, taking pride that it was our own. But if proposals were the springboard into marriage. If they were the beginning of a story yet to be written, then Nash and I have some missing pages.

As we pull back into the country club, a few members mingle around the lobby talking in small groups while others sit in the carpeted bar and drink beer out of tallboy glasses. But there's no sign of Thad or the groomsmen. Allison sends a quick text, and Thad responds right away, telling her they are on the 18th hole and headed back soon.

It's enough time for Allison to walk us down to the wedding venue.

The 500-seat chapel is situated in a wooded area behind the golf course. It's made from the framing of an old barn, and it has been renovated into a premier Dallas wedding spot. Remnants of the old barn wood hug the large A-frame glass facade as it towers over us. The gorgeous rays from the setting sun blast oranges and pale pinks through the open sanctuary making small rainbows in the corners of the windows. It's romantic in that classic ambiance meets Dallas chic. As Allison shows everyone around, pointing out each detail and brags about how her wedding decorator is the best in Dallas—it's hard to push the emotions away. With Nash and I in ghosting mode, I wonder if we'll ever find ourselves in such a place.

Falling in love isn't complicated, but after three years, Nash and I have managed to find every pitfall there is in a relationship. The moments of absolute joy helped mask the dark times, and as I stand in the chapel, I have to believe that giving up isn't just wrong—it's weak and a failure I don't want.

A few moments later, a text from Thad comes through telling Allison the boys are back. As we make our way to the lobby, an unexpected pair of hands wrap around my waist.

"Guess who?"

I turn around. "Nash! What are you doing here?"

"You're not happy to see me?" He asks, planting a kiss on my lips.

"I thought you were staying home. I thought—"

"I wanted to surprise you," he says, pulling me close. "And I missed you."

I'm hesitant at first as I feel his chest solid against me.

But the comfort of familiarity outweighs the anger from our fight as I give in and sink into his embrace.

"We need to talk."

"You're right, and we will. I love you, babe," Nash replies.

"I love you, too. I'm glad you're here. And I missed you, too."

"Even though I snore—which I don't."

I laugh. "You do snore, but yes, I still missed you."

"I hate when we fight, and you know how that sappy five things text gets me every time."

4
———

AFTER AN INCREDIBLE NIGHT of makeup sex, I sleep in late while Nash works out in the hotel gym. I shuffle through my suitcase and take inventory of what I've packed. Black pants, a different, looser pair of black pants, a black sweater, my black Converses, a gray Banana Republic cardigan that I wear for special events, and—no fancy clothing curated by Julia. As I rub my head and try to strategize, I realize I have to make a trip to the mall.

The three stores I've wandered into don't offer anything spectacular, so I give up, order a pretzel, and call Julia, hoping for some inspiration. Malls are not my thing. Large groups of people are also not my thing, nor shopping in general, but I have to get a dress, and I don't have much time.

"Hey, Julia," I say. "You're going to hate me for asking this."

"Did you meet a hot guy, and you need my help to kill Nash?"

I smile. "No. I do need your help, but not because of a hot guy or murder. I'm at the mall."

"You forgot my outfits, didn't you?"

"Yeah, I'm kind of a moron."

"Yes, you are. What do you need?"

"A casual dinner dress for meeting Thad's family tonight and maybe another outfit for tomorrow."

"Have you found anything yet?"

"No."

"What store are you in right now?"

"I'm not in one. I'm eating a pretzel," I say as I stare at the cinnamon and sugar coating my fingers.

Julia takes in a deep breath, and I can hear the heaviness of her exhale on the other end of the phone. "Leah, I just—" she begins. "Stay there. Don't move. I swear, you and your fashion illiteracy..." her voice trails off as she hangs up.

Twenty minutes later, a text comes through,

*Julia: Go to BCBG and ask for Marcie*

*Me: Ok, thanks! Julia... I seriously owe you*

*Julia: I know. I'm also having a local Dallas jeweler send some stuff to your hotel. Don't freaking lose it because it's a loaner! You will buy me lots of wine when you get back for doing all of this*

*Me: I will buy you all the wine! THANK YOU!*

I pick up the outfits Julia has arranged, head back to the hotel, and jump in the shower. The hot water is soothing, running down my body, and I let it linger just a bit longer, pressing my forehead against the wall.

Julia has picked well as I slip into the long-sleeved BCBG wrap dress. The contrasting hem makes my legs appear longer than they are, and the black and white print accentuates my best features. The necklace she sent over is elegant and perfectly matches the dress, and the gold diamond-shaped earrings stand out beautifully against my fair skin. I let my hair hang in long, loose curls and apply a matte red to my lips, a move Julia would be proud of.

"Damn, you look incredible," Nash says as he kisses my neck. "Are you sure we have to go to this thing? I can think of a better way to spend the evening," he whispers, slipping one hand under my dress.

I giggle and block his hand from advancing. "Yes, we have to go."

Before walking out, we stop in front of the mirror. His gray fitted slacks and black polo accentuate his muscular physique, and my patterned dress matches him perfectly. I can't help but stare at our reflection and admire how broken pieces seem whole in the right light.

Pulling into the gated entry at Thad's parents' house, I fill Nash in on the agenda for the evening. "Allie said it was just family and a few close friends. We're going to have dinner, and I'm sure we'll hear stories about how amazing they are."

Nash rolls his eyes as the giant cedar trees guide us down the winding driveway.

The blacktop gives way to cobblestones as we pull up to the house. The mansion is impressive, but the number of cars around the circle drive and parked on the grass shocks us.

"Unless you've gained a hundred new family members, I don't think this is going to be a small family dinner," Nash says, taking in the line of cars. "It looks like a dealership."

Inside, a butler points us in the direction of the party and hands us both a flute of champagne. Soft piano music plays through the surround sound speakers as Nash and I make our way into the sizable den where people are mingling and snacking on plates of assorted sliders. I search the room for Allison when I feel a hand on my shoulder.

"Is this her?" A portly, older man asks.

"Yes. Leah, this is Mr. Worthington, Thad's father. Mr. Worthington, this is my cousin, Leah, and her boyfriend, Nash."

"It's nice to meet you, hon," he says, kissing me on the cheek and shaking Nash's hand. "Darling, we should probably get started," he says, switching his attention to Allison as Pastor Jon joins us.

Pastor Jon is not a typical clergyman. I had visited his fancy Dallas church with Allison and Thad once before. He was nice enough, but his megachurch was more like a red-carpet event and less like a place Jesus would want to visit. The stage setup had more lights and sound than a Christian music festival, and the elaborate coffee bar served an assortment of options. It was not the tiny, one-room church Allison and I had gone to with our grandparents at Sugar Creek.

Brother Raymond was Grandpa and Nana's pastor, and his worn cowboy boots, old Levi's, and brown blazer with elbow patches were a stark contrast to Pastor Jon's fitted black blazer, black polo, and sleek pair of designer denim jeans. Pastor Raymond's Bible appeared to have survived the first World War—tattered, torn, and stuffed with notes—and the church pews resembled the same.

Standing beside Pastor Jon, I wonder what his Bible resembles. A few images enter my mind—all of them inappropriate.

"Ladies and gentlemen," Pastor Jon's voice booms over the sound system. Heads turn in his direction, and I spot a beige wireless mic hooked around his ear and running the length of his cheek.

"Is he giving a free concert later?" Nash jokes. I nearly spit out my champagne. Pastor Jon's need for a wireless mic does seem excessive, but it captures the attention of everyone in the room as we all walk into the formal dining room. I spot Grandpa and Nana, who are already sitting with Kate and her husband, Greg.

"Hey, Grandpa," I say, kissing him on the cheek.

"Hi, Cricket," he replies, squeezing me tight.

"How was your trip?"

"The flight was a little bumpy, and I had to keep Nana from crying, but other than that, it was fine."

"Oh, Leon, you did not," Nana scolds. She swats his arm and smiles as Grandpa lets out a hearty laugh. "You kids sit down," he demands.

"Oh, these are saved," Kate announces. "Sorry, Granddad, I should've said something. Our friends from church asked if they could sit with us."

"Isn't this a family event, Kate?" Nash challenges.

Kate glares at Nash and folds her hands in her lap. "Thanks for understanding, Nash."

"It's fine," I insist.

Nash tended to take things too far, especially if he was annoyed—which he was. He had exchanged harsh words with Kate before, and while I enjoyed it sometimes, I don't want him to cause a scene. Grandpa gives me a frown as Kate focuses her attention back on her phone and scrolls through social media.

"You sure? We can move," Grandpa suggests.

"No worries, Grandpa. It's fine. I'll talk to you later," I say.

Kate glances at me and gives a smug smile as we walk away.

"You shouldn't let her do that," Nash groans.

"I'm not going to fight over seats, Nash. She's childish, and it's stupid."

"She needs to be put in her place."

"Let's just enjoy the night," I plead, kissing him on the cheek as we sit down.

"Well, if it isn't the golf king himself," Lily's husband, Peter, says. Nash smiles as he leans over the table to shake his hand.

"Golf king?" I ask, confused.

"I shot a sixty-eight yesterday with these guys."

"Is that good?"

"Babe, it's a par seventy course. I was perfect."

"Alright, rub it in again," Peter says.

Nash shrugs. "Beginner's luck."

"Come on, man. Don't 'beginner's luck' me. You posted your scorecard online," he laughs.

Nash pulls out his phone to show me the post. "500 likes and sixty-four comments, and it's only been up for a day."

Nash's constant use of social media is annoying. He lives on his phone and often brags about the likes, loves, comments and DMs that the various platforms give him. I'd lost count of the times he showed me his increasing followers on each one or how many people commented and liked a random post he'd made. I'd educated my high school students about the detriments of being consumed by the hollow attention social media gave its users but overlooked the same behavior from Nash. It was endearing at the beginning of our relationship, but three years later, it's just weird.

As Nash shows off his social media accounts, Lily and I make small talk, and I try hard to act interested, nodding and raising my eyebrows on cue. If I had to guess, Lily is the leader of Allison's friends. She organizes the spa dates, the specific coordinated coffee orders, and has just enough disruptive information about everyone that they fear her. I have experienced her type before and maneuvered my entire life to stay away from people like her. She was the mean girl in high school and a total bitch as an adult. As she continues to spill gossip about everyone in the room, I try to find an escape, but Nash is fully engaged in a conversation with Peter, the two of them scrolling through his phone. Lily is mid-sentence with the latest gossip at table six when I excuse myself to the restroom and text Julia.

 *Me: I literally hate everyone*
 *Julia: Same girl*
 *Me: No, these people...you know I can't handle small talk*
 *Julia: You're so awkward*
 *Me: I know! And I have the worst poker face*
 *Julia: The worst. I can't believe I'm missing this shit show*
 *Me: I know. But...the dress is perfect!*
 *Julia: I know*
 *Me: You're the best!*
 *Julia: I know*
 *Me: I feel so fancy!*
 *Julia: That was the point. If there are any single guys there, you'll get laid tonight. But take the jewelry off first. It's too expensive to lose*

 I smile and start to tell her Nash surprised me but opt against it. Julia will be angry that he showed up, and it's probably a conversation best left in person. As dinner ends and desserts are served, Lily asks Kate and the bridesmaids to meet outside.

 "Let's take Allison out tonight," Lily insists. "A pre-bachelorette party. It'll be fun since we're all here."

 "We have Caroline's christening tomorrow," Kate says.

 "It's one night, Kate. Come on. Go out with us," Lily begs.

 It takes less than a minute for Lily's idea to win Kate over, and the decision is made. We are in a Dallas nightclub an hour later, ready to watch a hotly anticipated male revue. As a marketing rep, Lily had all the connections and scored VIP tickets to the sold-out show along with free bottle service. I'm already buzzed from dinner, but that doesn't stop me from ordering two Manhattans. As the lights dim, five shirtless males walk on stage to "Sex and Candy," and the audience goes wild. Their tight denim jeans hang low on their well-defined hips, and as much as I want to remember the incredibly sexy, choreographed pelvic thrusts, the alcohol has taken over. I don't remember the ride back to my hotel, but the way my head throbs the next morning, I am sure I've been hit by a baseball bat.

I pull up to St. Vincent's church with five minutes to spare. The previous night's mascara is still smeared under my eyes, so I lick my finger and rub the black makeup, but it only worsens. My dark sunglasses will hide my raccoon eyes, so I leave them on and hope for the best. I've managed to pull my hair into a messy side braid, careful not to put too much pressure on my pounding head, just as the church bells start to ring.

Growing up as a Baptist, the only thing more sinful than premarital sex had to have been showing up to church hungover. As the bells ring, I apologize for my ratchet appearance and remind myself that Kate and Allison are inside—and the church is still standing. Rummaging through my purse, I pop a stick of spearmint gum in my mouth and spray a vanilla body scent on my wrists and hair before running in. Down the long center aisle, I spot Lily and glance at my watch, but instead of seeing the time, I notice the purple eggplant stamp on my hand.

"Just in time," Lily whispers. "Where's Nash?"

"Hungover," I reply and roll my eyes.

Nash had gone out with Thad and some groomsmen

after we went to the male revue. He had fallen into bed sometime after I did and barely moved when I had tried to wake him up for church.

"I threw up in the parking lot," Lily groans as we all stand for the start of the service.

I flash my hand in front of her. "Penis stamp."

She cups her hand over her mouth and tries to keep from laughing. "Are you going to keep those sunglasses on?"

I lower them down, revealing my eyes. "Yeah, you better," she advises.

Six altar servers dressed in white robes enter from the back of the church as they carry long, golden candlesticks, a thurible, and a crucifix. Making their way up the aisle, I observe Kate, Allison, and our grandparents sitting in the front row. A moment of guilt sweeps through me as the first altar server passes by my pew. He is the age of my students with floppy brown hair and black-rimmed glasses. Moved by his stoical poise, I take my sunglasses off and turn my attention to the others. They decrease by age as the last two have to be in grade school. But it's the last altar server that catches my attention. His icy blue eyes and blond hair stand out from the rest. They are almost familiar—like I've seen them before. I jerk my head back around to the front as my heart starts to race.

Alcohol had caused massive headaches for me in the past, but I'd never hallucinated. I rub my eyes and turn back around to glance at him just as he passes by me; his eyes are focused straight ahead. At the front, the altar servers light candles and prepare the service, but I can't take my eyes off the boy with the blue eyes. He lights each candle with purpose and careful technique and takes his place with the other boys. Their large bodies almost hide him, and I realize he can't be much older than fifth grade. He looks toward the opposite side of the sanctuary a couple of times, and my eyes follow, but all I can see are the backs of heads. Several minutes into the service, I start to feel nauseous, and I need some air, so I sneak down the aisle and outside to a small wooden bench. Digging through my purse for my phone, I find a bottle of water instead and take a long sip. The hydration helps, but I can't calm my mind, and then an unwanted memory surfaces. In an instant, I am transported back to that awful day.

The cold, bare waiting room, the *Time* magazine on a table, my Converses that tapped nervously on the floor, and my pink nail polish I had peeled off waiting for them to call me back.

I close my eyes as the water slips out of my hands and drops to the ground. Weakened by the moment, I find my phone and text Julia.

*Me: Have you ever hallucinated with a hangover?*

*Julia: Did you do drugs?*

*Me: LOL...no, we got really drunk last night*

*Julia: And drugs?*

*Me: Answer the question*

*Julia: How many times have I told you that you HAVE to cover your drink at a bar? Like we've been over this so many times. It's literally in the rule book of bar hopping*

*Me: So that's a no?*

*Julia: No, because I cover my drink*

A few minutes later, a text comes through with a link to a website on ways to safely bar hop. I shake my head and toss my phone back in my purse, but I can't sit still. The altar boy has triggered something in me that I can't stop thinking about. But it wasn't just that. It's the shame that comes with silent baggage—the kind that's worse than being hungover at church.

Everyone had a past, and the transgressions of life seemed to flash like neon signs inside the walls of the holiest of places. Uncle Jack used to say the All-Knowing didn't care, but I had my doubts.

As the sun peeks in and out of clouds, I walk down the sidewalk past the church hoping the exercise will clear my head. But with each step, the heaviness drags in my heels. I make it to the edge of the block before ducking into a coffee shop and taking a seat.

As I sip on a cappuccino, my anxiety slows, recalling the times I feared the worst. When Justin Timberlake started making more solo tracks, I predicted the NSYNC breakup was imminent. And when Peyton Manning missed the entire 2011 season, I feared the Colts would trade him—and they did. Whether a conditioned response from the premature death of my mom, I sometimes slipped into the mindset that life was fighting against me. It was a trait Uncle Jack hated and had addressed with me on more than one occasion. I was better at catching it as an adult, but there were still times I let it get the best of me. That's what's happening. I'm fearing the worst and the altar boy is is just my imagination playing ticks.

As I finish my drink, I walk back to St. Vincent's and see Lily outside looking around the building.

"Hey, girl," she says.

"Hey."

"The service is over. I've been trying to find you. Are you comin' back in?"

"The christening is over?"

"Yes. They're greeting the family. Your family. Allison said to find you."

Lily and I hurry back in just as the parishioners are greeting Kate, Greg, and baby Caroline. I jump beside Grandpa and Nana, embarrassed by my hangover. Through hugs and handshakes, I search for the young altar boy but can't find him. Relief and disappointment fill me as I listen to Grandpa and Nana talk with an elderly lady about how beautiful the service was. I smile and nod in agreement as I shift my attention to the pews, and that's when I see him. His face is older than I recall, and his hairline has receded, but I could never forget his face. Standing next to him is the small altar boy with icy blue eyes. I freeze in disbelief, and my body goes numb as I witness my abortion doctor wrap his arm around the boy whose eyes remind me of a man that had left me at his clinic.

"Are you okay, Cricket?" Grandpa asks. "You're pale as can be." I squeeze his hand and try to find the words.

## 5

"I'm okay. I just need some air," I finally say. "Grandpa, I'm
going to go. Tell Kate and Allison I'll see them later."

As I hurry out a side door, I duck into a small room
and try to catch my breath. Sweat droplets form on my
nose as every awful memory pours out of my heart. In the
shadows of the small room, I think about every terrible
choice I've ever made and wonder why that list hasn't
buried me six feet under. Death had taken my mom and
Uncle Jack—two of the kindest souls to ever live—but
somehow, I was left with a half-assed life and a laundry list
of unforgivable mistakes. There had to be some unspoken
code that awful people lived longer so their terrible decisions could loop on replay. As my head pounds in my ears,
I call Julia again.

"Are you still hallucinating?" She asks.

"Worse. I need to ask you something." I turn my phone
on speaker and take in a few deep breaths.

"No, we don't drug test at work," she says.

"Stop. I'm serious."

"Okay, what?"

"Do you think there are some things in life that are unforgivable?"

There's silence on the other end of the phone. "Julia? Are you there?"

"I'm here."

"Well?"

"I mean, I don't know. I'm confused. Are we talking about wearing socks with sandals, unforgivable? Or is it worse? Socks and sandals are a low bar unless you killed someone. Leah, did you kill someone? Are you in jail?"

"No, I'm not in jail. Answer the question."

"Yes, I believe that. I mean, I think if you do something to kids or animals, there's a special place in hell for you."

"What do you mean about kids?"

"Well, I think if you hurt kids—like if someone hurt one of our kids at school, then they don't get a pass. It's a straight ticket to Hellville."

I smile and wipe the sweat off my nose as I recalled Julia's appearance in court regarding three of our students at Hazelwood. Her testimony had helped send three 'Hellville' adults to jail and had solidified her reputation as an advocate for kids. It was a title she never talked about and never wanted, but something she had zero tolerance for.

"So those are the only two instances?"

"I mean, there might be others, but jail is always an option, too, which is the bigger question right now. Are you in jail? Your voice has an echo. Where are you, Leah?"

I glance around the tiny space and observe the closet-like features, wooden panels, and intricate screen on one side.

"I'm still at St. Vincent's, but—"

"What?" Julia says.

"Oh, no," I whisper.

"Leah?"

"I think—" I stammer as I look through the small screen. "Julia, it's the confessional."

She bursts into laughter. "Only you, Leah. Literally only your dumbass walks into a confessional to make a phone call."

"I'm getting out of here."

"Wait, is someone in there?"

"What do you mean?"

"Is someone waiting for you to confess, Leah?"

"I don't know."

"Knock."

"No!" But before I can hang up and walk out, the screen slides to the side.

"Julia, I gotta go," I say, my voice panicked.

"Oh my gosh, he's there, isn't he?" Julia gasps. "Hey, ask him what he thinks of socks and sandals."

I hang up and stare at the screen. "Father, I'm sorry. I didn't know—" I stutter. "I mean, I was just— I thought— I'm so sorry. I was looking for some privacy."

"It seems like you were doing more than that, my dear," he responds.

"No, it's just—" but the words fail. I didn't even know where to start. How can I tell a man of God that I almost had an abortion ten years before, and the doctor who agreed to do it is in his church with his arms around a boy I think is mine. Maybe Julia is right. Maybe I was drugged because as the story plays out in my head, it sounds worse than crazy.

"Come," he instructs. "Step out with me." As the two of us stand in the hallway, I can't help but feel small in his presence. The guilt of my past consumes my mind as he cups my hands in his. It's the first time I realize they are shaking.

"Father Michaels."

"Leah McKinney. It's nice to meet you."

"And you. Your family is here today?"

"Yes. Kate and Greg Williams. It's Caroline's christening."

"Oh, yes. Lovely family."

"Thank you. I'm Kate's cousin. Please don't tell her about this. I'm so embarrassed, and she'd never forgive me."

"Seems like forgiveness is something you're struggling with."

My face flushes, and for a minute, I wish I was in the shadows of the confessional again.

"Let me tell you something about forgiveness, Leah. It starts by accepting that we are flawed. We make mistakes, and we try again with a better understanding the next time. We were never meant to do this life on our own. And once you understand those two things, the unforgivable thing will seem less scary."

"But some things are worse than others. I'm not sure forgiveness would be enough."

"It's always enough. And you're asking the right questions. Trust yourself enough to find them."

Moved by his words, I thank him and apologize again for crashing his confessional.

"It's okay. It happens more than you think."

"It was a beautiful service today, Father. Thank you."

"I'm glad you enjoyed it. And tell your friend something."

"Sure, what's that?"

"Tell her she's right about socks and sandals," he grins. "Very low bar."

As I arrive back at the hotel, Nash has gone to work out, and the room is empty. Exhausted from the night before and the emotions of the morning, I fall into bed only to be woken up four hours later.

"Hey, you gotta get up," Nash says.

I glance at my watch; it's almost 5PM. I take a quick shower and wash the hangover off my body, dreading Kate's post-christening dinner. I could've laid in bed the rest of the evening and skipped the unnecessary event, but Grandpa insisted I go in his absence after he and Nana decided to skip the dinner. Plus, after the riot at Uncle Jack's funeral, he thinks the more time Kate, Allison and I spend together will help heal some wounds. I don't have the heart to tell him he's wrong. I change into a black button-down t-shirt dress —a staple piece Julia had requested at the mall. "All I'm saying is that dress is classy enough for fancy events but hides the fact that you've had three beers and ten dinner rolls," she'd said.

She's right. With a forgiving waistline, the dress fits perfectly after a night of drinking, but my head is still pounding, and it's making me more irritable by the minute.

"Did you withdraw $200 last night?" Nash asks in the car.

"I think so."

"And you spent all of it on male strippers?"

"It was a male revue," I correct.

"Strippers. You blew $200 on strippers last night. Did you get laid, too?"

"Nash, stop. Don't talk to me like that. And what I do with my money is none of your concern. If we were married, maybe that would be different. Or, I don't know, maybe if I had a ring, that might help, too."

"With that shitty attitude, Leah, you'll be lucky if you ever get one."

As we pull up to Kate and Greg's, I can't get out of the car fast enough. We walk in separately, and I rush to the backyard. Nash's mood swings are nearing my last nerve, and the two times I've tried talking to him about our fight; he's shoved it to the side. And with the stress from the morning, I am in no mood to deal with his childish behavior.

Kate and Greg's two-acre property is the perfect place for entertaining, and as I walk out, guests are sipping on fruity drinks under the oversized pergola. The pool and hot tub veer off to the left, and a couple of guests have taken seats on lounge chairs overseeing a handful of kids swimming. Others are standing around a large fire pit and drinking beer. It looks like a picture out of home magazine. The elaborate backyard, fancy people laughing—it's a snapshot from every reality housewife show.

Kate and Greg have rented a massive white tent for dinner, and several other guests are already seated under the string-lighted canopy. Finding an empty table, I sit down as Nash walks over to a group of guys around the fire pit.

"Hey, girl. Are you okay?"

"I'm fine," I snap as Lily takes the seat next to me.

"What happened at Mass?"

"Excuse me?"

"I mean, you left and were gone forever. It was just strange."

"I was hungover," I answer.

"Oh, girl. Me too," she laughs. "I haven't been that drunk since my own bachelorette party."

I doubt that. Lily is not the kind of girl to pass up a party or an opportunity to drink. She enjoys the attention, which was evident by her eagerness to volunteer to be tied up, blindfolded, and spanked during the male revue.

As more people start to fill the tables, Lily gives me the details about each person. It's like a game of socialite bingo.

Mark a square if the person at table 9 has had an affair with someone in the room. Mark a square if a woman at table 17 tokes up occasionally because her stay-at-home-mom life is awful. Half of me is interested, and half wants her to shut up, but my heart stops when she points to the couple four tables away from us. The same familiar face from earlier in the day.

"That's Dr. Clive Stewart. He goes to St. Vincent's with Kate and Greg. He's delivered half the babies in Dallas," she explains. As Lily talks, Dr. Stewart pulls out a chair for his wife, who Lily describes as "the sweetest southern woman you'll ever meet."

"Seriously, Susana is precious."

But my focus is on Dr. Stewart. There is no doubt he's the doctor who I'd known ten years before. As my stomach knots, I tell myself I've changed so much in ten years he won't recognize me. Doctors have many patients, and at his elderly age, surely, he's forgotten. Before I have time to process what I see, Lily makes eye contact with him and waves. He acknowledges her with a smile I once found so comforting and waves back, but not before making eye contact with me. His smile fades, his hand lowers—he remembers.

## 6

The shock from the morning takes over my body again, and heat rushes to my face. I reach for my water as my hand shakes while Lily continues her guest trivia. A business partner of Greg's, a Dallas socialite friend of Kate's who Lily thought was only at the dinner to "act slutty" and a few other pointless couples, but I can't take my eyes off Clive, and he is staring, too. The confusion and worry on his face unnerves me as Nash sits down.

"Hey," I say.

Nash doesn't respond. But, with traces of my past sitting four tables away, I can't handle the anger from Nash, too.

"I'm sorry," I whisper. "You were right. I shouldn't have spent that much money last night."

"Whatever."

Nash's voice is cold, but his behavior is worse. In a move of manipulation, Nash flips a switch and starts to entertain our table. He cracks jokes and makes everyone comfortable —everyone except me. I've seen it before. We would have a fight, and instead of canceling plans, he'd sit around a table and give everyone else attention except me. *"He's so funny, you're so lucky, he's the life of the party,*" they'd tell me as I'd smile and nod, but underneath we were a couple holding pieces of a thread. He was the best liar I'd ever seen, and as familiar as I am with his tactics, I find myself as an actor in his game, again. I laugh when I'm supposed to and pretend we are happy while he wins over strangers and feds his ego. It's a part of Nash I despise the most—even worse than his ghosting. Our therapist had talked about giving each other space when those ugly parts surfaced, and recognizing them in ourselves and holding each other accountable. Nash and I agreed to give those ugly parts a code name if they appeared in public, but after two failed attempts of saying, "this dressing is funky," and "this salad could use more dressing," Nash isn't taking the bait.

As dinner ends, Nash's audience disperses to other tables, and the attention is over. But he's gotten what he wanted. He finishes off his wine and informs me he's going to the car. His tantrums are so stupid. Even though they don't always last long and he usually apologizes after—I wonder if there's a way to deprogram him. Can I cut out the asshole part of his brain and make that part into something better? Maybe turn it into someone who makes me dinner when he's angry. But based on the times Nash has been an asshole recently, I would've gained fifty pounds by now.

"I'm going to tell Kate and Allison, and I'll meet you there. And, Nash, we need to talk when we get back to the hotel."

He rolls his eyes and the dinner idea is gone—maybe fifty pounds is too generous.

Clive has disappeared for the moment—a temporary relief— as I pull out a chair. Kate is talking to a woman I recognize from Mass, and Lily and Allison are whispering about the slutty socialite Lily pointed out earlier.

"She's just so desperate," Lily says.

"Well, she's older. I mean, her options are limited now."

"True."

"Hey," I interject.

"Hey, Leah. Lily was just telling me about how much she *loves* Nash."

"Seriously, Leah, he's so hilarious!" Lily gushes as Allison rolls her eyes.

"Yeah, he's never met a stranger," I laugh.

"Or refused to go to bed with one," Allison whispers under her breath. I glare at her and immediately regret my confession about Nash's infidelity. She'd mentioned it a few times in the past, always emphasizing how she'd *never* stay with someone who cheated on her, which wasn't surprising. Allison wouldn't dare risk her precious reputation with a cheater, or at least if Thad ever did, she'd never tell anyone. The comfort of Thad's money wouldn't allow her to. "Anyway, don't forget your alteration appointment tomorrow," she adds.

"I know. Lily, it was nice to meet you."

"Oh, you, too! We'll see you soon, girl."

But, as I start to get up—something stops me. At the next table, Greg is talking with a man whose voice sounds familiar, but I can't see his face. After the long day, I assume my mind is so full of the past that every male voice has to be someone I used to know. But the man's voice booming over Greg's shoulder is different. Unmistakable different. I take a step back to get a clearer view but only catch the back of his head as my heart begins to race. The familiarity sends chills down my spine. Then, as Greg moves to the side, I see him. The man I'd fallen in love with ten years before. His voice opens every crack in my heart, and as I stare at him, his icy blue eyes meet mine. I can't move. My stomach turns, and I think I'm going to puke. He nods his head as Greg talks, but he never takes his eyes off me, and I can't turn away. I need to. I need to leave immediately, but he holds too many pieces of my life in his hands. A life that he ended abruptly on a parking lot in Little Rock, Arkansas. As he and Greg continue their conversation, a tall, slender woman stands next to him. Her thin lips are pressed into a hard line, and the Botox is doing its best to hide the fact that she is much older than he is.

"Leah?" Kate interrupts.

"Sorry, what?" I choke.

"This is Ethan Erickson and his wife, Piper."

"Ethan, Piper, this is my cousin, Leah McKinney."

As Ethan stretches out his hand, I try to keep it together.

"It's nice to meet you, Leah," he says.

My name sounds uncomfortable in his mouth. I can't speak but manage a half-smile as I turn my attention to Piper.

"It's nice to meet you," I squeak.

"Likewise," she responds.

"Ethan is an attorney. He does litigation for Greg's business," Kate explains. "And I was just telling him that Allie and Thad still don't have a ring bearer for the wedding and how perfect his little brother would be," she adds, searching Allison for approval.

"Oh. Well—" Allison starts, thrown off by Kate's suggestion. "I mean, I didn't think about that, but maybe," she shrugs, trying to hide her annoyance.

"We can talk about it later, but it's a thought," Kate insists.

I shift uncomfortably, and Ethan hasn't taken his eyes off me.

"I'm going to get some water," Piper says.

"Are you okay?" Ethan asks. "We couldn't come this morning since she gets these bad headaches and—"

"Migraines," Piper sharply corrects. "I get migraines."

"Oh, no worries," Kate sympathizes. "I totally understand."

As Piper leaves the table, it's my cue to run. I give Kate and Allison a quick hug and hurry out. Some guests are standing around the fire pit as I rush by, still sipping on dark whiskey, smoking cigars, and laughing in gruff voices. I stop suddenly to adjust the strap on one of my wedges just as someone bumps into me.

"I'm sorry," the young boy says. I turn around as the altar boy stares back at me. Up close, his nose freckles stand out against his pale skin.

"Spencer!" Clive shouts, appearing behind me. "I thought we agreed you were going to stop running around," he scolds.

"I wasn't running around," he complains.

"Tell her you're sorry," Clive says, his eyes fearful and panicked.

His face flushes. "I did."

"It's okay," I whisper, taking in his every feature.

"Introduce yourself," Clive says.

He fidgets with his hands and glances at Clive, then back at me, his wavy blond hair reminding me of my own at his age.

"I'm Spencer," he says. I try to smile, but Spencer's sticky hand and tiny nose freckles are too much. Clive sees the tears forming in my eyes.

"Spencer, go find your mom," he instructs. I didn't want him to go, and I try to memorize his face as he runs back into the tent and disappears.

"Spencer?" I ask, my voice trembling at the name I'd given my own son—the one he delivered.

"Leah, it's not what you think," he starts to explain.

"How old is he?" I ask.

"He's almost ten."

"When's his birthday?"

Clive pauses. "Leah, just let me explain."

"When is his birthday?" I repeat, but I don't want to know his answer.

"May 11," he whispers.

I back away from him as the knots in my stomach tighten. I can't speak, but he continues anyway. "Just let me explain. The adoption fell through and—"

But before he can finish, I run inside, rush through the house, and out to the front. I search frantically for Nash and the car but come up empty. As the tears start to fall, I reach for my phone to find a missed text from Nash.

*Nash: Had to leave. Business thing. Sorry.*

"Leah!" Clive shouts.

"No, stop. Please."

"Listen, it's not what you think. Just let me explain."

"How you stole my child? That's what you want to explain? How you tricked me into believing you, and you kept him for yourself? I trusted you!"

"It's not like that. Where's your car? Let's go talk," he suggests.

I don't want to talk. No explanation will matter. I'd trusted him with the most delicate part of my life, and he'd lied, but there was a part of me that wanted the truth. As we walk to his car, my insides have twisted themselves into a pretzel, and I lose my dinner in the grass.

"Here," he says, opening the car door. "Get in." He hands

me a bottle of water and some napkins from the console as I sit crippled with shock.

"I can't imagine what you must be thinking," he starts.

"You don't want to know."

"Leah, your adoption plan was always the plan. I never intended to keep Spencer, but the adoptive parents backed out shortly after you gave birth. It happens, and my wife—" his voice cracks. "We'd just had a miscarriage, and I thought—"

"So, he was a band-aid?" I yell.

"No. He wasn't a band-aid, Leah. But I knew we could give him a great life, and he'd be loved. And he is. He's the sweetest—"

"Stop. Don't," I say, tears running down my face. I can't hear him talk about my son and how amazing he is. I can't know the details of his life or how I'd missed every milestone.

"I'm so sorry. This was never what I wanted."

"Stop. Okay? Just stop!" I scream.

It wasn't what I wanted either. I didn't want to get pregnant, but I did, and at eighteen, my life hadn't even started. So, I chose a different path, but there hadn't been a day that I had forgotten about Spencer. Every birthday, every Christmas, every single day, the thoughts of him would haunt me, and I'd wondered if I'd made the right decision. I understood what it was like to grow up without two parents, and as hard as the decision was, I did the best I could at the time. But as I ugly cry in Clive's car, the reality of that decision shatters me all over again.

"Do you want me to drive you home?" He asks.

"What?"

"Do you have a ride home? I'm not sure you're okay to drive."

*Shit*, I think to myself. Nash has the car, and I don't have a way home, but I am not about to let Clive shuttle me back to the hotel. He's done enough damage for one day.

"I have a ride," I tell him.

"Okay, but take this," he instructs, handing me his business card. "You're going to have more questions once this sinks in. I want you to call me when you do."

I want to rip it up and throw it in his face, but he's right. I am too numb to process what has happened—with him, with Spencer, with Ethan, the whole night is a blur, so I take his card and shove it in my purse.

The Uber drops me off at the hotel, and I fall into bed, but I can't sleep. I toss and turn all night as I replay Spencer's face over and over in my head. His fair skin, freckles, and blond hair are identical to mine, but his eyes and smile match Ethan's. As the images burn holes in my heart, I think about the worst part of the whole night. I never told Ethan that I didn't go through with the abortion.

## 7

I CALL Nash six times on my way to the alteration appointment. The first time it rings, he doesn't answer. The next five times, it goes straight to voice mail. With the chaos from the night before, I've barely processed the fact that Nash left me at Kate's house with no way back to the hotel. The first voice mail message I leave, I've only called him an asshole twice, but the number has tripled by the third message. Frustrated, I pull into a parking spot at the bridal boutique and slam the car door. Between the wedding cake smell still pouring through the vents and the happy tunes playing through the speakers, my mood is sour as the sales associate hands me the awful yellow dress. Standing on a platform, she asks, "Are you wearing those shoes for the wedding?"

I glance down at my black Converses and consider for a second that they might make the dress better. "No, unfortunately, I'm not," I respond.

"Why don't you go pick out a heel, and I'm going to grab a few more pins."

I peek my head out to the sales floor, hoping there aren't many customers. My mid-October skin is not doing me any favors, and I don't want anyone to see me parading around in a dress that should've been donated to a recycled fabric store. As I look around, an older lady is going through a rack of flower girl dresses, but the rest of the store is empty, so I duck out to the small shoe section. Staring at the options, I'm not a six-inch heel woman, but I'm not a one-inch heel either. I am confident in a four or five-inch, but a three-inch heel is usually safe. I hold the three-inch heel in one hand and the four-inch in the other, but I can't decide. Conservative or sexy? Comfort or style?

"I'd go with that one." I glance up as Ethan is pointing to the four-inch heel. "Hey, Leah."

"What are you doing here?"

"You look—" he pauses, his eyes running up and down my body.

"Oh, god," I gasp, realizing the dress. My face flushes bright red. "It's terrible, I know."

"It's definitely yellow."

"Right. Thanks, I'm aware."

Ethan smiles, and for a moment, we are back in my apartment in Arkansas, making sarcastic jokes with each other as if time never stopped.

"The dress is beautiful. It probably has something to do with the person wearing it. I didn't know what to say last night. I wasn't prepared—"

"It's fine, Ethan. Really. It's been a long time."

"I'd like to catch up. Maybe we could have a drink later?" He asks. But before I can respond, the sales associate appears.

"Did you find a pair, sweetheart?" She asks.

I give Ethan a thin-lipped smile and return the four-inch heel to the shelf as I walk back to the dressing room. She goes to work pinning my dress, but I can't focus. *Why is he here? Did he say I was beautiful?* None of it makes sense. As the sales associate pins chiffon pieces, I stare in the mirror and recall the last time I saw Ethan. It takes only seconds for me to be back on the parking lot with him.

The Arkansas air was cool as I slammed his car door shut and sobbed when he pulled away. He'd left me alone in front of the abortion clinic after he'd promised to love me forever. Of all the things I'd been through, even the death of my mom, I'd never been more alone than when Ethan left me that morning.

"All done," the sales associate says. "Are you okay, honey? You're all flushed and splotchy."

My heart races and my body is burning up as red patches appear on my chest, neck, and arms.

"Could I get a bottle of water?" I ask.

"Of course, and let me unzip you so you can change. This fabric can sometimes be suffocating."

I sit in the dressing room in a heap, taking a few slow, deep breaths, sipping on the water, and wondering how the weekend has turned into a disaster. With the red patches starting to go down and my heart beating a more regular pattern, all I want to do is get out of Dallas.

But, as I walk back out to the sales floor, Ethan is sitting on an oversized white chair reading a bridal magazine. He smiles as I place the heels back on the shelf, but I'm too angry to care.

"So, what do you say?" He asks.

"About what, Ethan?"

"Catching up? Let me take you to lunch."

"No."

"Come on, Leah. I know—" he starts.

"What do you know, Ethan? Really. Tell me what you know?"

"Sir, here's the tuxedo brochure you asked for," the sales associate interrupts.

"Thanks," he replies, shifting his focus back to me.

"Leah?"

"I have to go, Ethan. It was good to see you."

He follows me outside. "Leah, stop. We need to talk."

"Do we?"

"Yes, we do."

"What would you like to talk about? How you left me? Or how you never checked on me to see if I was okay? Which part of that would you like to talk about, Ethan?"

"That's not fair, Leah. I was an idiot."

"Asshole. You were an asshole. Let's not get it confused."

"You're right, which is why we need to talk. Please."

"I'm leaving today, and I don't think catching up is a good idea. There's not much else to say."

"Fine. If that's what you want, then I understand," he responds, slapping the tuxedo brochure against his hand in frustration.

"Why do you have that?"

"Your cousin was pretty persistent last night about needing a ring bearer and having my brother do it, so I stopped by to get some tux suggestions."

"You just happened to come to the same place I was going to be?"

"I knew you were going to be here. I overheard you last night."

"Stalking isn't really your style. And pressuring me into a conversation isn't okay, Ethan. You of all people should know that."

Standing at our cars, I want to get in, drive away and never look back, but inside I have so much to say to him, and none of it is coming out. He's right, we do need to talk, but I don't know where to begin. Our love was unlike anything I'd ever experienced before, and I have never forgiven him for ruining my life.

"At least tell me you'll think about it. Please, Leah."

"Fine. I'll think about it," I reply, wondering if I'm serious or just saying it to get out of the situation. "I gotta go, Ethan."

"I do, too. I gotta get him back," he says, pointing at the backseat.

The young boy is playing something on his iPad when he stops and glances at me with his icy blue eyes. My heart stops as I make eye contact with Spencer. He gives me a sheepish wave and starts playing with his iPad again.

"Who's that?" I manage to say.

"My brother. Well, stepbrother technically, but we don't call him that. His dad married my mom when he was a baby," he explains.

"Ethan—"

"I know. I'm going. But think about it, okay?"

As he gets in the car, I stand in shock at the three of us— the missing pieces of a family that was never supposed to be —in a parking lot once again. I jump in my car and dig through my purse, pulling out Dr. Stewart's business card. My hands tremble as I type out a text.

*It's Leah. I need to talk to you*

# 8

CLIVE RESPONDS, but I don't know what to say. I've never shared the details about Spencer's biological dad with him, and the ten-years-too-late explanations sound worse with each attempted response. I need time to think and strategize before sending Clive a text back. But as the plane engine hums, I wonder if it's even worth it.

Avoidance is easy. I've done it most of my life. If an uncomfortable situation presents itself, I avoid it. It's an atrocious coping skill, but it's better than dealing with the consequences of my unforgivable mistakes. I'm sure my therapist disagrees, but she'd also have to know the truth of my past to form that opinion—which she doesn't.

And then there was Nash. I have waved the banner of honesty at him so many times after his affair with Mika, always demanding that our life together has to be sealed with our word. Except I haven't kept mine. He'll never look at me the same if he knows that all along I've kept a secret like Spencer from him. We had our own battles to fight, and as the plane touches down in Louisville, I'm not going to text Clive back. In fact, I'm going to forget the whole weekend happened. Avoid—it's what I know best.

Our apartment is empty as I arrive home. Throwing my suitcase on the bed, I walk to the kitchen. A bottle of Moscato sits unopened in the fridge, so I pour a glass, crash on the couch and turn on the TV, trying to drown out the weekend. But the distraction is futile. Deception only has one outcome, and there are too many players in the game. Keep Nash away from Dallas, keep Ethan away from the truth, forgive Clive for stealing my son, and never think about Spencer's nose freckles. It's an unrealistic plan, but a bottle of Moscato later, I've convinced myself it's possible.

The following day, I can smell the paint fumes in the hallway. I'm not aware of any weekend painting, and confusion turns to worry as I round the corner to the office. The odor engulfs me as I open the door—orange walls on every side. I cup my hand over my nose and quickly open every window in the office, but the smell is dreadful. Down the hallway, I spot Miss Kay, a few dry paintbrushes and rollers in her hand.

"Good morning, Miss Kay," I say as politely as I can.

"Mornin', hon."

"Did you paint the office?" I ask.

"Yes, ma'am. Those walls needed some touching up. I was so pleased with how the auxiliary gym turned out last week that I figured the office could use the same. And I always thought that the school should have some fun colors, you know? Kids love it. It makes 'em happy."

"You painted the auxiliary gym?"

"Yes, honey. Well, the equipment closet. It just felt like time, ya know?"

"No, Miss Kay, I don't know. Did you fill out a maintenance request?"

"We've never used such a thing here, Miss McKinney. Now, if you'll excuse me, I've got to go wash these brushes."

I stand in the hallway for a minute as Miss Kay waddles off with her paintbrushes, trying to grasp what just happened.

"Leah!"

I turn around, making eye contact with Julia.

"What in the holy hell?" She shouts.

"I know."

"It looks like a pumpkin had an orgasm in there."

"I know."

"You realize Dr. Bradley and the board members are coming by this afternoon, right?"

"Shit," I sigh, dropping my head into my hands.

"He emailed a reminder last night. They're coming by to present—"

"The soccer team with their state banner. Dammit, I totally forgot," I say. "What are we going to do?"

"I don't know what *you're* going to do, but I'm going to take a half-day. So, good luck with that."

"You are not leaving. We're going to fix this."

We close the office and mobilize in the hallway while we air out the fumes. With each passing period, students cough and cover their noses as they pass by the office. It's chaos and by lunchtime, three teachers and a handful of students have left school with unbearable headaches. I make three phone calls to Dr. Bradley's secretary to see if we can move the presentation to another day, but they deny the request.

"Julia, we're going to have to keep Dr. Bradley and the others in the gym. We can't let them in the main entrance."

"And how do you think we're going to do that?" She asks.

"I'll meet them out front and walk them over."

"And you think that's going to work?"

"I don't know, but we don't have any other options."

As two o'clock inches closer, our plan is officially in motion. With Julia positioned in the gym, we dismiss students from class. Moments later, as I wait on the steps outside, the rain starts. Dr. Bradley runs from the parking lot with three board members up to the steps—none of them have an umbrella. In the worst rain I've seen in six months, I realize there is no other way to the gym than through the school. He immediately gets a whiff of the awful paint fumes as we pass by the office and pulls a handkerchief from his pocket while he leans in.

"Did we do some painting, Miss McKinney?" He asks, appalled at the explosion of orange covering the walls.

"There was a miscommunication over the weekend," I reply, trying to sound like I have it under control.

"Our district has a policy on the uniformity of our schools. We don't just paint whatever we want when we want. There's a process. We can talk about this later," he informs, shaking out his handkerchief aggressively and folding it back into his pocket.

The blood rushes to my cheeks as I usher them down the hallway, the embarrassment heavy with each step I take. Entering the gym, Coach Douglas is escorting the soccer team to the locker room and I meet Julia's wide-eyed stare.

"You took them through the school?" She whispers.

"I had to. The damn rain."

"Did he see?"

"Yes."

"And?"

"Not good," I reply, shaking my head.

As Coach Douglas raises the banner, the gym erupts in applause, but I notice two board members whispering and then exiting to the hallway. I glance at Julia.

"Where are they going?" I ask.

"Evidence."

"Seriously?"

"Probably."

The following morning, as Julia and I sit in her office, I read her the email I've received from Dr. Bradley along with a few parent emails and one from a teacher. The stench has led to a worker's comp complaint and a conversation about latex allergies. And more importantly, Dr. Bradley has received some complaints, too. Julia and I labor over his email, searching for any signs of positivity just as Trista Miller's voice cuts through.

"I can't deal with her right now," I say.

"I'll handle it," Julia responds, getting up from her desk, but Trista is already at the door.

"Dear heavens, ladies. I had to see it for myself. Looks like we got a little festive with the Halloween decor."

"It's not a good time, Trista," Julia quips.

"Okay, well, just a heads up. I talked to a few friends of mine, and as long as we get it repainted, there's no harm done."

"I'm sending in the work order now," I say.

"Just a little bump, Leah. No biggie. I mean, the talk is a little worrisome, but things happen. It's so new for you, and a little accident like this can happen. We understand, and you've got so much on your plate, hon. Repaint, and it'll be good as new. But dear lord, this color. I mean, why such a hideous shade?"

"It wasn't—"

"Oh, it's fine. You're a millennial," she laughs. "I mean, it's understandable. We just certainly don't have the *same* taste."

"Thanks for stopping by, Trista. We've got it taken care of," Julia snaps.

As Trista walks out, burying her nose in her hand, Julia rolls her eyes.

"Should I tell Dr. Bradley it was Miss Kay?"

"No. Passing the blame makes you look out of control. But firing Kay seems inevitable. She's destructive, and if you don't address it, it'll only get worse. The last thing you want is for your boss to think you're an idiot."

"Does he think that?" I ask.

"I mean, I don't think he has a great opinion of you right now if that's what you're asking."

"This is a mess."

"It is. But, Leah, if we're having an honest moment here, I think I need to say this, too," Julia starts. "You've got to do a better job of checking your email and keeping track of your calendar. You couldn't predict that Kay would be a dumbass and paint the school, but you should've known that Dr. Bradley was coming. It can't be my responsibility to keep you informed of what's happening here. You're better than that."

"I know, and you're right. I think I've been distracted lately."

"You have, but that can't be an excuse to let things slip."

"I know."

"Speaking of distractions, you haven't said a word about Dallas. Give me all the details."

"It was fine."

"Fine? That's it?"

"I mean, I told you about Kate and Allison's snotty friends. It was mostly just more of that. Oh, and Nash showed up."

"Of course he did. You mean the bastard couldn't stand a

weekend where he wasn't the center of attention? You don't say."

"Stop. He wanted to surprise me, and I think he regretted our fight."

"No, he didn't. He doesn't care about anyone but himself."

She isn't wrong. That morning, Nash left before I got up, and the cycle continues. He still hasn't apologized for leaving me at Kate's, and I am too consumed with the wreckage in Dallas to push the issue further.

As I retreat to my office and submit a maintenance order for the office, I call our therapist to schedule an appointment. But as I sit on hold and wait for an available date, a faint memory of Uncle Jack creeps in. More importantly— his words—"you can't just jump into the canoe with the first boy you see." My mind wonders back to Wyatt Simpson and how exhausting it is to pull people downstream—or jump into canoes with them because they're charming.

The receptionist comes back on the line and I schedule our therapy appointment, hoping the session will look less like drowning and more like progress.

Two weeks later, we arrive separately. With his business trip to Ohio, we almost had to cancel, but I insisted Nash take a later flight and sitting in the waiting room; his mood is foul. The first five minutes of our session, I fill in the pieces of Mika's text and what occurred in Dallas and listening to my own words linger in the air, the tension mounts.

"So, the woman you had an affair with texted you late at night. Leah, can you tell Nash how that made you feel?"

"Like I wanted to kill you."

"See?" Nash exhales sharply.

"Leah, with less sarcasm."

I understand what she means, but I did want to kill him and her that night, too. But, I try again. "I felt like it was starting again, and I was angry that you promised it was over."

"It's over, and I've told you that."

"Leah, what would give you peace about this situation?"

"He works with her. He sees her every day. She's not blocked on his phone or anywhere else, and he has access to her whenever he wants," I say.

"So, if Nash found a new job?"

"I'm not leaving my job. That's stupid."

"I'm asking hypothetically, Nash," she says, turning her gaze back to me. "If he found a new job, would that give you peace?"

"I don't know. Just because he leaves his job doesn't mean he can't communicate with her."

"I'm not leaving my job."

"Not even if it was better for our relationship?" I glare.

"No."

"It doesn't sound like that would give you peace anyway, Leah. But there are other solutions. Nash, you could block Mika's number and have no contact outside of work. You could unfollow her on social media and block her there, too. Both are reasonable options and don't involve you uprooting your career. What are your thoughts about that?"

Nash looks away but pulls his phone from his pocket. We watch as he arranges the settings to block and unfollow Mika, and there is relief in his actions.

"Leah, how does it make you feel watching Nash take those steps?"

She acts like he just erected a national monument in my honor, and I instantly become defensive.

"It takes a second to unblock her. He could do it when we leave here," I snap.

"It's never good enough. Anything I do for her, it's never good enough."

"There's definitely a level of trust that has to occur between the two of you. Leah, small steps are still steps as long as they are going in the right direction, but it still seems like you have some anger that we need to address. Let's hit that when you and I have a chance to talk again."

She's right. I am angry, and it will take more than one session with her to unravel that web, but to make any progress in our session, I want to keep going, especially before he leaves on his trip. So we move on to Dallas, and as sour as the session started, Nash begins to open up toward the end. He apologizes for leaving me at Kate's—a moot point but still a step according to our therapist. But the biggest step of all is Nash's overwhelming commitment again to our relationship. He agrees he's made mistakes and hasn't treated me well. And more importantly, he promises to uphold his word and work on putting our relationship above anything else.

"Nash, tell Leah again what you just said."

"You're the most important person in my life, Leah, and I give you my word that you—this, what we have—is what I want. I'm not going to jeopardize that."

The hour-long session is over too quickly, but as we stand in the parking lot, Nash reiterates what he said inside. But somewhere in the back of my mind, I wonder how long it will last. It's the worst thing to think after therapy. Some progress is made and then a voice taps my shoulder and says, "*But, when will it happen again?*"

The following morning, as I sit in my repainted office

and work on an agenda for our curriculum team, a text comes through from an unknown number.

*Leah?*

I stare at the 469-area code. I don't give my number out to parents or students, and the few 469 area codes I have in my phone belong to Kate and Allison. Hesitant to text back, another message appears.

*Is this Leah McKinney?*

I respond. *Yes, who is this?*

*It's Ethan*

I sit back in my chair, staring at the blue text as the three bubbles appear.

*Ethan: I'm sorry. I know you said you didn't want to talk, but I was wondering if you changed your mind?*

My hands begin to sweat as I stare at the screen and then a wave of guilt. I just spent an entire therapy session calling out Nash for staying in contact with a former lover, and here I am in my own predicament. I click on the arrow by his number and scroll down to the block contact button but stop. Blocking someone's number is two things—impulsive or forever. The impulsivity occurs out of temporary anger because the caller no longer deserves access for a while. It typically lands on exes, annoying acquaintances, or gossipers who are searching for information. The forever blocked numbers occur for narcissists and telemarketers. I have blocked two people in the past —an old boyfriend turned stalker and a former coworker who swore she had an obscene picture of Nash but never produced the evidence. Both are in the forever blocked category, and even though Ethan is an ex-boyfriend, I can't make him the third, so I go back to his message. He's sent another one.

*Ethan: Hello?*

*Me: I'm here*

*Ethan: Are you up for talking?*

I consider his question and wonder how I'll even begin to tell him the truth. Our conversation will ultimately lead to the abortion clinic, and if Ethan finds out I didn't go through with it, how will he react? How can I tell him I've kept a secret from him for ten years? So, I offer him the vaguest response.

*Me: Maybe*

It's not a guarantee, but it's not a *yes*. It's the truth. Maybe at some point in my life, I'll have a conversation with him, and perhaps I won't. His response is immediate.

*Ethan: I'll take maybe. And Leah...*

*Me: Yes*

*Ethan: It was really good to see you in Dallas*

## 9

OVER THE NEXT FEW DAYS, I go back to Ethan's text twice, three times, and then a fourth, reading and rereading each word in my head.

"Why are you smiling like an idiot?" Julia asks, entering my office.

I close the message and set my phone down. "Just something funny on Twitter."

"What is it?" She sits down, waiting for the funny thing.

"It was just this meme about teachers. I'll send it to you later."

"You're a terrible liar, Leah. Like it's awful. Anyway, I just came in to remind you that we have the first-semester data stuff coming up in a few weeks. It'll be here before we know it, and we need to make sure it's ready to go after Christmas."

"First of all, I'm not lying. Second, I know about the first semester data. The surveys are completed, and the only thing we still need to collect is the department chairs' datasheets. We have a meeting with them next week before

Thanksgiving break. We can work on putting them together when we get back."

"Look at you being all responsible and principal-like," she laughs.

"Like a real adult and everything," I joke.

"All right, well, go back to texting whomever you were."

"I wasn't texting anyone."

"Liar."

That evening, Ethan checks in, again, to see if that *maybe* has manifested into a *yes*, which it hasn't, but it's hard to turn away from the attention he's giving me. Nash has returned from his trip, but the hangover from therapy has started to wear off. He's moody and snaps at the slightest thing. The pressure from his job is mounting, and in the few conversations I've had with him, the stress of trying to land a client in Ohio is spilling over into our relationship. I try to support him and be encouraging, but with each passing day, his frustration increases, and Ethan's texts fill in the space where Nash's avoidance is seeping out.

Over a quiet breakfast, Nash says, "I'm going to see my uncle at Thanksgiving."

I nearly choke on my oatmeal. "Next week?"

I wait for an answer, but there isn't one. "You're ditching me on Thanksgiving?"

"Yeah, Leah. I just need some time to think." Nash gets up from the table and washes his bowl.

"What exactly am I supposed to do? We made plans to spend Thanksgiving together."

"I don't know," he says. "I'm sure you'll figure it out."

"Why are you doing this, Nash? What's going on with you?"

"I don't know. I'm just going through some stuff, and I need to take some time for myself. To figure things out."

"Figure things out?"

"Yeah. Listen, I love you, and I don't want to lose you, but I need some time alone."

"So you're breaking up with me?"

"I didn't say that. I just need some time alone."

"I'm not ready to be done, Nash."

"I didn't say we are done. I just need some time."

But I know better than to believe him. The *I need time alone* speech is always the precursor to a breakup, and hearing Nash say those words only fuels the story I'm telling myself in my head. That night, he sleeps on the couch—by choice—and we are at a breaking point. So, in a last attempt to save our relationship, I ask him to dinner the following evening to determine if there's anything left to salvage. But things don't go as planned.

Ten minutes after we arrive at O'Shay's, Mika Templeton walks in. My head almost explodes as she leans against the hostess stand and laughs too hard at something clearly not funny. As I fidget in our booth, I consider making a scene.

In my head, dramatic theme music plays as a narrator's voice describes the tension between the two of us in great detail. Then, I stand up, point across the room, and tell every patron just exactly what kind of girl is requesting a table for three. Everyone is in shock. They kick her out and award me some sort of trophy. There's applause as she exits. Someone posts it on Facebook with an insulting caption, and the likes pour in. Wives and girlfriends give me sympathetic hugs. An honorable husband buys the whole restaurant a round of drinks in my honor, and I get a free meal for enduring such trauma.

The scene fades to black in my mind as Nash searches my face for a reaction. She knew we'd be here. I take a deep breath in, slowly letting it out, as I stare at her and wait. I know what's coming next. Girls like Mika are predictable in every way. And true to form, she gets up to use the bathroom, purposely walking by our booth.

"Nash, oh my goodness! I didn't know y'all would be here," Mika says, turning up her thick Kentucky accent a few notches.

She has squeezed her body into a black off-the-shoulder mini dress that barely covers her ass and doesn't compliment her small chest. I can't understand what Nash ever saw in her other than easy sex and potential AARP benefits—maybe that was enough. She doesn't stay at our table for long, insisting she is meeting some friends for drinks, but it's long enough to ruin our evening again. As Nash walks over to the bar, I text Julia.

*Me: Mika Templeton is at O'Shay's*

*Julia: Is it half off whore night?*

*Me: LOL*

*Julia: Nash is a piece of shit. Also, did she come in the backdoor? I hear it's kinda her thing...*

*Me: She's such a whore. Do I set her on fire now or later?*

*Julia: Neither... you are too pretty for jail*

*Me: I'd never make it*

*Julia: But I'm down to cut Nash's dick off. I know some people... super cheap. And even if it's not super cheap, it would be money well spent*

*Me: JULIA! Stop*

*Julia: Just saying. You have options*

*Me: Ugh, it's just complicated*

*Julia: You know what's not complicated?*

*Me: What?*

*Julia: Cutting his dick off*

As Nash returns with my drink, Mika joins two friends at a booth across the room, her stringy, brown hair lays lifeless down her shoulders, and for the first time, Nash repulses me. Our therapist said cheating was never about the attraction to the other person, and initially, I thought she was lying. But as I watch her across the room, I start to believe there may be some truth to that as my anger switches back to Nash. If he can cheat with someone like her, there's no bottom floor for him, which is dangerous.

I recall a conversation with my doctor shortly after Nash's affair with Mika. As I laid in the exam room, tears running down my face, explaining how he'd cheated, and I needed to be checked for every STD known to man, the doctor took my hand and assured me that I was doing the right thing and promised to do a full lab. I'd never jeopardized my sexual health, and waiting for the results of my blood work was a painstaking three days. The results were clean, and somehow I'd dodged a bullet, but after Nash and I got back together, I refused to have sex with him without a condom. He hated it, and eventually, I caved—I wish I hadn't now.

"Are you okay?" Nash asks.

"Is there someone else, Nash?"

"What do you mean?"

"Are you breaking up with me because there's someone else? Just be honest. I saw the way she looked at you. You can tell me."

"Leah, stop. No, this doesn't have anything to do with her, and we're not breaking up. I just need some space."

"That sounds like a breakup. I don't want to hang on while you screw around on me and then decide I'm what you want. That's not fair, and we both deserve better than that."

"I love you, but I've got some stuff to figure out about

myself. Stuff that you can't help me with. That's all this is. I'm not screwing around with anyone."

As we drive home, I think about the past three years. The happiest moments were always the ones I leaned on when everything else was crashing in around us, but even those moments have faded. Nash isn't the same person I loved three years ago, and fighting for breadcrumbs in our relationship has pushed me into a dark place. But for some reason, I still believe in the fight. To revive something that's on the brink of collapse is heroic and beautiful, and it's the right thing to do. Stay. Work it out. Trust that the effort will produce results, but I am slipping faster than I can keep up with. The happiness I'd had for life is gone and in its place is a complex set of issues that have reshaped my existence. I no longer recognize what I'm fighting for—and more than that, I don't recognize myself anymore.

We don't accomplish much over dinner, and even though Nash says it's not about another woman, I have my doubts. I don't have clarity over where we stand other than we are taking space. The uncertainty hangs on my body as I walk into work the next day.

"How was dinner?" Julia asks.

"Terrible."

"Leah, just end it with him. You know he's not going to change. You're wasting your time."

"It's been rough. But does that mean we just throw it away like it never existed?"

"Yes, it does. He's a selfish asshole, and he'll never be able to give you what you want. So you part ways, wish him well, and move on."

"I'm not ready for that, Julia. Maybe the space is right for us. Maybe he's right."

"And maybe he's full of shit. Either is possible, and you shouldn't wait around to find out."

I glance across the table at Julia. "Do you have Thanksgiving plans?"

"You mean other than Granddad De Loughrey creating factions at the dinner table and causing political warfare? No, not really," she says. "Why?"

"We should go to Sugar Creek," I suggest. "We could leave Friday. I'm sure my grandparents would love to meet you. Hanging out in the cabins for a week. The peace and quiet. It'd be fun. And I really need to get away and think about all this stuff with Nash. You can help me with it."

"I already helped you with it—leave him. Problem solved. You're welcome. And it's a hard *no* on traveling to that village and living off the land for a week. I don't pee in the woods or sleep on the cold ground. Thanks, but no."

"Come on, Julia, please?" I beg. "The cabins are nice, and they have bathrooms. Showers, too. And my Nana's cooking—it's the best comfort food you'll ever have. I'd let you choose the tunes for the drive."

Julia raises an eyebrow, considering. "Both ways?"

"Both ways."

She makes a dramatic exit for the bathroom but stops and gives me her deadly RBF stare. "Okay, fine. But I am not going to love it, and if any of your redneck friends try to hook up with me, I'm out."

I squeal, and Julia rolls her eyes, giving a half-smile before walking out of the room. I call Grandpa later in the day and tell him we are coming down. He assures me he'll have the cabin ready, and Nana says she'll pick up groceries.

On my way home, I am giddy about the pending trip with Julia but still concerned about Nash's last-minute change of plans. As I pull into the apartment, he isn't there. I blow it off and do some laundry, but he still isn't home by the time I climb in bed, so I send him a text.

Me: *Where are you?*

Nash: *At my uncle's*

Me: *You already left?*

Nash: *Yes*

Me: *Cool*

No response back. I slam the phone on the bed and turn the light off, pulling the covers up close to my chin. My phone buzzes again, and I quickly turn over. It's a text from Ethan.

Ethan: *You up?*

I stare at the words fighting the urge to respond. A few minutes pass and another message pops up:

Ethan: *No worries. I just wanted to check on you. I'll catch ya another time*

But the loneliness of the evening has taken over, and I decide to text back.

Me: *I'm up. Can you talk?*

As always, his response is immediate.

Ethan: *Yes! Can you take a call?*

I hesitate, knowing that hearing Ethan's voice in such a vulnerable state will be more than I can handle.

Me: *No, but I can text*

Ethan: *Are you okay?*

Me: *Stressful day*

Ethan: *I'm sorry*

Me: *It's okay. What are you doing?*

Ethan: *Sitting outside*

Me: *Nice*

Ethan: *Do you remember?*

Me: *Remember what?*

Ethan: *Sitting outside*

Shifting under the covers, I'm shocked at Ethan's question. Sitting outside was *our* thing. We had done it a thousand times when we were together. The night sky would fill with stars, and we'd spend hours talking about life. It was the place we retreated to when our days had been chaotic, or when we just needed to connect. The simplicity of the fresh air and the magic of our love had always given me comfort and a sense of indescribable beauty that neither of us could understand. It was uniquely us, and as I reread his text, I have to know if that's what he means.

*Me: Looking at the stars?*

*Ethan: Yes*

My breath hitches and my heart starts to race, unsure where the conversation is going.

*Me: I'm glad you still look at them*

*Ethan: It was my favorite thing to do with you*

*Me: Mine too*

*Ethan: Go outside*

*Me: Now?*

*Ethan: Yes*

I get out of bed and put my robe on, unable to stop myself from needing the comfort of a nighttime sky. As I open the balcony door, I step outside.

*Me: I'm here*

*Ethan: Look up*

*Me: I am*

*Ethan: Do you see them?*

*Me: I do. They're beautiful*

*Ethan: Like you*

*Me: Ethan*

*Ethan: I've never stopped loving you, Leah*

## 10

I DON'T RESPOND, but Ethan has sent several apologies and even attempted to call, a clear sign he regrets what he said and, more importantly, was probably drunk when he texted. But that still doesn't stop me from reading his text repeatedly as I pull into Julia's driveway.

"We're going to the creek, Julia. Not a Hamptons getaway," I scold.

"Well, a girl needs to be prepared for all occasions, right?"

"Is this necessary?" I ask as I pinch the fabric of her beige, monogrammed Louis scarf.

"A Louis is always necessary."

"Are those your Gucci boots?"

"Leah, we are going to the woods. Do you expect me to rough it in some basic everyday lumberjack boots? I'm not an idiot. I've seen *Naked and Afraid*."

"Oh my god," I say, laughing hard and dropping my head in my hands. "Let's just go."

We take the interstate toward St. Louis as Julia and I

scream along to *The Miseducation of Lauryn Hill,* then *Crazy-SexyCool,* then *August and Everything After.* From there, Julia cobbled a bunch of nineties hits together that we sing along to while stuffing our faces with chicken nuggets.

"I have to go to the bathroom," Julia announces, squirming in her seat.

"Again?"

"Sixty-four-ounce Dr. Pepper, Leah."

"The next rest stop isn't for fifteen miles. Can you hold it that long?"

"Ugh. I guess."

"There's a gas station two exits away. We could always stop—"

"If you want to get herpes from a nasty toilet seat, then go right ahead, Leah. Everyone knows gas station toilets are disease-infested cesspools."

"And rest stop bathrooms, aren't?"

"No, because people don't realize that rest areas have bathrooms. They think it's a place to rest and relax, not use the restroom. Less traffic, fewer germs. It just makes sense."

Julia's logic does not make sense, and pulling into the rest area alongside seven parked cars seems like the right time to spoil her theory that rest stop bathrooms are some type of secret society, but I resist.

"Nash left early," I confess, washing my hands in the bathroom.

"What?"

"Remember I told you he was going to his uncle for Thanksgiving?"

"Yes."

"Well, he left early and didn't tell me."

"When?"

"He wasn't supposed to leave until today, but he's already there."

"He's lying."

"Just because you don't like him doesn't mean he's lying."

"No, Leah, he's lying to you. He posted something on social media yesterday, and the idiot had his location settings on. He was in Louisville last night. So, if he told you something different, he's lying to you."

I pull up Nash's account, scrolling through his recent posts, and there it is. A geotag from the previous evening, at 10:52PM from Louisville, Kentucky.

"What the hell?"

"I told you," Julia sighs.

"Should I text him?"

"Why? So, he can lie to you? Red flags will always look pale in rose-colored glasses, Leah."

As we pull back onto the interstate, I listen to Julia paint a grim picture of my relationship—interjecting every so often with excuses for Nash's behavior.

"Failure is only failure if you don't learn anything from it, Leah. You gotta let go of that thinking."

"And when have you failed, Julia?"

"Well, I haven't, but that's beside the point," she grins.

"Exactly. So, you don't know what it feels like to fail."

"Bullshit. We've all failed before. But I'll tell you this much. Staying trapped inside a relationship with someone who doesn't give a shit about you is a miserable existence. And more than that, it's abusive. Just because he doesn't put his hands on you doesn't mean he's still not abusing you in other ways. The lies, manipulation, mood swings, all of it, Leah, those are all reasons to walk away. And it doesn't mean you failed. It just means you are choosing to live instead of drowning with someone who can't swim."

"You sound like Uncle Jack."

"Good, maybe you'll actually hear me instead of making excuses for staying with that asshole. You're smarter than this, Leah. You can't let fear dictate what you should do. Like Alanis always says, *if he doesn't change his ways, you cut his dick off.*"

"Those are not the words, Julia."

"Well, they should be, and we should probably give her a listen to just make sure."

As Julia blasts *Jagged Little Pill*, I think about Nash's post—becoming angrier with each screeching Alanis lyric. Tolerance is a badge I wear proudly, always believing the trait somehow puts me in a different bracket. But when does tolerance become a gateway to abuse? Maybe Julia is right. Just because I don't have a black eye doesn't mean Nash hasn't left deep wounds everywhere else. And maybe those rose-colored glasses are starting to lose their shine.

After a few more rest stops due to Julia's infinitesimally small bladder, we arrive at Sugar Creek around 8PM. Nana and Grandpa are standing in the driveway, waving us down eagerly.

"Hello, hello!" Grandpa greets us, wrapping me in a hug. His flannel shirt smells like popcorn, and his Cardinal hat sits barely on the top of his head.

I hug Nana next. "Hello, sweet girl."

As I pull away, I bring Julia forward. "This is Julia, and she's never been to a creek."

Grandpa laughs as he shakes Julia's hand, and Nana gives her arm a slight squeeze.

"Nice to meet you, Julia," she says.

"The pleasure is all mine. I've heard so much about y'all, and I'm so grateful you let us stay at this beautiful place so last minute," Julia responds.

"Oh, no problem. We're so happy you two are here."

"You know, the weather will be unseasonably warm this weekend," Grandpa says. "We should catch some crawdads and have a boil."

"Really?" I ask.

"The water might be chilly, but Nana's crawdad soup sounds mighty good."

It does sound good. Nana usually makes her famous crawdad soup in the early fall and then keeps the extra in frozen bags to eat in the winter. But Grandpa tells us she took the last of it to church the weekend before, and catching crawdads with Julia will be hysterical.

"Sounds fun," Julia mumbles.

"For now, though, you two girls should get some sleep. Leah, the cabin is ready."

I smile at Julia. "Perfect."

I give my grandparents a hug and kiss as Julia and I hop back in the car and drive away from the house. A half-mile down the road, the old, wooden Sugar Creek sign appears. The black, stencil-painted letters are hardly visible in the dark, and the orange arrow pointing drivers toward the campground has faded from the sun.

"Looks like someone needs a new sign," Julia says.

"I know. My grandparents put that sign up when Allison and I were kids."

"Did the dinosaurs help them hammer the posts in the ground?"

I laugh. "Maybe. It was one of the things on my uncle's list before he passed."

"Seems like that might be your first job as the new

owner," Julia remarks, reminding me of the weighty responsibility I have.

Rounding a curve that runs alongside the creek, the
wood cabin appears at the bottom of a small hill. Grandpa
has left the porch light on; the fixture was a new addition
Uncle Jack added to all the cabins in the past year. As we
open the door, the smell of cedar hits us. The two twin beds
sit opposite each other, splitting the room down the middle.
Baskets of snacks are on top of the beds, and Nana has left a
thermos of her famous chamomile tea on each small
nightstand.

"Well, isn't this cozy," Julia says, surprised at the cabin's
charm.

"See."

"Whatever."

We claim our spots on opposite sides of the cabin as
Julia unzips her suitcase and puts her clothes carefully in
the small chest of drawers. I laugh at her weirdness and the
bizarre idea that some people unpack their suitcases when
they travel. Julia is one of those people; I am not. I grab a
pair of shorts and a t-shirt, lay them on the bed, and leave
the rest in my suitcase—like normal people.

"Holy cow, this bathroom is huge."

I follow her as she admires the walk-in shower, another
addition Uncle Jack had installed. *Campers are easy guests,
Leah. They don't need a fancy five-star room, but everyone likes a
big bathroom with a nice shower,* he'd told me the year after
he renovated the older cabins. The showers and bathrooms
were constantly reviewed well.

"Nice, huh?"

"It's different from what I imagined," she says, placing
her moisturizer and makeup bag on the large vanity.

"And this tea," she adds. "It's freaking amazing."

"Nana swears by it. She says it'll put you to sleep in twenty minutes."

"Well, that's probably a good thing since the last time I slept in a twin bed, I was in diapers. I'll need to be passed out quickly to sleep in this thing." She forces herself dramatically on the bed., but to her shock, the memory foam mattress cups her body.

"Comfy, right?"

Julia rocks back and forth on the mattress feeling its cloud-like comfort. "I mean, it's okay." Five minutes later, we are both fast asleep.

The next morning, I wake up before Julia. Tiptoeing around the cabin, I try not to disturb her as she's curled up in her black flannel pajamas and matching eye mask. It makes me laugh. I don't know a single camper at Sugar Creek who packed an eye mask.

I change into a pair of comfortable jeans, a long-sleeved t-shirt, and my Converses, throwing on a light jacket as I step outside.

The lingering warm front makes the cool November air feel more like spring, but the bare trees indicate otherwise. Missouri's unpredictable weather is familiar to everyone, and it isn't abnormal to experience all four seasons in one day.

I walk around to the side of the cabin and unlock the shed. My red Honda ATV barely fit in the tiny space, and as I back it out, I send Julia a text and take off toward the creek, deciding to take the scenic trails before going to my grandparents' house.

The morning sun peeks through the trees as I follow the trails that run alongside the creek. I love the peacefulness of Sugar Creek, and I miss the early sunrises. Uncle Jack had driven me around the trails on early mornings more times than I could count. I'd hold on tight as he squeezed the ATV through trees and across small bridges explaining the flood zones and pointing out the best swimming holes. And on my thirteenth birthday, he'd bought me my own ATV, the red Honda, so that we could ride together.

Those mornings we waited for the sunrise were my favorite, and as I park at the top of the bluff overlooking Sugar Creek, it's hard not to feel his presence. The bluff was another addition Uncle Jack had made to the property. With the free advertisement social media provided, he realized if he cleared the hiking trail leading up to the bluff, the views from the top would sell themselves. Posts started appearing on social media as visitors flocked to the bluff to snap their sunset proposals, graduation pictures, and my favorite—the best-friend-jumping-mid-air picture.

The more likes each image received, the more visitors Sugar Creek attracted. But the picturesque bluff was so much more to me. It was the place Uncle Jack and I came after my mom died. It was where we cried and cursed at life for taking so much from us too soon. And it was on the bluff where we learned to forgive and love again.

I turn the engine off and process, for the first time, that this place I love so much is mine. A gesture I'm still not sure I deserve. Following the trail back down, I pull up to my grandparents' house to see Julia sitting on the porch with Grandpa.

"Leah!" She waves. She and Grandpa have maple bar donuts in their hands. "Your grandpa just took me to the cutest donut shop I've ever seen in my life!"

"Yes. The Donut House is legendary around here. Damien owns it. And their maple bars—nothing even comes close. They're to die for."

"Damien?"

"My prom date," I say coolly.

"That's who that was?" Julia stammers.

"Yes. He's cute, right?"

"I mean, he's fine," she says, taking another bite.

Grandpa smiles. "I have a box of twists and more maple bars. Why don't we go inside, and I'll make us some coffee to go with them?"

As Julia and I stuff our faces with donuts and coffee, Grandpa watches the news in his brown recliner. The weather report is calling for seventy-five degrees by noon.

"How 'bout that? We'll set another record," he touts proudly.

"Sounds like global warming," Julia quips. "A little climate crisis in the Bible Belt."

"What?" Grandpa asks.

I fake cough toward Julia and shake my head. Grandpa is a staunch Republican, and the climate crisis is not an argument Julia wants to have with him. I recall a tense conversation he'd had with Uncle Jack—a proud Democrat—about global warming. When Uncle Jack started explaining to Grandpa how it would affect the creeks, rivers, and ecosystems he loved so much, Grandpa got up from the table, told Uncle Jack he was "full of shit," and refused to talk politics with him ever again.

"Oh, nothin'. Record-setting temps in November is pretty impressive, Mr. McKinney," Julia corrects, rolling her eyes at me.

After breakfast, we put a bucket, hot dogs, and two nets into Grandpa's truck and head toward the creek. Making small talk about the weather and donuts, I'm excited about our crawdad adventure.

"Grandpa, why did you bring the fishing pole?"

"I wasn't sure little missy would catch 'em by hand," he jokes.

"Oh, I'm just going to watch," Julia answers. "Thanks for the offer, though, Mr. McKinney. I'm not really the fishing kind."

Grandpa and I laugh, figuring Julia will sit on the rocks while we do the work, but I'm still glad he brought the *princess pole*—which is the name he gave it when Allison picked crawdads with us.

At the creek, the water is much colder than I had anticipated.

"Ah!" Julia yelps as she gets in.

Grandpa laughs. "Crawdad picking ain't for the faint of heart."

As we start our search, Julia has taken the package of hot dogs out from the truck. Under a large rock, I find my first crawdad, a fat one, and grab it. It wriggles in my hand. "I got one!" I shout, placing it in the bucket.

"One down," Grandpa says.

"Hot dogs are so gross," Julia whines, hooking a piece of the meat onto the princess pole.

Grandpa and I stare at each other and burst into laughter.

"What?" Julia asks. "Have you eaten them? They're made from a bunch of different meats, all combined together. A mystery meat specialty. Puke."

"Did you tell her?"

"What?" I ask, searching Grandpa's face. But his smile indicates I should play along. "No, I totally forgot, Grandpa."

"Tell me what?" Julia demands.

"She's not going to be happy," he says.

"No, she definitely will not be happy," I follow.

"Tell me what?"

"Nana is making spaghetti hot dogs tonight," he finally says. "A McKinney favorite."

"It's delicious, Julia. I promise," I say, trying to hold it together.

Julia sighs. "I thought we were having crawdad soup. Isn't that why we're catching them?"

"Crawdads have to be kept overnight before we boil them," I explain as Grandpa nearly doubles over.

"Leah's right," he says. "A full twenty-four hours before we can cook 'em."

"Spaghetti hot dogs?" Julia groans.

"You'll love it," he says, turning his focus back to the creek.

"I mean, I guess I could pick out the hot dog parts and just eat the pasta," she says as I laugh hysterically.

"Why are you laughing?"

I can't breathe, let alone answer her, and Grandpa isn't any better. With his head thrown back, small tears start to roll out of the corner of his eyes.

"You two are awful. Do you hear me? Awful, terrible people," she yells, stomping off through the water.

That evening, as we sit around the table and eat crawdad soup, we listen to Grandpa and Nana tell stories about Sugar Creek and talk about life. It's the season of thanks, and even though so much has gone wrong in the past two months, as I sit in the company of my grandparents and my best friend, I also have a lot to be grateful for. It's easy to find life's failures when the focus is always on the next thing that can go wrong. And plenty has gone wrong, but being at Sugar Creek is different. Life is simple and moves at the pace it's supposed to. There's an unmistakable peace in picking crawdads and laughing around a dinner table. One that I've forgotten because I've been too distracted with everything else. After dinner, we go outside by the fire.

"Stay as long as you want. Enjoy what's left of the hot chocolate I made earlier."

"Thank you, Mrs. McKinney," Julia says with a smile. "And thank you for dinner. It was delicious."

We sip on homemade hot chocolate and watch the fire crackle in front of us. Julia insists that Nana's crawdad soup is the best she's ever tasted, noting she's dined at the finest New Orleans restaurants and never had anything close to what Nana had cooked. Another minute passes before Julia glances at me.

"We need to talk about Dallas."

"What do you mean?"

"I mean, you've acted strange ever since you got back, and I know you better than you think. So, something happened that you're not telling me."

I can't hold it in any longer.

"Julia, if I tell you something, you have to promise me you'll never, ever say anything to anyone about it."

The smile fades from her face, and besides the crackle of the fire, everything else is silent.

"Never mind. That was dramatic. I think I'm just stressed about Nash."

"No, Leah. What were you going to say? You can't drop a pinky swear moment like that and then say, *never mind.*"

I take a deep breath and begin. "When I was a freshman in college, I got pregnant."

"Hang on."

She walks away from the fire and disappears into the house. A few minutes later, she returns—flask in hand and pours liquor into our hot chocolate.

"Spiced rum?"

"Absolutely. I never leave home without it, and this is too big for non-alcoholic hot chocolate. Continue."

I tell Julia how Ethan was the graduate assistant for my college business class and how we had fallen in love. But it was more than that. The love Ethan and I shared transcended the deepest parts of our souls. We couldn't even explain it, but we both understood it was rare, beautiful, and unique. And then I got pregnant. I explain how he didn't want to have the baby and ultimately convinced me we shouldn't keep it, so he took me to the clinic.

"He dropped you off?"

"Yes."

"Like, so he could go park the car?"

"No. He left me in the parking lot. He said we were done, that he was sorry, and it was over. Two days later, when I came back from Little Rock, he was gone. He left Arkansas, and I never saw him again. But I never told him I didn't go through with the abortion. The doctor at the clinic, Dr. Clive Stewart, said he'd help me find an adoption agency. That spring, I had a little boy, and I named him Spencer."

"Did your grandparents know?"

"No. Uncle Jack did, and I made him swear never to tell them. He drove me to the hospital when I had Spencer, and he took care of me after."

Julia is on mug number three when I explain the details about Clive and how he was one of the top-rated OB-GYN doctors in Dallas but did contract work at a clinic in Little Rock.

"I agreed to a closed adoption, and after Spencer was born, Clive told me the agency would handle everything. I never thought I'd ever see or hear from them again—until," I stop.

"Until what, Leah?"

"In Dallas—" I start again, the knot in my throat tightening.

I tell Julia about seeing Clive.

"Did he recognize you?"

"Not at the christening, but he did that night."

"This is unreal," she says.

"There's more, Julia. There was a boy at Mass with Clive. His eyes were so familiar, and he reminded me—" I stop again, tears starting to rise.

Julia puts her hand on my shoulder. "I can't imagine. I mean, naturally, he would, Leah."

"And it's the craziest thing, right? After all these years. So, I shrugged it off and assumed I was insane. But that night at dinner, I was leaving and bumped into this boy again. Clive ran up to us and called him by his name."

I take a deep breath, recalling that night. The silence engulfs us both before Julia's voice breaks through.

"What name, Leah?"

"Spencer," I whisper.

"No," Julia gasps.

"I mean, his eyes are exactly like Ethan's, and his face turns red like mine. Clive and I were standing there, and he was terrified. He was frantic, and I realized there had to be more, so I pressed him, and he confirmed what I thought. He adopted my son."

"That son of a bitch."

"But it's worse, Julia."

"It can't be any worse."

Through tears, I tell her about seeing Ethan and how he was Greg's business attorney. She's in disbelief. Hanging onto every word, eyes wide, mug number four half empty.

"So not only was Clive at dinner but Ethan as well."

"Ho-ly shit," Julia says quietly.

"I know. And the next morning, when I was getting my dress altered, Ethan showed up."

"What?"

"Yeah."

"Why?"

"He was getting a tuxedo brochure for his brother. Kate suggested the night before that since Allison and Thad didn't have a ring bearer, Ethan's younger brother could do it. I thought it was weird, and Allison did, too, but you know how Kate is."

"Awful nice of her."

"Exactly. But when I walked out to his car," I continue, the tears rolling down my face. "Sitting in Ethan's car—" I try again.

"What, Leah?"

"Spencer," I sob. "Spencer was in Ethan's car."

Julia leans back in the chair, crosses her arms, and stares at me. For several minutes neither of us say anything as the tears fall hard.

"So, Ethan's brother is really his son?"

"Yes. I mean, it's his stepbrother. Ethan said his mom married Clive eight years ago, so it would've been after Spencer was born. And Clive told me that his first wife died, but I never thought—"

"I mean, how could you? And you never told Clive who Spencer's biological dad was?"

"No."

Julia takes my mug, pours the last bit of spiced rum, and tops it off with more hot chocolate. She leans over and wraps one arm around my shoulder as I lay my head against her and cry harder.

"So," Julia whispers. "Are we kidnapping him? Is that what this conversation is about? We're kidnapping your son, right? I mean, I'm in. I just wanted to make sure we are on the same page."

"Julia!"

"Listen, I know people. We can pull this off, and no one would know. It's like rescuing a dog from a bad owner. So easy," she jokes.

"No, we are not kidnapping him."

"Okay, well—I'm just saying we have options, and my family has a place in Mexico."

"I appreciate the offer," I say, wiping my eyes.

"That's why you called me from the confessional. You weren't on drugs or hallucinating."

"I told you that."

"I know, but with you, you never know. Who doesn't cover their drink when they go out?"

"You're right."

"So, what are you going to do about this situation, Leah?"

"I'm not sure," I reply, thinking about the messages Ethan and I have exchanged since Dallas.

"Clive gave me his number and said I could call him if I had questions."

"Have you called him?"

"No. I mean, I sent him a panicked text message after seeing Spencer in Ethan's car, but I never called him. I'm not sure what I would say."

"Maybe start with the truth. Tell him about Ethan."

As Julia and I drive back to our cabin, I consider her suggestion. I pull Clive's card from my purse and place it on the nightstand, hoping I'll know what to do after some rest.

We collapse in our twin beds, the effects of the spiced rum running through my body, but I am relieved my secret is out.

"Julia?"

"Yeah?"

"Thanks for letting me tell you that. It means a lot."

"All the things."

I smile. "All the things."

## 11

JULIA STAYS one more night at Sugar Creek before she gives up, packs her stuff, and goes back to Louisville.

"Tell your grandparents I had a great time."

"You want me to lie to them?"

"No. I did have a good time, but I'm just not a camper, Leah. You know this," she says, taking a bite of a donut.

"I'm actually surprised you stayed as long as you did. Are those Damien's donuts?"

"Am I just supposed to starve on the plane, Leah? It's not like I had a ton of options."

I smile. "They're so good."

"Freaking delicious. Let me know how things go with Clive. I'm proud of you for calling him. It's a big step, and that matters. Remember what I said. Just be honest, and everything will be fine. Call if you need anything."

"I will."

My flight to Dallas leaves early the following day, and with two days until Thanksgiving, the small Arkansas airport is packed. After my talk with Julia, I texted Clive, and he's agreed to meet me, but first, I'm having lunch with

Allison after she insists she needs to talk about the wedding. I wonder if she's going to drop a bombshell and tell me she and Thad are calling off the engagement—not that I want that to happen, but it'd be nice for life to dump all over Allison for once. However, when she and Kate arrive, the news is not a called-off engagement but rather a bridesmaid brawl.

"Andrea's new boyfriend is Vanessa's ex-boyfriend," she explains. "And Vanessa just found out and left the group chat."

"Oh, I saw that," Kate responds.

I scroll through my texts to find the group chat Kate and Allison are talking about—but nothing.

"There's a group chat?"

"Oh, it's like our Dallas ladies' group. Nothing wedding-related, really. I mean, we do talk about some stuff, but it's nothing you'd be interested in, Leah," Allison says, rolling her eyes.

She's probably right but being left out of the group chat bothers me. I hate the idea of them. It's the new snotty, girl lunch table. Exclusive to only certain people, and when drama ensues, someone is forced to eat by themselves or removed from the group chat—or in my case, not included, to begin with.

As Allison explains more, I figure out that Vanessa, pink bridesmaid dress, is angry at Andrea, green bridesmaid dress, for dating her ex-boyfriend—whom she dated a year before. According to Allison, the two had been at the spa when the ex-boyfriend showed up, and the drama that followed was "ugly." I envision Vanessa and Andrea throwing hot towels, eye masks, and body wraps at each other but refraining from pulling hair. Extensions are a last resort for socialite fights because hand-sewn wefts will most definitely hurt like hell being yanked out. While Kate and Allison discuss the travesty of the unspoken rule of dating exes, I wonder what life would be like if I only had to worry about who my friends were dating and what days worked best for my spa retreats.

"I'll be right back," Kate says, pulling into the country club. "Greg forgot his golf glove."

"No worries. I need to check something out in the chapel, anyway, so we'll go with you," Allison says.

As we enter the dining area, Greg is having lunch at a small table. I don't recognize the man sitting next to him, cutting into a well-done steak, but Ethan is seated across from him. His blue polo hugs his muscular biceps and matches his eyes perfectly, which are locked on mine. It has been almost a week since Ethan's text—the one I still haven't responded to—but the intensity in his eyes makes me wonder if the drunken text was actually a sober confession.

"What are you ladies up to today?" Greg asks.

"We're on our way to lunch," Kate replies, handing Greg his glove.

"Lifesaver. Thanks, babe."

"What would you do without me?"

"I'd die a lonely man," he jokes.

"Leah, you remember Ethan?" Kate asks.

"I do. Nice to see you again."

"Nice to see you."

"And this is Robert, one of Greg's business partners."

I give a small wave noticing Robert's hands full. "It's nice to meet you," I nod.

"And you," he bellows, wiping his mouth.

"We're going to the chapel, so we'll leave you to solve the world's problems," Kate winks.

Ethan shifts uncomfortably in his seat, still burning a

hole through me when my phone rings. As Nash's name appears on the screen, I excuse myself to the terrace to take his call.

"Just meet us over there," Allison whispers, walking out of the dining room with Kate.

"Hello?"

"Hey, babe," Nash says.

"Hi."

"What are you up to?"

"I'm in Dallas."

"I thought you were in Missouri."

"I was but—" I pause. I can't tell Nash why I'm actually in Dallas, so I lie.

"I came to see Allison for some wedding stuff."

It wasn't a total lie—just not entirely the truth.

"Oh, okay. I miss you, Leah."

After our last conversation and Nash's abrupt departure, his revelation throws me. "You do?"

"Of course, I do. I miss us. And I'm getting my shit together, but I want you to know that I love you, and I miss you. I miss us."

I pace the terrace, unsure how to take Nash's sudden change, but wonder if the whole 'give him space' thing is working. Maybe Nash has finally realized that he wants a life with me, and time away was what he needed.

"I can't wait to see you when I get back," he adds.

"We need to talk, Nash," I say, glancing into the dining area at Ethan's table.

"I know, and we will."

"Like in person without distractions."

"I agree," he says, and I think he means it as I walk closer to the terrace door.

Greg and Robert have left the table, but Ethan is still

there and has turned his chair toward the terrace as he stares at me.

"Oh, hey, before I go. Some guys in the office talked about going camping at Buck Island this weekend, and I was telling them about your place. How many acres is Sugar?"

Still staring at Ethan, I barely hear Nash's question. And as Ethan gets up from the table and starts walking toward me, my heart begins to race.

"It's ten miles. Like 6400 acres, I think. Nash, I gotta go. Allison needs me. I'll call you later," I say, hanging up as Ethan stands in front of me.

"So, your phone does work?"

"It does. Where are the other two?"

"They went ahead. I'll catch up. Why haven't you texted back?"

"Ethan, don't. I have to go."

"Have dinner with me. Leah, please. I'd like to catch up."

"Just like that, huh? We just go to dinner and pretend—" but I stop.

"Pretend what?"

"Nothing. I gotta go, Ethan."

"Meet me tomorrow. I'll text you an address."

Later that night, Ethan's proposition consumes me as Kate and I snack on a charcuterie tray. At the same time, Allison combs through her online wedding registry, scrolling through items already purchased. Her sprawling Highland Park home she shares with Thad has more china and kitchen appliances than I've ever seen before, but I'm not surprised that someone who already has so much registered for more.

"Kate, someone bought the Tiffany flute glasses," she chirps.

"The flute glasses that Thad said you couldn't register for?" Kate giggles, raising an eyebrow.

"Well, what else are we supposed to drink champagne out of?" she scoffs.

"Leah, did you buy those for Allison? Now that Uncle Jack made you a millionaire and everything," Kate quips.

"Really, Kate? We're going to talk about that again after the spectacle you made at his funeral?"

"You know I'm joking with you. Allie and I are both happy you inherited that place. We told you that. I mean, it wasn't a surprise. Everyone knew you were his favorite."

I take a long sip of wine and count backward from ten. It's a trick the therapist said to use with Nash when I felt like cussing him out. It sometimes worked, and with my grip tightening on my wine glass, I figure it won't hurt to try it with Kate. After her explosive outburst at the reading of Uncle Jack's Will, Grandpa demanded an apology and ordered the entire family to respect Uncle Jack's wishes.

"Kate, Uncle Jack, and I had a special bond because my mom died. It wasn't because I was his favorite. My mom died, so try to remember that. You and Allie had the same opportunity as I did to spend time at Sugar Creek, but you chose not to. And honestly, I'd give it all back; the money, Sugar Creek, all of it if it meant he was still alive. Can you say the same?"

"Leah, she was kidding. You don't have to get so defensive about it," Allison sneers.

"Just because Allie and I didn't love that place doesn't mean we didn't deserve his inheritance, too. We were just as much his family as you were, and it's not our fault your mom died, but somehow we always get punished for it."

"You're right, Kate. You and Allison have such terrible lives and grew up so horribly punished. Have you ever thought for one second that he was looking out for both of you? He didn't want to burden you with Sugar Creek because he knew you wouldn't want the responsibility, so he left you money instead. And don't talk about my mom like that. You and Allie have no idea what that was like, and you've certainly never been punished for it."

"Don't act like a victim. All I'm saying is we loved Uncle Jack, too, Leah. And your mom. It's silly for you to think otherwise."

But, I don't believe her, and as I down my wine and snuggle in to Allison's 3000 thread count bed sheets, I note two things. First, Kate and Allison are more selfish than I can even comprehend, and second, Nash doesn't have any office friends that camp.

## 12

THE FOLLOWING MORNING, I meet Clive for brunch at a local cafe. With nervous energy, I have accidentally arrived fifteen minutes early. I am never early, and there is a reason. Most of the time, it's because I can't find anything to wear, or the humidity has turned my hair into an untamed lion. But this morning with Clive is different. My hair is fine and my outfit, too, but I've given myself too much time, and I realize the longer I sit in the car, the more my anxiety is increasing. I have worked out parts of the conversation over the past two days, but as I rehearse my lines, none of it's making any sense. I am stumbling over explanations and running through excuses before I realize it all sounds like garbage. As I walk in, I order a mimosa hoping the alcohol will bring some truth to the conversation, but twenty minutes in, the liquid courage is nowhere to be found.

I listen to Clive explain that a representative from the adoption agency was waiting for him outside my room seconds after Spencer was born to tell him the adoptive parents had filed for divorce and backed out of the adoption. It infuriates me.

"Why didn't you tell me?"

"Leah, you were too emotional and upset to handle that news at the time. I didn't think it was in your best interest."

"That's a great professional opinion," I snap, glaring at him. "He was my son. I had a right to know."

"It's a choice I've always thought about. But if I had it to do all over again—" he pauses and looks down at his breakfast wrap. "I'd make the same decision."

My anger intensifies, and as I stare at him, the memories of Spencer's birth comes flooding back.

I was hysterical. After a scheduled appointment of being induced, I assumed things would go smoothly, but after twelve hours in labor, I was exhausted, scared, and alone. As agreed, Clive took Spencer out of the room minutes after he was born, and as much as they prepared me for that moment—the silence in the room was overwhelming.

"You weren't looking out for me because if you were, you would've told me the truth. I trusted you."

"Leah, I did what I thought was best for you and Spencer. I gave him a life he deserved with a family who has loved him unconditionally from the second he was born."

"And you think I don't love him unconditionally? Do you think I haven't thought about him every single day?"

"No, I'm not saying that. But what if I had told you the truth? Would you have taken him and raised him?"

His question startles me. I wasn't prepared to raise Spencer, and as Uncle Jack and I drove home from Little Rock after Spencer was born, the selfish relief I had knowing my life could continue despite my poor choices of getting pregnant was still something I hadn't forgiven myself for. As much as I want to think I would've raised Spencer, I realize the answer is no.

"It's hard to say. Maybe I would've, but you took that choice away from me," I fume.

"And I've thought about that since you first walked into the clinic, which is something I need to talk to you about."

Clive takes a drink of water before explaining the main reason he is there. After his wife died when Spencer was a year old, a colleague referred him to a grief counselor at St. Vincent's. He met Ethan's mom, but she didn't know about Clive's side gig as an abortion doctor.

"I stopped working at the clinic when Susana and I started dating. It would crush her if she knew that. Do you understand what I'm saying?"

"You want me to keep it quiet."

"Yes, Leah. I know that's a lot to ask, considering."

We are two flawed humans asking for trust in a world where it barely exists. Secrets are the worst. The heaviness of carrying around my own for the past ten years is suffocating, but holding onto Clive's, too, is a responsibility I don't want. I wish he hadn't told me, but he did, and his truth is out—unlike mine.

"I'll keep it quiet, but—" I stop as a young girl approaches our table.

"Dr. Stewart, I'm sorry to interrupt, but Mrs. Stewart said you'd be here. I was on my way to take Spencer to get his tux measurements, but my brother just had a car wreck, and I have to go to the hospital."

"Oh, Ashley! Is he okay?"

"Yes, I think just some scratches, but his car is totaled."

"Go, sweetheart. I'll take Spencer. It's fine."

"Okay, I'm sorry. I would've taken him home, but Mrs. Stewart already left for Waco."

"No worries, Ashley. Go check on your brother and text

me when you have an update. Also, tell your parents if they need anything to let me know."

"I will. Thanks," she says, rushing out.

"Who's that?" I ask.

"Babysitter. Sweet girl," Clive remarks, leaving money on the table as we walk out.

"What about Waco?"

"There's an unbelievable farmer's market. She goes every year before Thanksgiving. She makes the best apple pie. Farm fresh. It's Spencer's favorite."

I smile, thinking about my obsession with Nana's apple pie, and I'm pleased that my fair skin isn't the only thing I've passed on to my son.

"Do you want to meet us there? I could probably use some help with the tuxedo stuff anyway," Clive suggests.

I should decline, but I'm in uncharted territory. I didn't rehearse this part of our conversation, and the hideous yellow dress *is* ready for me to pick up. So those two reasons are enough. Also, I don't trust Clive to pick out the right pants for Spencer. A man of his age probably hasn't worn tuxedo pants in thirty years.

"Sure," I tell him.

On the way to the bridal boutique, I call Julia.

"How's it going? Did you tell him?"

"Not exactly. I'm on my way to help him get Spencer fitted for his tux."

"Tell me you're lying."

"I'm not lying."

"I mean, you really know how to blow a plan. This isn't a damn family reunion, Leah."

"It wasn't the right time, Julia."

"It'll never be the right time. That's why these things are hard, but they still have to be done."

"I know," I sigh. "I'll call you later."

I hang up as I pull into the boutique. The wedding cake smell hits me as I enter, and I inform the sales associate that I need to pick up my dress, just as Clive and Spencer walk in. She directs me to the back to try on the dress for a final time, and a few moments later, I can hear Clive and Spencer in the room across from me. The sales associate asks Spencer if the tuxedo pants are too tight, and as she goes back out to the sales floor, I pop out. He is standing on the platform, trying to button his tuxedo shirt. I observe him for a few seconds as he struggles to get the small buttons in between the tight holes.

"Want some help?"

He glances up at me in the mirror and furrows his eyebrows.

"No, I got it," he says, but he is still struggling. He works each button until he gets down to the last one and then realizes that he's missed one in the middle. A small smile spreads across my face wondering what he will do next. Unbutton the shirt and redo it or leave it the way it is. In a matter of seconds, he realizes his mistake and starts unbuttoning the shirt to fix it.

"You look like Belle," he says, working the buttons again.

"Belle?"

"*Beauty and The Beast*," he says, checking the mirror each time he finishes a button.

"Oh, Belle," I laugh. "Yeah, I guess I kinda do."

He finishes the last button; all aligned the second time; he looks proudly in the mirror. I push back the emotions and force a half-smile. It's incredible how small feats seem so beautiful seeing them for the first time.

"Is *Beauty and The Beast* your favorite?"

"No, I like *Star Wars*."

"*Star Wars?*"

"Yeah, my brother lets me watch it with him," he explains.

My heart drops remembering Ethan's obsession with the George Lucas films. He'd seen all of them multiple times; he had them practically memorized. It was the first movie we watched together.

"How's everything going back here?" Clive asks.

"Spencer, do you remember her?"

"Kinda," Spencer says, tugging at his pants.

"You ran into her at Mr. Greg's house, remember?"

"Oh yeah," Spencer laughs.

"I think this shirt works for him," I say, trying to be helpful.

"Oh, good. Spence, go try these pants on, and then we'll go."

Spencer jumps off the platform, does a weird shuffle, and runs back to his dressing room as I walk into mine. There's a strange calmness as I watch a part of my life—a part that I had worried about for ten years—try on pants and button his own shirt. He is healthy and beautiful and can light candles in a church and jump off platforms. He has likes and watches movies, and most of all, he seems to be okay. I had done what I thought was best for Spencer, and as I watch him bounce around the fitting room, I am thankful that I didn't ruin his life.

As I walk out, the sales associate is adjusting the length of his pants when I notice the t-shirt he is wearing—a Chicago Cubs t-shirt. It has to be a joke. There is no chance I could've produced a child that liked the one team every Cardinal fan hated. On second thought, maybe I have ruined his life.

"The Cubs?" I ask.

He glances down at his shirt and smiles. "They're my favorite."

I have failed. Somehow, against all odds, I have given birth to a Cubs fan. It was undoubtedly a form of punishment for all the wrong I've done in my life.

"Do you like them?" Spencer asks.

"I'm a Cardinal fan," I answer.

"They're okay," he says, shrugging.

"We're not sure where his love for the Cubs came from, but he does like them. He loves baseball, and he's got a great arm," Clive says.

"Oh yeah? Maybe you can show me sometime?" I suggest.

Spencer smiles and does a fake wind up in the mirror, giving his best pitcher face.

"I bet he'd love that," Clive adds.

We walk out of the boutique, and Spencer jumps in the car while Clive walks over to mine.

"I'm glad you reached out, and we had a chance to talk today."

"Me, too," I say. "Thank you for letting me spend some time with him."

"Of course, Leah. I'm not going to pretend to know the emotions you're feeling or the pain you've endured, but I will tell you this. You'll always be Spencer's mom. You got him through the most crucial part of life, and don't ever think what you did wasn't brave."

Brave—it's a word that doesn't describe me. If he knew what secret I was keeping, he wouldn't think the same. As I wave goodbye, Clive agrees to follow up with me, and I figure the time will give me space to process my emotions from our meeting.

I have a missed text from Ethan as I drive back to Allison's. He'd sent me the address and time for dinner, but after the morning with Clive and Spencer, I'm not sure I can handle an evening with Ethan. That, and I can't get the image of Ethan and Spencer cuddled on a couch watching *Star Wars* out of my head. I pull into Allison's, thankful no one is home, and grab a bottle of wine from their built-in wine cooler. The guest bedroom is fully equipped with a large soaking tub, so I draw the blinds, light some candles, and jump in, hoping the lavender bath bombs and wine will give me clarity as it does in the movies. But it's hard not to think about Spencer. As the bubbles build around me, I wonder what my life would've looked like if I had kept him. Would I have finished college and been able to provide him with a good life? I wouldn't have let him become a Cubs fan, but could I have given him a life he deserved? And how would he have fared without a dad? I obviously had my own issues without mine, but I always felt loved by my mom and others. Could I have given the same to Spencer? As I take a sip of wine, an ugly thought creeps in. What if I resented him for being the thing that broke Ethan and me up? Or worse—what if Spencer resented me for having him when I knew his dad wouldn't be around? Working at Hazelwood, I knew plenty of kids who resented their own parents for less, and I couldn't imagine carrying that weight around.

I have enough guilt as it is for lying about it all. I can't imagine adding Spencer's hypothetical resentment, too. But there's a curiosity that's building as I sit in the hot water. I want to know if Ethan has regrets. He said he was an idiot but did that mean he regretted his decision? I wasn't able to come clean with Clive, but maybe I can with Ethan. As I finish my wine, I decide to find out, and I send him a text back confirming our dinner plans. But not to reconnect. I hope it looks more like closure, and if the meeting with Clive has taught me anything, it's that some things are better left in the past, and that's exactly where I need to leave Ethan.

## 13

As my senior year ended and summer officially began, Sugar Creek had never been busier. I had registered to take a summer college class after my counselor suggested the idea. With my two college classes in high school, the summer class—intro to business—would put me almost a semester ahead of everyone else.

The night before my first class, I had spent all day on the creek, helping floaters, campers, and canoers become acquainted with the property. Uncle Jack had hired me as the guest relations manager, and that night, I had worked almost thirteen hours. I fell into bed sunburned and exhausted and forgot to set my alarm. The next morning, I woke up late, the campfire smell heavy in my hair as I looped my ponytail into a top knot. I raced to change into something decent and sped down all the backroads I knew as I crossed the Missouri-Arkansas border. The student lot was mostly empty as I pulled in at 8:55AM, ran into the gray building, and up three flights of stairs, barely making it with two minutes to spare. The lecture room was U-shaped with three rows of tables. I glanced at the second and third rows, but both were full, so I found a seat in the front and settled in. Dr. Early walked in after me, coffee in hand, leaning heavily on one crutch. His mustache was scraggly and unkempt, and he dressed more like a guy on vacation than he did a business professor. He greeted us as he put his book and coffee on the small brown table at the front of the room. Then, using the crutch to sit down, he took out a handful of papers and tipped his black-rimmed glasses to the front of his nose. I took out my spiral notebook just as the door opened again.

"Good morning, Ethan," Dr. Early said.

"Morning, Dr. Early."

Ethan Erickson was Dr. Early's graduate assistant and the hottest guy I had ever seen. His icy blue eyes stood out against his early summer tan, and his light facial stubble made him appear older than he was.

"I heard he's related to Brad Pitt," a girl behind me whispered.

"Are you serious?" The girl next to her asked.

"Yep. Total hottie."

I could see it. The boyish good looks, the eyes, the scruff; there was a resemblance, and I couldn't take my eyes off him.

Dr. Early explained that Ethan, who had just finished his MBA, would be teaching our class after an unexpected surgery prohibited the elderly professor from being able to teach full time.

"So, really, he's doing me a favor," Dr. Early told us. "In eight weeks, this ol' thing will be good as new," he added, patting his heavily braced knee.

"Does Mr. Erickson have office hours?" The girl behind me asked, her voice breathy and annoying. "I just didn't see them listed here."

*Slut*, I thought, shaking my head. But I waited anxiously to hear the answer.

"Ethan will have the same office hours as me," Dr. Early replied. "He's basically me. I just have to be here, so they give me a paycheck." I took out my highlighter and traced over Dr. Early's office hours as he continued with the syllabus.

"And I wanted to add this," he announced. "Ethan comes to us from the University of Texas where he just received the award for Outstanding Master's Thesis/Report in the subject of Business. So hell, he's probably more qualified than I am to teach this class. It's a distinguished award."

I clapped. I didn't mean to clap, but I figured everyone was going to clap. It was impressive, and the standard protocol was to clap. But no one else was clapping—just me. The whole room was silent, but Ethan was staring right at me. My cheeks were burning as I grabbed my syllabus, trying to avert his gaze.

"So embarrassing," the slutty girl behind me mocked. She was right, though; I was mortified.

Twenty minutes later, hoping to leave with a bit of dignity still intact, Dr. Early asked everyone to write down their lowest grade from their last semester of high school and give it to Ethan. He explained we would use the results for the next class. I panicked, thinking about the 'D' I had received last semester in math. Most of the time, I was a straight-A student, but my high school math teacher was another matter. I quickly scribbled down the 'D,' realizing that lying on the first day of college was foolish and Dr. Early had access to my transcripts, but I did write down that I had some *focus issues* in class that attributed to my low grade.

My math teacher was also our handsome football coach

who wore jeans on Fridays. It wasn't fair since those were our quiz days, and it was distracting. One cannot simply change from track pants four days a week into tight Levi's and expect high quiz scores.

Everyone was walking down to the small brown table to hand Ethan their slips of paper. The two boys in front of me both gave Ethan theirs, which both read "A." Flustered, I folded the small paper as many times as I could until it resembled a spit wad and handed it to him, but my fingers got stuck on the hand off, and I wound up dropping the paper on the floor. I squatted down to pick it up and apologized, but not before realizing I was eye level with his crotch. I should've stood up immediately, handed Ethan the paper, and left, but I didn't. Instead, I lingered in a crouching position, my nose almost touching the zipper of his jeans for an uncomfortable number of seconds before finally realizing the awkwardness. I shot up and handed the paper back to Ethan, who was smiling and laughing at my nervousness.

"Sorry."

"No worries," Ethan replied. "What's your name?"

"Leah."

"Ethan," he said, holding his hand out to shake mine. "It's nice to meet you, Leah."

I shook his hand, the overwhelming heat in my face taking over. I had to get out of there. "It's nice to meet you too. I'll see you tomorrow."

"Wednesday," he corrected.

"What?"

"Wednesday. You'll see me Wednesday. That's how college works, Leah," he said with a wink.

"Right. Wednesday, sorry." It took me walking past four

classrooms and two flights of stairs before I could breathe again.

The following two classes were filled with lectures and doodling on my class notes while staring at Ethan drawing a generic business model on the whiteboard. His slanted, small, all-caps writing fit perfectly around the arrows he was drawing from one section to the next. I tried to copy his font on my notes, making a heart out of the "O's" in each word I wrote. But that following Wednesday, things would take a dramatic turn.

As I walked out of class, I had a million things on my mind. I needed to clean four cabins at the creek. I needed to help Uncle Jack repair two canoes. I needed to eat. My mind was anywhere but in class, and when I got to the parking lot, I realized I had left my textbook. The classroom was empty as I walked in, except for my book lying on the table. The front cover was open. But when I started to close it, I spotted the purple post-it on the inside cover. The blank post-it was in my book when I bought it, and I had since doodled all over it while Ethan had been lecturing. Squiggly lines, a softball, a heart, a peace sign, my last name, and the words "Ethan is hot" traced repeatedly. Next to those words, in slanted, small, all caps writing was, "So is Leah. Room 617." My heart was pounding as I read it again and again as Ethan walked back into the room. I closed the book immediately, but it was too late.

"You left your book."

"I know, sorry. I realized after I got to my car."

He inched closer and said, "I'm glad you came back for it."

With his six-foot frame towering over me, his eyes were searching mine as he waited for my response. I couldn't speak, and as much as I had probably fantasized about having a moment with him, I needed him to know I was not *that* girl.

"Listen, Ethan. I think you are handsome. Not to mention that long sleeve raggedy-red shirt you had on the other day with jeans about made me die. But I can't just show up to your room and have sex with you. Just hooking up on the off chance, you'll give me an 'A' for the class. That's not something I want to do."

"That's good information, Leah," he smiled. "Also, room 617 isn't where I live. It's the tutoring lab. I wrote it down because your quiz score from today was pretty low, and I thought you might want some additional help."

I wanted to die, and my tomato-red face was impossible to hide. I couldn't breathe.

"I'll work on not wearing raggedy clothes anymore, as long as you work on your face turning bright red. It's really endearing. Think about the lab, okay?" He said, leaving the room.

I left class and walked over to the registrar, determined to drop the class, quit college, and never talk to another guy again, but somewhere between the business building and the registrar's office, I remembered it was too late to drop without a financial penalty.

The following few classes were painfully uncomfortable, and I did my best to hide until I got back my second quiz and failed miserably—again. The two guys sitting next to me got perfect scores, and I even overheard the slutty girl behind me brag about only missing two points. However, I had missed seven out of the ten questions. I groaned, knowing my GPA was slipping each time Ethan lit up with his gorgeous smile. I crumpled the piece of paper, jammed it in my backpack, and slumped out. Through the weekend, I tried to figure out how I would save my grade, and by

Monday, I'd decided to picture Ethan toothless and fat and focus only on passing. It didn't work, and by the end of class, I was daydreaming about us in bed for the fortieth time.

But over the next two weeks and two trips to the tutoring lab, I had turned a corner and raised my grade to a B-. So, I needed to celebrate. One of my best friends from high school was getting ready to leave for college, and we wanted to send her off properly before we all went our separate ways.

We had planned parts of the night for a few weeks. We were going to end our last summer together with a party and memories we'd never forget. But with zero party houses available, we agreed to meet at Roadside Park, a small rest area ten miles down the road from Sugar Creek. What should have been a small group of girls multiplied as ten of us turned into thirty, then forty before I lost count. With copious amounts of alcohol, we sat in lawn chairs and on tailgates talking about high school and promising each other we would always stay close, and that's when I smelled it—someone had brought pot.

I followed the smell to a group sitting around a picnic table where some were already high. Red eyes and deep conversations were occurring when I joined my friend, Bailey, and took a long hit off the bong. A few guys were discussing conspiracy theories and how our government had too much power. As the circle of people encouraged the guys to enter politics, the bong made its way around a few more times, and before I realized it, I was stoned.

At 5AM, hungover and smelling of pot, I pulled into Sugar Creek. Taking the keys to my cabin, I fell onto the twin bed, hoping to sleep off the night. An hour later, Uncle Jack was standing over me.

"Leah!"

I opened one eye. "Yeah?"

"Need your help today," he said.

"It's my day off," I whined.

"I know, but it's going to be a busy one," he said sharply.

"But—" I started.

"Now, Leah. Get up. And wash that dope off you," he said, slamming the door.

There were two times in my life that I let Uncle Jack down; that was the first.

I took the fastest shower of my life and made my way down to the canoe rentals. Out of all the jobs at Sugar Creek, renting canoes was the worst. Uncle Jack understood that, and I had a feeling he'd assigned the task on purpose. It was exhausting work. The experienced canoers would typically lift their own off the racks, but the first fifteen rentals were all first-timers, as karma would have it.

I lifted the first canoe, my body exhausted from the night before, and by the third, fourth, fifth, and sixth, my back and arms were burning with pain, and my head was throbbing. I had stopped twice to run behind the building and throw up before being called back by Uncle Jack. In the middle of handing off my fifteenth canoe, I heard a familiar voice.

"Leah?" Ethan asked. "What're you doing here?"

"You know this chick, bro?" One of Ethan's friends asked. "She's a hottie."

I tried to laugh off the remark, but it was slimy and offensive. "My family owns this place," I said. "I work here."

"Whoa," Ethan said. "That's awesome!"

"Get her number later, E," another friend of his chimed in. "Can you get us our stuff? We're kinda in a hurry."

I forced my best customer service smile. "Five canoes, coming up."

"Here, I'll help you," Ethan said, walking with me to the racks.

Ethan helped me take the first one off. "Are y'all here just for the day?"

"No, we've rented a couple of cabins. We're going to stay the night and head home tomorrow."

"E! Let's go, man," his slimy friend called, cracking open a beer. Ethan smiled and put on his black sunglasses, which somehow made him hotter than he already was.

"Y'all have fun today and be careful," I said, watching them walk away carrying their canoes over their heads.

I had tried to avoid Uncle Jack all morning, but by lunch, I needed some food if I was going to make it through the day. So I left the canoe rentals with Damien, hopped on the ATV, and headed to my grandparents' house. The kitchen was empty, but Nana had left out some turkey and cheese for sandwiches. Scarfing it down with two Tylenol and ice water, the food was delicious. The sun had already started to burn my arms, and I made a mental note to reapply sunscreen before going out again just as Uncle Jack and Grandpa walked in. Their faces were stern, which told me a lecture was coming, and I was angry that Uncle Jack had brought in a reinforcement.

As Grandpa sat down next to me, Uncle Jack made a sandwich, and I knew what was coming. "Leah," Grandpa started.

"I know," I said, "And I'm sorry. I really am. We don't have to talk about it. I know I messed up."

"Life is about messing up. This isn't your first time, and it won't be your last, but what you did last night wasn't just stupid; it was dangerous."

"I know. I'm sorry."

"No, you don't know! Dammit, Leah, you could've died last night!" Uncle Jack shouted.

"Jack," Grandpa warned.

"Well, she could've, Pops. So, stop babying her and tell her like it is. You of all people should know better, Leah."

"That's enough, Jack."

Uncle Jack took his sandwich and walked outside, slamming the screen door. The knot in my throat grew bigger, and I could feel the tears build.

"He's scared, Cricket. He made a promise to your mother before she died that he'd take care of you. He told her he'd always protect you. We both did. She never wanted you to have the life your dad has, and she trusted us with the responsibility to not let that happen. You can't be messing with that stuff. Addiction, Cricket—" he paused. His face hardened, and I believed for a minute he was going to cry, "It ruins lives, and your mother recognized that, and I'll be damned if we're going to let her down. She deserves better, and so do you. Things aren't always what they seem, even if you think they're harmless."

As the tears rolled down my face, I knew he was right. My mom and I had countless conversations about the dangers of drugs and the dead-end outcomes. I could only imagine what she would've thought about my wild night, and as much trouble as I was in, I wished she was at the table ranting about my stupid decisions.

"Finish your lunch and then get back to work. And Leah, understand that every decision you make affects the people who love you the most."

With a full belly and enough guilt to last a lifetime, I relieved Damien as the day canoers checked in their boats. The last part of my shift consisted of checking cabins and ensuring the campers had everything they needed. As I made my rounds and offered reminders of quiet hours and campfire protocols, Ethan's cabins were the last two, but they weren't there when I arrived.

"Are you looking for those boys?" A dark-haired woman at the next cabin appeared as a small, blonde toddler ran around at her heels.

"Yes. Well, I was just checking to see if they needed anything. Are y'all okay? Do you need anything?"

"We're good. But those boys seem rowdy. Hollerin' and yellin'. They drove off down the road like there was no speed limit," she said with a shrug.

"Thanks for letting me know. If it gets out of hand, don't hesitate to call. Our number is in the cabin."

"Thanks, sweetheart," she said, picking up the young girl and walking inside.

By the next morning, the woman's concerns had turned into real life.

"Leah! We have a problem," Uncle Jack said.

After taking stock of Ethan's cabins, it was clear that the $25 security deposit would not cover all the damages.

"Do you know who stayed here last night?" He ran his hand along a significant hole in the wall.

"I do. I'll handle it."

I searched the creek for Ethan, hoping the walk would cool me off. Finally, after fifteen long minutes, I spotted him and his boys across a low water bridge, setting up their canoes.

"What the hell?" I screamed. "You trashed the cabins and put holes in the walls! What's the matter with you?"

All of Ethan's friends laughed. "Uh oh," the slimy one said, "you're in trouble with your lady."

"Do you even know how much this is going to cost my family? Or do you care? You're a bunch of entitled brats who don't give a shit about other people's property. You're disgusting. All of you," I yelled, glaring at Ethan.

He sighed. "Leah, I'm sorry. Things got out of hand. I tried to find you this morning, but I didn't know where you were."

Ethan's slimy friend burst into laughter. "Those cabins can't be that expensive. I'll have my dad send a check. $100 should cover it, right?"

Ethan turned to him. "Shut up, Colin."

"Classy friends, Ethan," I said, fuming. "Keep your money and go turn in your canoes. You're not welcome here anymore."

"Leah!" Ethan shouted, but I was already gone.

I worked tirelessly through the day, trying to rearrange guests who expected to stay in the wrecked cabins. Uncle Jack said we'd deal with them after the holiday because we didn't have time to fix them before the Fourth of July crowd. But two days later, on the eve of the holiday, a gift basket arrived with a note written in small, slanted, all caps writing: "I'm sorry. The cabins are fixed. Please call me—Ethan."

I jumped on the ATV and floored it to the ransacked cabins. The holes were patched with hardly any evidence of damage, and Ethan had replaced both air conditioning units.

"Gotta hand it to him," Uncle Jack said, standing in the doorway.

"Did you know about this?"

"I'm not sure I would've been as dedicated. I think he might like you."

"When did he do this?"

"He came to me that night with tools, and he worked until it was done."

"Where is he now?"

"I sent him home," Uncle Jack said.

"I should call him," I said.

"Give it a day or two. Let him think about it a little longer. He made it right, but don't rush just because he did the honorable thing. A man who truly cares for you will wait no matter how long it takes."

As the Fourth of July celebration rang out across Sugar Creek, the Saturday fireworks spectacular was always a favorite, and that year didn't disappoint. On Sunday, I determined I had waited long enough and called Ethan—a day sooner than Uncle Jack had recommended.

"Let me take you out," he said.

"You've done enough."

"Please, Leah, it's the least I can do."

We made arrangements to meet up the following evening.

"So, where are we going?" I asked.

"I know a little spot," Ethan said.

We pulled up to the bar, and Ethan escorted me inside. A few small booths hugged the exposed brick walls, and ten barstools were packed in tight at the counter. Local beers were the highlight, but the historical photos, Arkansas memorabilia, and small tube TV made the place feel like home. It was charming, a forgotten gem that the locals took care of, and the vibe was chill as soon as I walked in.

"You are not twenty-one," said the husky voice behind the counter.

"Barry, she's with me. She'll be fine," Ethan said, putting his hand on the small of my back.

"How do you know this girl, Ethan?"

"She's in one of my classes."

"Well, she's underage in my bar. Get her out of here."

"I'm going to take her to a booth, and you can bring us

some of that famous goulash," Ethan said. "She won't drink anything. She'll just be enjoying your fabulous food."

Barry scowled, mumbled something under his breath, and with a sigh, he disappeared in the back. Ethan grabbed my hand as I followed him to an empty booth. He waited for me to go first and stood as I took my seat.

"Goulash?" I winced.

"If you want to stay here right now, you're going to have to eat some," he said smiling. "There is nothing that pleases him more than when people eat his food. So, how's class going?"

"Really? You're going to ask me about class?"

Ethan laughed. "Yeah, it seems like your grade has come up the last few weeks, and I was hoping my new teaching style helped."

"You mean the unattractive, monotone lecture you give each class or your too small, slanty, all caps writing that no one can see on the board?"

"My lectures are monotone and unattractive?"

I laughed as Barry came by with waters for us, still glaring at me for being in his bar.

"Does your family hate me?"

"My uncle took down the wanted poster, but there's still a lifetime ban in place."

"Damn," Ethan groaned, rubbing his hand through his hair. "I guess I deserve that."

"You guess?"

"You're right. I was an asshole."

"Yes, you were."

"That place is unbelievable. It's really cool that you grew up there."

"I think so, too. It's kind of a shame that you're banned. The hiking trails and bluff are a sight to see."

"You like rubbing this in, don't you?"

I smiled. "I do."

"I am really sorry. I never should've let those guys get out of control like that."

"I know you are. But I think it meant a lot to my family that you fixed the cabins."

"Your uncle's a great guy."

"He is," I said.

"I bet he'd let me see that bluff." Ethan winked and took a drink of his water.

"Don't push it."

"So, tell me about yourself."

My mind went blank. What could I tell him about myself that would be remotely interesting? That my dad was in jail? That my mom passed away? That the list of my high school boyfriends consisted of one? That I was suddenly terrible at business and his examples on the board were only beneficial for the everlasting debate in my head of whether he's a boxer briefs or boxers guy? That I was crazy attracted to him? None of those things were appropriate conversation starters.

"I don't like goulash," I said, staring at the chunky noodles in front of us.

"I'm not surprised at that. You don't strike me as a goulash girl."

"Oh, really? And what do I strike you as?"

He paused, chewing carefully. "You strike me as a girl who loves her family and cares deeply about things. Someone who would do anything to protect the people most important in her life. And as far as I can tell," he said, leaning across the table, "I've never met anyone quite like you."

My heart was doing somersaults in my chest. There was

a comfort about Ethan that I'd never experienced before. Like I had known him in another life. There was something deep in his soul that penetrated mine. A connection I couldn't describe, yet it existed between us. But instead of admitting that, I panicked and changed the subject. "What about you, Ethan? What are you doing in Arkansas?"

He smiled and sat back in the booth.

"I'm taking a gap year until I figure out if law school is right for me."

"You want to go to law school?" I asked, shoveling goulash noodles from one side of the bowl to the other.

"I don't know. But that's why I'm here. To figure some stuff out."

"So, you're having like a quarter-life crisis?"

He nearly spit his goulash out.

"I mean, I get it. The stress at your age is probably massive," I joked.

"Massive," he laughed, taking a drink of water. "So, tell me about Sugar Creek. Do you like working there?"

"I do. I think people are fascinating, and I love seeing how relationships exist between them. Every year, the creek brings an interesting crowd, but I've learned valuable things from being around people who don't think like me. Some of the best conversations I've ever had have been around a campfire with someone who sees life differently, and I think that's important. People have different attitudes at Sugar Creek. They're relaxed, and the atmosphere provides an escape that I've experienced myself. There's something peaceful—almost spiritual—about it, and I love when people discover that, too. I believe we all have purpose and a reason we're here, and while I don't have it all figured out yet, I think my purpose might be to help people somehow because I hate to see others suffer. I hate social classes and when people are taken advantage of. I'm trusting, probably to a fault, but I feel like giving everything to someone is the best way to live."

I should've stopped there, but I didn't.

"I love the idea of falling in love and spending nights staring at the stars and talking about life. I'm a giver, and I'll go out of my way to see someone else happy. And I love this. Sitting in this booth with you in this empty bar talking— and feeling whatever the hell this moment is with you."

He didn't say anything, but somewhere in my rant, Ethan grabbed my hand, and he was stroking the top of my knuckles with his thumb. Then, he leaned down, never taking his eyes off mine, and kissed my hand.

"You're beautiful, Leah. Unlike anyone I've ever known. There's something about you I can't get out of my head. And I don't want to."

His hand slipped up to my wrist just as Barry came by to check on our goulash. Our hands retracted, but I locked away that moment for the rest of my life. If I never experienced anything else, that night would've been enough.

"You better like my goulash," Barry threatened.

"We're actually gonna take it to go, Barry."

"Good, get her out of here," he said.

"We're leaving?"

"I wanna show you something."

He held my hand as Barry packed up our goulash. Ethan thanked him, patted him on the back, led me to the bar's back entrance and up a very narrow flight of stairs.

"The fire escape?"

"You'll see," Ethan smiled.

We reached the rooftop as the warm Arkansas air hit our faces.

Ethan grabbed my hand, "Look up." Above us, the dark sky was littered with a million stars.

"It's beautiful."

"It sure is," Ethan said as he stroked my face. "We have that in common—the stars. My dad used to take me fishing at night. It was one of his favorite things to look at. The way the stars lit up the night."

"Was?"

"Before he died," Ethan responded, his words burying themselves deep into my heart.

"I know the feeling," I mumbled.

"What?"

"My mom. She passed away three years ago."

And in the silence, we were two people peeling back the layers of unimaginable loss.

"My dad passed away when I was in middle school, but when you said that tonight, about the stars, it reminded me of something he said."

I turned toward him, noticing the tiny freckle on his lower lip was even sexier up close.

"What did he say?"

"Fall in love with the girl who looks at stars. That's what he told me. If a girl can love something as simple as the stars, imagine how she'll love you."

I grabbed Ethan's hand as we both stood on the rooftop, staring across the dark Arkansas night.

"I'm glad I'm here with you, Leah."

"Me too."

And a second later, Ethan's lips were on mine. It was sudden but welcomed; I opened my mouth, and the kiss deepened. As much as I wasn't *that* girl, I went to Ethan's apartment that night and made love on the first date. We spent the last few weeks of summer stargazing on the roof of the bar, and even though I'd banned him for life from Sugar Creek, I gave in. We made love in the cabin he destroyed— and fixed— and watched the sunset on the bluff.

When the fall semester started, there wasn't a day we weren't together. And as our connection deepened, I had fallen in love with him. We went to Barry's bar on Tuesday nights after Ethan discovered a deck of Uno cards and challenged me to a game. The first night we played, he lost four times, and every Tuesday after, he kept score on a bar napkin. He was terrible at the game, and I took pleasure beating him over and over. But it was in those moments playing Uno, stargazing, and sitting around a campfire that my love for Ethan grew into something neither of us could explain. We were two halves that just fit together. No one ever saw me the way Ethan saw me.

At Ethan's encouragement, I had taken a job at a local youth shelter as Sugar Creek hit its slow season. I told him stories about kids from broken homes and kids coming in with addictions, and we shared our own experiences with the loss of a parent and how devastating it was to always feel like a part of us was missing. Our relationship flourished, but it was more than sex; we had fallen in love without even trying. We celebrated the good days, tried harder on the bad, and weren't afraid to love each other despite our flaws. He was swimming beside me and became my best friend, and I couldn't imagine life before I met him.

But by late October, something was off. Nauseated and dizzy, I figured I was coming down with a cold. I stayed home from school for a few days, throwing up too often in the mornings and completely exhausted at night. Ethan checked on me every day, but I wasn't getting any better, so I went to the doctor. The on-campus health center was stuffy and filled with feverish students and runny noses. As the nurse took my height and weight, she began asking me routine questions. What were my symptoms? When was my last period? That's when it hit me. *When was my last period?* I thought. Ethan and I had been careful to use condoms, but my last period had been in August.

"Are you pregnant?" The nurse asked.

"No," I answered.

"Well, let's take a urine sample just to be sure," she instructed, handing me a cup.

Ten minutes later, she came back into the room with the words that would change my life forever.

"You're pregnant. Twelve weeks to be exact."

Ethan met me at my apartment, and I could barely get the words out before I was puking and crying over the toilet. But it was Ethan's reaction that shocked me the most.

"I need to think about this, Leah."

"Ethan—"

"I'm sorry. I just need to think."

The next few days were some of the most painful of my life. I skipped several classes, consumed with fear. Phone calls and texts to Ethan went unanswered, and the silence was starting to take a toll. So when I finally got a call from him a week later, I was relieved.

"Where have you been?"

"I've been figuring things out. Can I come over?"

I agreed, and ten minutes later, he was sitting on my couch.

"Leah, I'm not ready for kids. And honestly, you aren't either. It would ruin both our lives, and I think you know that." The rest of his speech was scattered with half-truths and selfish statements that didn't make any sense. The first words were all I needed to hear anyway—Ethan did not want our baby—and that admission said everything. I had grown up with a single parent most of my life, and I didn't want that for my own child. After crying, fighting, and begging Ethan to change his mind, termination was the only thing he wanted.

The drive to Little Rock was tense. Neither of us spoke for the first hour. Being in my second trimester, finding a clinic was near impossible in Arkansas. The deep red state had closed most clinics except a few, and I was lucky to find one that would accept me. As we checked into the hotel, my mood plummeted when I realized he purchased two rooms.

"Really?" I asked after he handed me a key.

"I thought it would be better."

Ethan walked into his room, four down from me, without saying a word. I was heartbroken, and more than that, his refusal to sleep in the same room was offensive. I didn't get pregnant on my own, but he had treated me like a disease since he found out. It was disgusting, and inside my own room, I fell on the bed, completely demoralized. I tried to sleep, but at 10PM, I knocked on Ethan's door.

"Can I come in?"

His boxer briefs hung low on his hips, and his bare chest still had a faint glow of summer. I crawled into bed with him as my mind raced through every moment we had spent together. Ethan wrapped his arms around me, and I buried my head against his chest, crying hard, knowing the next morning, my life would never be the same. We held each other for a few hours, but I couldn't sleep. Somewhere in the middle of the night, I tried to talk to Ethan one more time.

"Are you still up?" I asked.

"Yes."

"What are you thinking about?" He was silent, but I knew."Ethan, we don't—" I started.

"Stop, Leah. Just stop. I can't be a parent, and neither can you. We're too young. We have our own dreams. We've talked about this, and a kid would just get in the way of that. For both of us. It would ruin everything we want in life."

He was out of bed and pacing in front of me, his jaw tight and lips pressed together.

"Go back to your room. I'll see you in the morning."

"But—"

"Go!" He demanded.

The next morning, neither of us said a word in the car. We pulled into a parking spot, and Ethan handed me an envelope. Inside was some money and a one-way bus ticket back to Fayetteville.

"What the hell is this?"

"You have the hotel for two nights, and there's a bus ticket in the envelope."

"Ethan—" I started, noticing his duffle bag in the backseat.

"Stop. Don't. I can't handle this, Leah. I'm sorry, I just can't!"

"So, you're just going to leave me here? You're not coming in? You're making me do this alone?"

"I'm sorry."

"I can't do this by myself, Ethan!"

"Leah, I'm sorry."

"I am, too. I'm sorry I ever met you. I'm sorry I ever fell in love with you. Here's this," I said, throwing a sonogram picture at Ethan, "I thought you'd at least want to know what you destroyed! I hate you, Ethan! I fucking hate you!"

Tears rolled down my face as I slammed the car door shut, sobbing in the parking lot. Ethan hesitated for a minute before pulling back onto the main road, leaving me alone in front of the clinic.

A few pro-life protesters stood between the parking lot

and the door holding signs, crosses, and shouting obscenities to the women who entered. As if my guilt wasn't horrible enough, their harassment disgusted me. Luckily, the protesters had surrounded a young girl and her mother, so I managed to sneak in with just one woman who handed me a pamphlet and told me I had *choices*, but her condescending tone said otherwise.

After checking in, I was escorted to a waiting room with three other women. It was silent. Stillness quiet, where nothing moves, not even air. The woman sitting next to me was wearing a gray t-shirt and cream-colored pajama pants. The t-shirt had a hole just under her arm, and I could see her white bra through it. Her hair was wild on top of her head, and she tapped her leg nervously as we waited. The older woman sitting across from me was with her husband. Their gold wedding bands were weathered and dull on their fingers. With a visible baby bump and hollowed-out brown eyes, she stared straight ahead as her husband gripped her hand tightly. I wondered what their stories were. How had they come to this place and this decision? There was an unspoken understanding in that small room. None of us said it, but we were all thinking it. What was about to happen would alter our lives forever. We'd be judged and ridiculed, called names and labeled, and we'd join a list of shamed women whose reasons would never be good enough for a judgmental society. It was sickening and unfair.

"Leah McKinney?" A petite nurse called as she glanced at her clipboard.

I didn't make it to the scale to check my height and weight before the tears started again. The nurse, Jessica, put her arm around my shoulder, comforting me.

"Hey, it's okay. This is hard. We'll talk about all of it," she said, leading me into an exam room. She asked standard questions about my pregnancy, health, and family history of diseases before doing a quick ultrasound—making sure to turn the screen away from me. She gave me another squeeze and said the doctor would be in shortly. The next ten minutes were excruciating. Alone in the room, I tried to think about anything other than terminating my pregnancy, but it was impossible. With tears rolling down my cheeks, the doctor opened the door. He was wearing a red and blue striped surgeon's cap, but his face was friendly, and his eyes were bright.

"Leah is it?" He asked. "I'm Dr. Stewart. It's nice to meet you."

"Hi," I said quietly.

Dr. Stewart and I talked for a few minutes, and my anxiety started to lower. He was personable, caring, and incredibly nice. He took my hand and told me he understood how hard the decision had to have been for me and that I didn't owe anyone an explanation for why I was at the clinic.

"The choices you make in life should always be yours, Leah. Of course, judgments will come, and opinions will always be shared, but if we all lived our lives concerned about the thoughts of others, we'd live a terrible existence. This choice you've made is undoubtedly hard, but it's your choice."

As Clive left the room, I considered his words. It was *my* choice, and I had a right to decide what was best for me. Ethan had taken control of the situation from the minute I told him, and out of fear of losing him, I went along with his choice. But he'd left me in a parking lot, and he was no longer in my life. As the seconds ticked by, I wasn't going to let a selfish man make a decision that I hadn't fully processed.

"Alright, hon," Jessica said, entering the room. "Why don't you lay back. We're going to do some labs. You'll feel a little pinch in three, two—"

"Stop!" I yelled.

"What's wrong?"

"Get Dr. Stewart, please."

Jessica retreated, and a minute later, he appeared.

"It is *my* choice, and I don't know what I'm going to do, but I don't want this. I'm having this baby."

## 14

I WALK into the dimly lit restaurant and spot Ethan nursing a dark whiskey at a small table. After the failed attempt to come clean with Clive, I need to be honest with Ethan. I have forgiven him for abandoning me, I think, and our lives can move forward in different directions. Or at least that's what I'm telling myself as I walk toward him. What happened in the past is over. It's time to move on.

"You look incredible," he says.

"Thanks," I reply.

The Italian restaurant has an authentic vibe with elegant crown molding, curved archways, and thick wooden tables. It's a first date kind of place and browsing the room, most tables have fancy couples laughing over bottles of wine.

"Can I get you a drink, ma'am?" A handsome, clean-shaven waiter asks.

"No thanks, water is fine."

"You sure?" Ethan asks. "You don't want a glass of wine or something?"

"No, I'm good. Thanks."

As the waiter walks away, I regret not ordering the wine,

but even one glass will lead to emotions I do not want to feel. I need to stay in control. I need to have a sober mind, and with our history, I'm not taking any chances.

"How are you?" He asks.

"I'm fine," I reply cheerfully. "How are you?"

The question is weird—all of it is, and shortly after sitting down, I am disappointed that I agreed to meet with him. Our past is too complicated for casual conversation, and I realize this instantly, but it doesn't seem to phase Ethan. He runs through the events of his day like we have been friends for thirty years and the ease he has of pushing the obvious topic to the side upsets me. I glance down at my phone and consider texting Julia for a fake emergency phone call just as Ethan starts to explain his business relationship with Greg and how he didn't realize the connection between Kate and me.

"My wife and I—" he stops.

"It's okay, Ethan. Go on."

"Anyway, we moved up from Austin a year ago for my job. We got acquainted with Greg through St. Vincent's, and he's been one of my clients for the past three months."

"You're Catholic?"

"Yes."

"You've always been Catholic?"

"Yes. Not always practicing," he shrugs.

"Oh," I mumble.

"I don't tend to make personal relationships with my clients, but I've gotten to know Greg through St. Vincent's and Kate, too. She seems," he pauses, trying to find the words.

"Aggressive? Annoying? Bitchy?"

He laughs. "I wasn't going to say that, but you were always a good judge of character."

"Well, I was wrong about you," I snap. It's an unfiltered reaction. I take a drink of water, trying to play it off as a casual statement, but judging by Ethan's callous stare, he doesn't think it's so casual.

"I didn't mean—" I start.

"It's fine, Leah."

The waiter brings over an appetizer of stuffed mushrooms, and I hope the distraction will reset the evening. As Ethan picks up three and puts them on his plate, the conversation does reset—to me.

"So, you're a principal?"

"I am. How did you know?"

"I googled you."

"That's sketchy."

Ethan shrugs and takes a bite of his mushroom. "And that guy you were with at the party?"

"He's my fiancé."

"You're not wearing a ring."

"Not that it's your business, but it's getting sized." I wasn't about to tell Ethan that Nash proposed without a ring.

"Greg said he's a jackass. He said he went golfing with him, and he was running his mouth the whole time."

"No, he wasn't, and I doubt Greg said that. Nash is competitive, and it's rude of you to even say that without knowing him."

"You're right, Leah. I'm sorry. If you're happy, that's all that matters."

"Why am I here, Ethan?"

He lets out a long exhale and says, "I can't stop thinking about you."

There it is. A confession ten years too late. In my head, I'm fantasizing about Ethan, Spencer, and I sitting on the couch watching *Star Wars* and planning family vacations. It wasn't like he said he wanted to marry me, but I still can't stop the thoughts from pouring out. My cheeks are burning as I grab my water. "Why?" I ask.

"Partly because your face is doing that thing."

"What thing?"

"You're blushing, Leah."

The red-faced curse. A DNA defect that targeted people and ruined their lives. My mom used to tell me to pretend it wasn't happening. Of course, it never worked, but I tried it anyway.

"I'm not blushing. What's your other reason?"

"There are things between us—"

"Ethan, don't."

"That I've never had with anyone else," he finishes.

I move my uneaten mushroom from one side of the plate to the other and beg his words not to reach my heart.

"Things worked out the way they were supposed to."

"You don't believe that."

"Yes, I do. Ethan, you're married, and I'm engaged. Even being here is probably inappropriate considering our past. But that's exactly what we are—two people who existed in the past. We are different now. And sitting here trying to pretend that it's anything more is ridiculous. We've both moved on."

I said it, and as I finish, I expect some joyful release. Like an Olympic stadium all chanting "USA! USA!" I look around for people wanting my autograph for setting a boundary with Ethan, but all I see are couples in love having dinner and making memories together.

"Leah, I understand that, but you don't think what we had was different from anything you've ever experienced?"

"I think our experience was beneficial for where we were

in our lives at that time," I respond, copying a line verbatim from my therapist.

"Bullshit," Ethan groans.

"Really? I like how you presume to know me. We haven't spoken in ten years, Ethan. I'll be more than happy to go into detail about why that is if you'd like me to."

"You're right. I'll stop." But it's too late. His words are already painting our bedroom walls and negotiating Netflix nights. I want to bring up Spencer and the clinic, but I can't. If he knew what I'd done, this moment would be over, and why am I even concerned about that? Who cares if I break the news that Ethan's brother is really our son? It would serve him right to know the truth after what he put me through. But somewhere deep down, I can't bring myself to tell him. I wish so badly that I was an asshole without feelings and could hurt people the way they deserved—but I'm not. So instead, I glance at my watch.

"Do you need to go?" He asks.

"Yeah, it's getting late, and I have an early flight."

As we head toward the door, a beautiful blonde woman stops Ethan. "I thought that was you," she says, giving him a quick hug. Then, her gaze shifts to me as she waits for an introduction.

"Kristen, this is a friend of mine," he says, but his voice is taut. He doesn't give her my name, and his use of the word 'friend' twists my insides. She fakes a smile, and I can sense her suspicion all over me.

"I'll meet you outside," I say, smiling politely and excusing myself. A few minutes later, Ethan meets me at my car.

"Who was that?"

"A friend of ours."

"*Ours?*"

"She's Piper's friend."

"Is that going to be a problem?"

"No. It's fine," he answers, reaching in his car and pulling out a cigar.

"Do you mind?" He asks.

"You smoke?"

"Occasionally. I feel like tonight is one of those exceptions."

I roll my eyes. "No, I don't mind."

"Here, follow me," he says.

Across the parking lot is a vacant strip mall, and we take a seat on a bench outside an abandoned gelato store. As Ethan puffs on his cigar, I run through our entire conversation again in my head.

"Is this weird?" He asks.

"What?"

"Sitting here. Us."

"No."

"It feels—" he pauses.

"Normal," I say.

"Comfortable."

I nod and know exactly what he means. My connection with him had always been deeper than anything I'd ever experienced before. As we sit on the bench, I search for anger, but my heart has turned into a puddle, and I'm pissed at myself for allowing Ethan's words to waltz back into my heart like they belong there. So, I try to hide what I'm really feeling. "It is comfortable, but I've sat on lots of benches with other people and felt the same."

"Oh, have you now?"

"Yes."

"Look up," he instructs.

"What?"

He moves a piece of hair away from my face. "Look up, Leah." Above, the stars illuminate the sky, and even ten years later, somehow Ethan has turned a regular night into magic. *Why isn't there a single cloud when you need one?* He puts his arm around my shoulder and pulls me close.

"Do you remember?" He asks. "Fall in love with the girl who looks at stars. I never stopped loving you, Leah. Not once. I should've never married Piper, and if I could do it all over again, I'd do everything differently."

I pull away from him. "What did you say?"

"I never should've left you at that clinic. The fact I took you there haunts me, Leah. It really does. I'm so sorry. We could've made it work."

I lose it. Ethan's confession of love is one thing, but his confession about a do-over is too much.

"It haunts *you*? *We* could've made it work? Are you kidding me? You're a selfish asshole! I tried to make it work, Ethan! You walked away. No—you drove like hell away from me and didn't look back."

"Stop, Leah. That's low, and you know that's not what I meant."

"No, Ethan, low is dropping your pregnant girlfriend off at an abortion clinic and giving her bus fare to get home. Never checking on her again. Never asking if she was okay or needed anything. And then showing up ten years later, professing your love and telling her if you could do it all over again, you would. That's low."

"But I do love you."

"Bullshit. Don't ever contact me again. Forget you ever knew me!" I yell as I start to walk away. "And Ethan, remember this, what you did to me was unforgivable, but somehow in all these years, I've managed to love you *still* and forgive you despite what you did. That's love. The kind that sees your flaws and still shows up for you. The rarest kind you'll ever find. You'll spend the rest of your life uncomfortable on a bench with someone always looking for what we had. And I want you to understand something. You had a chance, and you threw it all away. This is your screw-up, Ethan, not mine. I hope no one ever treats you the way you treated me."

## 15

I HAVE seven unanswered texts and three missed calls from Ethan as I arrive back in Louisville a day after Thanksgiving —but I delete all of them. We are over, there isn't going to be any closure, and as hard as that is to deal with, I have to let it go. I am done reliving the past with everyone—Ethan, Clive, and Spencer. They are three pieces of a puzzle that don't fit any longer. Clive is taking care of Spencer, Ethan is married, and I'm with Nash. Our lives are running at different speeds, and there isn't any reason to intersect them.

I walk into our apartment as soft music plays from the Bluetooth speaker. A vase of two dozen red roses sits next to a card and a glass of wine on the counter. The aroma of lasagna fills the room as I search around for Nash. In the bedroom, he is buttoning a black shirt.

"You made dinner?" I ask, wrapping my hands around his waist.

"God, I missed you," he moans.

Nash's lips meet mine, and as the kiss deepens, his tongue is in my mouth. My thighs tighten as his hands tangle in my hair. Our breathing increases and I can't recall the last time Nash has been so eager to touch me. His unbuttoned pants hang low on his hips, and as I move my hands down his chest, he shivers with goosebumps, but my hands don't stop there—and this time, he has no problem being ready. We fall onto the bed, and I pull Nash's shirt off as he quickly removes my pants.

"What about dinner?" I laugh.

Nash smiles as his lips travel down past my navel. As we find our release together—twice—I am thankful for how valuable taking time apart is for a relationship. And after the events with Clive and Ethan, reconnecting with Nash is exactly what I need. We all have baggage, but at least I know Nash's baggage, and the familiarity of that is something I can count on. As we sit by candlelight, eating heaping amounts of lasagna and drinking wine, it feels like our relationship has taken a turn—but this time for the better. It's been a long time since the two of us had an intimate dinner at home and his attention and desire toward me is comforting. We laugh about how food always tastes better after sex, and Nash swears it has to do with our zodiac signs.

"I'm telling you, it's because you're a Scorpio, and I'm a Libra. I read it in one of those men's magazines at the gym."

"I'm not sure that's the best source of information. I think it's more biological than the zodiac." I wink at Nash and take a bite of lasagna. "But sex or not, this lasagna is amazing, babe!"

"My mom's recipe," he says proudly.

"Thank you for making it and for the flowers. They're beautiful."

"I love you, Leah. I realize things have been rough, but this is what I want. A night like this eating lasagna with you sitting there in my t-shirt and sexy panties."

He smiles, his dimples lighting up both sides of his

cheeks, and I glance down at the extra-large Louisville Cardinal shirt I have on. Nash's shirts are worn and more comfortable than mine, but I love wearing them even if they come down to my knees.

"Your hair's a mess, you're sitting here barefoot with no make-up, and you're the most gorgeous woman I've ever seen."

"Nash."

"I'm serious. I was a jackass. Scared of committing because I didn't think someone could love me like you do. I'm sorry, Leah. I swear to you—I give you my word—that all I want in this life is you. I love you, babe."

There is relief in his words and a hope that had been missing in our counseling sessions. Finally, something has changed, and Nash is choosing our relationship as I've always wanted him to. We clean the kitchen and make love again that night and the following morning.

I realize there will be more low moments to come in our relationship, but with Nash fully committed, I have a partner, again, and someone to fight those battles with.

On Monday morning, I pull into work more energized than I have been the entire year. With three weeks before Christmas break, I am determined to motivate my teachers and students to finish the semester strong.

"Good morning," I say, sticking my head in Julia's office.

"Morning," Julia responds.

"Let's meet in ten minutes to talk about Dr. Bradley's email."

"In your office?" Julia asks.

"No, let's go to the conference room."

"It's full."

"What?"

"The conference room is being used. Let's just meet in your office."

"Who's in the—" I begin but overhear Trista Miller's shrill voice outside the office door.

As she walks in, I'm dreading whatever complaint has caused her to show up this morning. "Morning, Mrs. Miller," I say, squeezing out a smile as best I can.

"Oh! Good morning, Leah. I didn't think you'd be here this early," she says, taking her monogrammed thermos out of her bag. "Don't mind me. I'm just sneaking in to grab some coffee."

"What are you doing here this morning?" I ask.

Trista fills up her thermos as she explains she's helping Cammie O'Neal set up the conference room for a scheduled professional development course she is leading.

"As the parent liaison, I just wanted to make sure that everything was set up like she wanted," Trista says.

"That's not your job, Trista," I snap.

"Oh, honey, I know. But I was here anyway, dropping off Trev, and since a few of the district administrators were going to attend the PD, I figured Cammie might need some help. You understand."

But I don't understand, nor do I recall a scheduled PD in the conference room or the fact that Cammie O'Neal is leading it. "Well, let me know if y'all need anything," I say, cautiously walking toward my office.

Trista nods. "Sure will, hon."

At my desk, I take a sip of coffee and stare at Julia.

"Did you—"

"Yes."

"But you didn't—"

"It was in the email."

"The email?"

"Dr. Bradley sent last night. The one a principal is supposed to read."

"I thought we'd go over it today. Is she—"

Julia looks up from her laptop. "I'm not sure, Leah. But, if I have to guess, I bet Cammie checks her emails and puts things on a calendar."

I try to stay clear of the conference room most of the morning, but the temptation to see my job slipping through my fingers is too much. As I peer through the glass, Cammie and an administrator are engaged in a conversation. She is so annoying. Others in the room nod and exchange encouraging glances with each other as Cammie seems to be explaining something. As an instructional facilitator, it wasn't uncommon for Cammie O'Neal to lead professional development. Still, she is too comfortable in my school, and the rumors of her wanting my job are becoming a harsh reality.

I walk into Julia's office before lunch and lay down on her small loveseat.

"I charge by the minute, and I'm pretty expensive," Julia says.

"I couldn't afford you," I laugh.

"That's true, but I do want to know how you shit all over the plan in Dallas."

"Now, Julia? Really?"

"Spill it, Leah. What happened?"

I give Julia the most important bullet points from my meeting with Clive, even telling her he called me out for keeping Spencer and asking me not to reveal his side hustle to Susana.

"I get why he's lying to his wife. Not that it's right, but I understand. What I don't get is why you told him you might have kept Spencer."

"I know," I reply.

"I mean, you wouldn't have, right?"

"No, and even saying that makes me feel like a terrible person, but honestly, Julia, I couldn't have given him the life he has now. He's happy."

"So, I should cancel the stand-by kidnapper I hired?"

I laugh. "Yes. Talking to Clive and then spending time with Spencer—" I pause. "I made the right choice."

"I agree, but I still think there are things you need to do. Forgiving yourself for the choice you made is one thing, but letting go of the other stuff," Julia takes a deep breath, "If you don't tell everyone the truth, you'll never get past this. The guilt will be too much, and eventually, karma will make you pay. That's just the way life works."

"I know."

"I don't think you do, though. What about Ethan? How did that go?"

"Not well. I haven't spoken to him since I left. It was bad. I blocked him."

I start to tell Julia about Ethan's confession when her phone rings. A panicked sub needs help with a student.

"I'll handle it," I say to her. "We can talk about this later."

"Okay, but you owe me like $400 for this session. And you're welcome," she says as I leave the room.

In the music room, Jason, a junior football player, is slumped over in his seat with his hoodie pulled up over his head. Ms. Hughes, the substitute, is almost in tears trying to over-talk the situation. I pull Jason in the hallway, and after several minutes of attitude and cussing, the truth comes out —he's had a fight with his mom last night and left his house. After calling a few friends, he couldn't find a place to stay, so he walked around the city most of the night, finding temporary refuge at a restaurant before being kicked out after not ordering anything.

"So, you haven't slept?" I ask.

"No, Miss."

"And you haven't talked to your mom?"

"No."

Jason and I walk back to my office and call his mom, who agrees to come in later that afternoon. Unfortunately, between Julia's lecturing and Jason's disruption in class, I'd missed eating lunch.

"Jason, are you hungry?" I ask.

"Yeah, I mean, if you're going to order something."

"I'll call in a pizza. Is that okay?" He nods, and twenty minutes later, a large pepperoni pizza arrives. I've never seen a boy so happy in my life. I leave to get some soda from our office fridge, and by the time I get back, he has eaten five pieces, but given his almost six-foot frame, I let him finish the box. As we wait for his mom to show up, he explains that their fight was over getting fired from his job. With only his mom's income, Jason's job helped pay for utilities. It was understandable that she would be mad, and when she arrives, the conversation proves just that. The stress of the lost income got the best of her, but she never wanted him to leave. With bags under her own eyes, she confirms the sleepless night she's also had. I tell Jason I'll check into some jobs for him if he doesn't run away again. He agrees, and his mom checks him out, so they both can get some much-needed sleep.

It isn't heroic, but as Jason and his mom leave, I wonder if Cammie O'Neal would've made the same decision. My color-coding and organizing skills might not be on her level, but could she diffuse a panicked substitute while empathizing with a struggling student? Those moments are never rewarded and rarely even known in education, but they matter just as much if not more than curriculum, testing, and organizing skills. The love given in classrooms and school buildings allowed students to have bad days and still be treated with respect and dignity. Cammie can impress others with her fancy presentations, but if she seeks public praise, shout-outs, and glory, those moments will all happen behind closed doors between a mom and a son who go home to tackle another day.

Later that night, I pick up dinner and wait for Nash to come home. As I sit down to check through my emails, the lock screen pops up. I rarely used our shared desktop, and after two failed login attempts, I recall Nash leaving the password on a post-it in the desk drawer. As I open the drawer and retrieve the password, a website appears up on the screen. There are several other tabs open, too, but the page on the screen is a glamping resort in Montana. The 30,000-acre luxury resort is nestled just north of Missoula, and the nightly rates are double our rent payment. I click through the pictures admiring how beautiful the place is. Rustic cabins with state-of-the-art features, creekside tent rentals, and too many amenities to even name, but Nash and I haven't talked about taking a vacation. As I click through the other open tabs, there are more resorts, one in Utah and another in Tennessee, all open to the contact pages. Finally, the last tab I open is an airline page. The dates and flight locations are empty, but my heart starts racing. I can hear Nash's keys jingling in the door and quickly turn the screen off. He walks in and wraps his arms around me, planting a kiss on my lips, but I'm freaking out. The few times Nash and I had talked about marriage, I'd told him I never wanted him to do it publicly. A moment like that should be private, and I wanted it to be special. As Nash changes out of his work clothes, I sit on the bed and wonder if he is planning something big.

Two days pass, and I still haven't confronted Nash about the websites.

"I don't know, Julia; I just feel like he might be ready." I pace around her office as she searches for something. "I mean, why else would he be looking at those resorts?"

"Maybe Mika is an avid camper. She did sleep with that married principal and broke up his marriage. What was his name?"

"Mr. Tackett."

"Yes, and they got busted at his little side piece cottage in Lake Tahoe. Maybe Nash wants round two with Tackett's sloppy seconds."

"Why do you always have to be so critical?" I snap.

"I'm joking, Leah," she says, opening another drawer and slamming it closed.

"What are you looking for?"

"I can't find our first semester data."

"What?"

"I had it on my desk before we left for the weekend, and it's gone."

"Julia. We have to find it. We're presenting it at the board meeting next month."

"I know," she groans, walking out of her office.

A few minutes later, she is calling my name. Standing at the paper shredder with her hands on her hips, she stares at the recycle bin full of shredded files.

"You've gotta be kidding me."

"Nope," Julia says, pointing to the mass of shredded paper.

"It took us forever to get those data reports done," I say in complete disbelief.

"Yeah, they're gone."

"Who would've done this?"

"If I had to guess," Julia starts.

"Why would Miss Kay mess with those?"

"Why does she do anything, Leah?"

"Okay, this is not a crisis. We have time. We can reprint," I say, trying to stay positive.

"We can burn the school down now, you know, like an accident. We can stage a heroic escape out of the second-floor window. Not only will we be seen as hard-core administrators, but we'll probably be compensated time off for enduring some sort of trauma," Julia suggests.

"It's scary that you've thought that out, and we're not doing that. We're fixing this, and I'm making coffee," I say, settling in for what's sure to be a long week.

Later that day, I confront Miss Kay about the shredded files, but she denies being in Julia's office. I can't reprimand her without hard evidence, but Julia isn't budging on whom she suspects destroyed our work.

Thanks to our technology teacher, who quickly finds and categorizes the files on other drives, we have half the report finished by Wednesday. With two days to go until Christmas break, Julia and I are determined to have the completed files reprinted and locked away where Miss Kay can't find them.

"I'm going to Sugar Creek this weekend. Wanna come with me?"

Julia gives me an evil side-eye.

"But Damien's donuts," I add.

"They are literally the saving grace of that town. I told him if he moved here, he'd be a millionaire."

"Wait, what?"

Julia smiles.

"Hold on. You've been talking to Damien?"

"It's not a thing. Stop freaking out."

"Um, it is a thing. How long?"

"We've just talked a few times. He's nice. Stop making it a big deal."

"I'm a little hurt you've been keeping this from me."

"I'm not keeping anything from you. It's nothing. Seriously."

"Well, it sounds like something."

"It's not. He's funny, and I like talking to him. And he makes great donuts. That's all. Drop it."

"I think you're flustered, Julia. And very defensive about your non-status with Damien."

"You're so ridiculous," she says, getting up to refill her coffee.

"I'll make sure to bring back some donuts for you when I get back."

"Shut up, Leah."

By noon on Friday, Julia and I have reprinted and finished the first-semester reports—again—and secure them safely away in her closet. In celebration of our feat, she takes out a bottle of wine and fills our coffee cups.

"I don't want to know why you have alcohol at work, but I'm pretty sure that breaks every code as principals."

"Fire me," she jokes.

I smile and realize that I've somehow made it through my first semester as an administrator. There's definitely been a few rough patches, but our kids are safe and cared for, and our staff has fulfilled the challenge we set at the beginning of the year—build relationships and teach to every learner in their classrooms—and that's exactly what has happened. It's a huge accomplishment.

"To badass bitches," Julia says, holding her cup in the air.

"I'll cheers to that," I smirk.

"Well, this looks fun," Trista Miller says, appearing in the doorway.

I pull my cup away from Julia's like my mom had just caught me stealing liquor from the cabinet. My eyes dart to Trista and back at Julia, and then I catch sight of the wine bottle sitting directly on Julia's desk. We're busted.

"Mrs. Miller," I croak.

"Oh, don't y'all worry. I won't say anything. Half days of school don't count anyway," she winks. "I just wanted to stop in and wish y'all a Merry Christmas and drop off this flavored popcorn Trevor is selling for baseball. I'm not sure it goes well with wine, but ya never know," she giggles.

"Thank you, Trista," Julia says. "You can't have too many cans of flavored popcorn at Christmastime."

Trista laughs and talks a few more minutes about her holiday plans eyeing the wine bottle the entire time.

"Well, I'll let you two get back to your little celebration. Have a blessed holiday."

"You too," Julia and I say in unison.

I drop my head in my hands as Trista walks away.

"We're screwed."

"Oh, stop. She's not going to say anything," Julia scolds.

"There goes my job. I can hear it now. *Principals were drinking at school.* Julia, they'll use our school pictures as mugshots on TV."

"Good. Mine is fabulous."

"Julia."

"I'm kidding. Trista has a big mouth, but the dirt I have on her—it would ruin her reputation in a matter of seconds, and she knows that. So, she's not going to say anything. Trust me."

"I hope you're right," I mumble.

"I am. Seriously, she knows better than to do anything that stupid."

Julia and I finish our cups and vow to take our celebrations next semester to a proper bar. As we wrap up the afternoon, we check off a few more items on our to-do list and triple-check the first semester data is locked in Julia's office before leaving for break.

"Should I bring Damien back with me? Maybe the four of us could all hang out on New Year's. Maybe you'll get married before me. I'll ask him if that's his plan."

"Stop it. I never should've said anything to you."

"All the things, Jules."

"All the things."

## 16

Nᴀsʜ and I arrive at Sugar Creek, ready for a relaxing week-end. As we unpack, though, Nash is anxious. He's pacing around the cabin and checking his phone, barely making eye contact with me. It's strange and sending up too many signals that are making me nervous.

"Are you all right?" I ask.

"Yeah, I'm fine. I haven't been here since the funeral, and I was wondering if you want to go for a drive?"

"In the car?"

"I thought we could take the Gator. It'll be warmer, and we can take the trails."

"Yeah, we can do that."

We drive over to my grandparents, and the strangeness of Nash's request starts to grow larger. He never wants to drive around Sugar Creek, and I can't help but think his anxious behavior earlier and desire to explore the trails is something more. I glance down at my fingers, thankful I spent the money on a manicure the week before—just in case.

We hop in the heated cab and take off, stopping every so

often for Nash to get out and move some debris off the trail. Blasting country music and zigzagging our way through the narrow paths coming to the foot of the bluff, he turns the ignition off and smiles.

"You wanna go up?"

"It's freezing, Nash."

"It's not that cold, babe. Come on."

We hike to the top as the sun is starting to set, and I anticipate what is about to happen.

Uncle Jack and I had mapped out the perfect time of day and the best sunlight in all seasons for proposal pictures. The 4PM time slot was the coveted time in December.

As Nash snaps a few shots on his phone, I take in the view. The pinks and blues of the dusky sky are bleeding into orange under the fading sun and the peaceful presence of the bluff—there is nothing like it. No matter how many times I've been to the top, the beauty is still overwhelming. Nash comes up behind me and wraps his arms around my body. His black puffer coat melts into mine, and we are two marshmallows admiring the setting sun.

"It's beautiful," I whisper.

"It is," Nash responds. He kisses my cheek as a cold chill runs down my body.

"You're freezing, aren't you?"

I am freezing, but I can't tell him that and ruin the moment. If Nash is going to propose, I need to tough it out, even if I can't feel my toes.

"I'm okay," I answer.

"Babe, you're shivering. Let's go."

There's no feeling worse than a crushed expectation. Confused and annoyed, I walk back down the trail, trying to figure out why the perfect moment has just vanished. As we drive back to my grandparents, my confusion and annoyance are slipping into anger, and all through dinner, it continues to build until I can't take it any longer.

"Nash, today at the bluff—"

"Yeah?"

"It's a special place. And—" I stop. I don't know what to say next. *Why didn't you propose to me? What the hell was that about?*

"Babe?" Nash presses.

"I'm just saying, I want to spend my life with you. I love you. You know that, right?"

"I do. And I want to spend my life with you, too."

"Then why take me up there today if you weren't," I sigh.

"Babe, everyone you know has been proposed to up there. You deserve something that's your own. *Our* own. I took you up there because that view is incredible, and seeing it with you again means more to me than anything. I wish you could see your face when you're up there. I've never seen you so happy before."

"It makes me happy because I'm up there with you," I say.

Nash turns the car off and grabs my hand. "Leah, we're going to spend the rest of our lives together looking at sunsets on that bluff."

"But you hate it here," I whine.

"I don't hate it. I don't love it, but hate is too strong of a word. I think we can find a balance where you can take care of what your uncle left you, and we still have our lives in Louisville."

"Will we get married here?" I ask.

"Do I have a say?"

"Nash!"

"I'm kidding," he laughs. "I do think there are other places more our style, but if that's what you want."

He leans over and kisses me. "Come on. Let's go in."

The following day, Nana has reheated the leftovers as we sit down for lunch, but Nash gets a call from work midway through. He steps into the other room to take it. As Nana asks if I want seconds, I strain to hear Nash's conversation. He's agreed to do something, but I can't hear the rest. Finally, he steps back into the kitchen, and I realize something is wrong.

"You have to go?" I ask.

"I'm sorry. They need me back tomorrow morning. We've been working with this potential client. It's a huge opportunity."

"Oh, Nash, we understand," Nana says, giving him a sympathetic smile.

"I'm really sorry. I hate to miss Christmas with y'all."

"No worries. It happens," Nana says, but I'm more than worried. I'm fuming.

Nash and I drive back to pack his things as he fills me in on the rest.

"I didn't want to say it in front of your grandparents, but I have to go to London."

"What?" I shout.

"Leah, I'll be back before New Year's Eve. Please. I need you to understand how important this is for me."

My heart is racing and I'm trying hard not be reactive, but it's impossible. I knew there was a chance he'd have to go back to Louisville early, and we might not get to spend Christmas with my grandparents, but I am not expecting him to be out of the country on my favorite holiday.

"I just don't understand. Why London? On Christmas? It doesn't make sense," I argue, as Nash packs.

"Babe, please. I don't need this right now. I need you to understand that I have to go, and that has to be okay. I promise I'll be back by New Year's Eve, and we'll be together."

"I don't want to spend it alone, Nash. Why can't you go after Christmas?"

"Leah, it's one holiday. Please don't act like this right now."

"I'm not acting like anything! But you know how much Christmas means to me. It's our holiday, and you're just leaving me like it's nothing."

"Stop. Please. I'm going, and I'll be back in a week. I promise."

We don't speak as we drive to the airport. I know if I open my mouth, I will cuss him out or push him out of the car. His behavior has been strange and I'm fighting the tiny voice in my head telling me there's more to Nash's story.

"I love you, Leah. I'll see you next week," he says, kissing me on the cheek as he exits the car.

I'm somewhere between furious and heartbroken, and as he walks inside the airport, my emotions are spilling over as I call Julia.

"Nash left."

"What?"

"He left for a work thing in London."

"Shut up."

"London, Julia. He's going out of the damn country."

"Leah, that sounds weird as hell. Are you sure he's not lying?"

My stomach turns at her question.

"I don't know," I stammer. "Things were weird when we got here. He took me up to the bluff, and I seriously thought he would propose, and then we just left. I asked him about it later, but he gave an excuse and—" I pause. "I don't know, Jules. I'm just really upset."

The following evening, my foul mood is still in full effect. After dinner, Grandpa asks me to come upstairs to his office. As he takes a seat behind a faded wooden desk, he's rummaging through a stack of papers before pushing them to the side and staring at me.

"Sit down," he says.

I take a seat and start picking at my nail polish.

"What's wrong?" Grandpa asks.

"Nothing. I'm just upset about Nash leaving. It's okay."

Grandpa leans back in the chair, his brown flannel shirt showing signs of wear at the cuff.

"I'm an old man, Cricket. But here's what I know. I love your Nana, and I tell her every day. But I also rub her feet every night. Not because she asks me to, but because her arthritis is painful, and I don't want to see her in pain. I'd do anything not to hurt her. A man's word doesn't go as far as it used to, but I've come to realize that if you watch him long enough, you'll see the words he didn't say. And you always gotta watch out for that undertow. The surface may appear fine, but you can't see what's underneath."

"You hate Nash?"

"No. But if his words don't match his actions, then I think you've got a problem."

"You think he should've stayed?"

"I think if I had to choose between Nana and my job, there wouldn't be a choice. She means more to me than anything, and you deserve the same, Cricket."

"Thanks, Grandpa."

"We love you, kiddo. Don't forget that."

"I know. I love you, too."

I walk downstairs and hug Nana before getting in the car and seeing a missed call from Julia.

"So, he flew out yesterday?" She asks.

"Yeah."

"So, there's no reason he'd be posting something on social media with a geotag in Louisville, right?"

"Julia."

"Check for yourself, Leah."

I pull up the app on my phone, but I can't find it when I check Nash's profile.

"Try again," Julia instructs, but the same error message appears.

"Did that asshole block you?" Julia hisses. "Here, I'm sending you the screenshot."

A second later, I check the message that comes through with Nash's post and the geotag location listed in Louisville. My heart pounds in my chest.

"Leah, are you there?"

"I'm coming home," I tell her.

I've never packed so quickly in my life. With the late departure, I leave my grandparents a note on their porch and start my drive back to Kentucky. Julia and I talk for the first hour of the trip, and I listen to her devise a plan on catching Nash cheating. The adrenaline gets me through the next seven hours—that and the murderous anger soaring through my entire body. At 4AM on Christmas Day, I pull into our apartment, unsure what I'll see as I unlock the door, but the apartment is empty.

Julia shows up thirty minutes later with coffee and bagels. "I'm just confused," I tell her. "His suitcase is gone, and some of his clothes and stuff are missing. It doesn't make sense."

"Has he called you?"

"No. He sent a text earlier wishing me a Merry Christmas."

"Well, he's a dumbass, and there's no way he didn't leave a trail behind. So, there's gotta be something here."

"I don't know, Julia. What if we're wrong. What if I'm jumping to conclusions?"

"You're not."

Julia and I spend most of the day searching the apartment for any traces of Nash's infidelity, but there isn't any evidence. We pick through drawers and scavenge through both closets, but nothing. Nash has called twice, but I deny his calls, and as the day rolls into the evening, we are exhausted but not defeated.

Julia's FBI skills are on another level, and even though we've hit a few dead ends, she is determined Nash has left evidence behind. As we sit on the couch and plot plan B, we hear a faint ding coming from the couch. Julia glances down between the couch and end table to see Nash's iPad sandwiched between the two. The ding sounds again, and she picks it up as an iMessage lights up the screen. It's from an unknown number.

*I'm at your office. You here?*

Nash's response comes next, *Almost*

"Do you want me to come with you?" Julia asks.

"No, I can do this," I tell her.

"Are you sure? We could get drinks after?"

I shake my head. "I think I'm going to need something stronger than a drink when I'm done with him."

"Recreational drugs are not my thing, but as your friend, I'll support your choices."

I force a smile. "I'm not talking about drugs, Julia. I just need to end this."

"I know. Call if you need anything."

"I will."

Pulling up to Nash's office building, the dusky Louisville

sky barely shows any light. Two cars sit in the parking lot: Nash's and a blue Volkswagen Tiguan. I get out of my car and examine the SUV. A small present sits in the passenger seat with a name tag that reads Taylor, but the handwriting is Nash's. I take a step back from the car and weigh my options. If I slit her tires, I can finish quickly and leave, but if I take a crowbar to it, it might take longer, and the noise will be a factor. But the absence of a knife and crowbar results in despair as I kneel beside the car. Sitting on the cold ground, I realize this is the end of our relationship. Three years down the drain. I wipe a tear from my cheek and walk back to my car. Pulling out my phone, I snap a picture of their cars parked side by side and send a text Nash.

*Me: Since you're in London, I know you won't get this until the morning, but I'm done. I'm heading home to pack my stuff, and I'm leaving. I hope Taylor was worth it. Merry Christmas, you asshole!*

I speed out of the parking lot, the adrenaline coursing through my body as I wipe the tears away. I have tried more times than I ever should've, and Nash isn't getting another chance to make things right. Between the lying and leaving every second, I've given him all I had, and nothing has worked. Grandpa's words ring loud in my ears—*"if his actions don't match his words, there's a problem."* I've excused Nash's cheating once before, but a second time—we are done. As I reach the parking lot of our apartment, a text comes through from Nash.

*Nash: It's not what you think*
*Me: It never is Nash*

I grab my suitcase from the closet and start throwing clothes, makeup, and shoes in as fast as possible. My head is spinning, and before I know it, I'm in the kitchen grabbing food. I'm not sure what triggered the food. I know I'll stay at

Julia's until I figure things out, and she has food, but I still grab fruit snacks and crackers anyway. As I start to leave the kitchen, I spot our fridge magnet. In a second, I rip it off and throw it against the wall as the pieces shatter on the floor. Nash walks in seconds after.

"Leah, don't."

"I'm done, Nash. Once was an accident. More than that is inexcusable. I should be used to it by now."

Nash grimaces. "Leah, stop. Please."

"We are done."

"Don't say that. What's gotten into you?"

"You've been lying for months. That's what's gotten into me. You say you're in one place, but you're somewhere else. You said you were in London, and you weren't! You're doing stuff on the computer and looking at resorts and airfare. For what, Nash? Or maybe I should say with whom? Mika or Taylor? Or maybe there's more. I know there's someone else. Just be honest and tell me."

I wipe my face and catch my breath, trying to calm down as he grabs my hand.

"Leah, stop. You've got it all wrong. I love you."

Nash kneels in front of me. "There's no other woman in the world for me. I've tried to tell you this, but you just won't listen. And you always think the worst. You're right, I haven't been where I said I was, but that's because I was getting this."

He pulls out a small box containing a four-carat diamond ring.

"I love you, Leah McKinney. I think you're the most beautiful woman I've ever known, and I want to spend my life with you. Will you marry me?"

## 17

I CAN'T MOVE.

As I stare at Nash on one knee, my heart is racing.

"What about Taylor and the gift and all the lying?"

Nash stands up and walks me over to the couch. "I've been planning this for months, Leah. Taylor is Eric's girlfriend."

"Eric from work?" I ask.

"Yes. She's a jeweler and helped me pick out the ring. She was dropping it off tonight, and I got her a gift for helping me."

"And the lies? Flying to London? And the resorts on the computer?"

"Taylor and Eric were going to visit her parents in New York. It was a family emergency, and I had to get back to pick up the ring. And I said London because I figured you'd try to come home with me to spend Christmas. I needed to be alone to get everything set up. I planned on proposing New Year's Eve. I reserved a table at that restaurant you love overlooking the city. It was going to be great."

"I don't understand. This doesn't make sense. What about the resorts on the computer? What was that?"

"I thought about doing it there, but none of them were *us*. I just forgot to close the tabs."

I glance down at the ring sitting perfectly in the box. *What the hell is happening?* My half-packed suitcase sits on our bed, and Nash is asking me to marry him. *Have I jumped to conclusions? Had Julia and I spent the day spinning the story?* Since Thanksgiving, he had made changes in every way I had wanted, but could his story be true? There *is* a ring. After three years, he's sitting in front of me, asking the question I've been waiting for. The moment has come for me to either trust in our relationship again or walk away.

I have blown so many chances in my life, too fearful of what others would think or say about me. Too afraid that life would somehow disappoint me again, but what if Nash's proposal is real, and I assumed he was cheating because that's how I viewed life. That it would always disappoint in the end. But what if it didn't? What if life is actually trying to work out for me, and I'm standing in my own way because of the past again? Love isn't perfect, and Nash and I have been through it all. I do love him, and I've fought so hard for our relationship. I can't let the past ruin another thing I love.

"Yes," I say, tears rolling down my face. "I'm so sorry, Nash. The ring is beautiful, and I want nothing more than to spend the rest of my life with you."

Nash lifts me off the couch and spins me around as I wrap both my arms around his neck and giggle.

"I know this is crazy," Nash says, "but . . . let's get married this weekend. On New Year's Eve. I was working out the plans with Taylor when you texted me earlier. We can go to Vegas. It'll be so fun, and it's where we first met. I don't want to wait any longer, babe. I love you, and I want to make you my wife."

My heart is bursting with a mixture of joy and shock— it's comical he wants to go back to Vegas. We'd always planned to visit again but never did. Our first encounter there wasn't sentimental.

After graduating from Arkansas, I struggled to find a teaching position, so I joined a teaching corps. With a 90% job placement, I had several options in a matter of months and ultimately was offered a position with a charter school in Louisville. Upon completing my first year, I went to Vegas to celebrate with three friends I'd met in the program. On our last night, I met Nash in a Vegas nightclub. We hooked up, and I assumed we'd go our separate ways, but Nash called a month later, and we've been together ever since. Nash always joked that one-night stands weren't supposed to turn into forever, but as I glance down at my huge ring— sometimes they do. The fact that he wants to go back to where it all began is surprising. Through some combination of joy, exhaustion, and delirium, I say, "Yes. Let's do it."

Nash nearly jumps for joy. He picks me up again and throws me on the bed, kissing down my neck, onto my body. As I pull his pants off, his hands are all over me, and as intense as he is—his arousal is missing.

"Are you okay?" I ask. "What do you need?"

"Just you, babe," Nash breathes in my ear. Finally, after turning hooker-like tricks, Nash's body springs to life, and as I throw his shirt off the bed, a faint smell of lavender fills the air.

"Did you use my shampoo?" I ask as Nash makes small, light kisses on my hip bones.

"I did," he answers. "I missed you."

"Babe," I moan.

"Yes," he says, sending my body into euphoria.

Somewhere in the middle of the night, exhausted and postcoital, I go to the bathroom for Tylenol and spot my shampoo bottle in the bottom of the trash. I'd used it all before I left for Sugar Creek, but knowing Nash, he probably, dug it out of the garbage and squeezed what he could to take a shower. He was always doing stuff like that. Toothpaste, shampoo, laundry soap—instead of buying more, Nash would pull the empty tubes and bottles out of the trash and extract the last possible amount he could.

Walking into the kitchen, I grab a bottle of water and down the pills as I glance at my sparkly diamond and think how far Nash and I have come. It's all finally happening.

The following day, I meet Julia for coffee anticipating her disappointment in what I have done.

"Jesus, Leah. I knew I should've come with you."

"Julia, it checks out. I looked up Eric's profile this morning, and his girlfriend is a jeweler named Taylor. So, Nash wasn't lying."

"Maybe he wasn't lying about that, but he does about everything else, Leah. You can't trust him. And you sure as hell don't a marry a guy like that."

"Well, we are. We're getting married. And I came here this morning because you're my best friend, and I wanted you to know."

"You're a grown woman, Leah. You can make your own choices, but that doesn't mean I have to agree with them. And, as your best friend—the person who can see this situation from the outside—I think you're making a huge mistake."

"I'm just asking you to trust me."

"I do trust you. It's him that I don't trust."

As Julia and I leave, I expected her objection to us

getting married. She's been an eye-witness to every argument, affair, and terrible thing Nash has ever done. It's hard for her to see him in any other light, and as I drive back home, I try to understand her frustration, and I know in time she'll see the changes in Nash and won't hate him like she does now.

Three days later, we land in Sin City. The Hollywood roman architecture of our hotel is impressive, and the iconic fountain puts on a fantastic show. Nash spares no cost as we make our way to the penthouse suite. A bottle of champagne is waiting for us as the Asian-inspired theme fills the three rooms. An outdoor balcony overlooks the Las Vegas Strip, and it has to be one of the city's best views.

"It's beautiful, huh?" Nash remarks, kissing my forehead.

"So beautiful," I say, turning and kissing his lips. In a matter of seconds, Nash is pulling me inside and unbuttoning my pants. There's something about hotel sex that I find so erotic. Maybe it's the idea of being in a new place, or maybe it's the fact that Nash and I haven't been able to keep our hands off each other since he proposed. As we make love, the lights from the Vegas strip illuminate the best parts of Nash, and I find myself in a place I've never been with him—comfortable. Finding our release, we lay in bed entangled with each other. I trace circles around Nash's abs as we talk about our life together.

"You make me feel like a man."

"How so?"

"Everyone I've ever been with mothers me. Like I can't do things on my own. You never do that. You let me lead and let me take care of you. You make me feel like I can do anything. And you're so kind, Leah. Incredibly kind."

"I love you," I say, kissing him.

"I love you, too."

I crawl on top of Nash and smile, indicating that I'm up for round two, but he stops me.

"We can't, babe. We have plans."

"Plans?"

Nash smiles. "Dinner plans above the city tonight. Come on. Let's get dressed," he instructs, getting out of bed and prancing naked in front of the open window.

At a rotating restaurant far above the Vegas strip, Nash and I order an overly priced bottle of wine and steaks. Over a candlelit dinner and unbelievable views, Nash explains the rest of the weekend—a spa day for me, a golf range for him, and a hot air balloon ride Sunday morning as Mr. and Mrs. Nash Sanders.

"I can't believe you planned all this," I tell Nash.

"Well, it was Taylor. She put the whole thing together."

"Blue Volkswagen?"

"So, you saw it when you followed me?" He is grinning, but his tone is sharp.

I start to apologize but stop. "I didn't follow you, Nash. I thought—" I begin. "Never mind. Anyway, she did all this?" I question, more suspicious than I intend.

"No, that's not what I mean. I planned it; she just gave some suggestions," he says, taking my hand in his, but there is a slight unease.

"Remind me to thank her. She did a great job. But we don't need her anymore, do we? Besides that, I wouldn't want to take her away from Eric," I laugh, but I'm not joking, and Nash isn't laughing.

The next morning, Nash pulls open the curtains. "Good morning, darlin'."

"Morning, handsome." I put my arms around his neck, and he runs his hand through my hair.

"You're the most beautiful woman in the world. I can't believe I get to marry you."

"I'm the lucky one," I beam, kissing Nash's lips and then down his neck. Pulling him back toward the bed, I waste no time tearing off his boxer briefs.

The bridal package is luxurious and consists of everything a bride-to-be could ever want, including a massage and professional hair and makeup. I consider snapping a picture and sending it to Julia to show her Nash's romantic side but opt against it. The moment belongs to us, and I want to keep it that way.

As the day turns to evening, Nash waits for me downstairs, letting me change into the blush-colored dress he's already seen. But walking out of the elevator, his wide eyes and huge smile turn my cheeks pink as he acts like it's the first time he's seen me in the beautiful gown.

"Babe, you're gorgeous," he says, planting a kiss on my cheek. "You better be careful, or else I'll take you back upstairs and have my way with you," he whispers in my ear. We walk together to a rented limousine and make a toast in the car.

"To the beginning of a beautiful life with an incredible woman."

"May we always be reminded of the love we have for each other and know nothing can break that," I add.

"You're incredible, Leah, and I love you."

"I love you, too."

We clink our glasses together and cheers to the moment, ready to start our lives together.

Pulling up to the wedding venue, Nash helps me out of the car. We walk into the gauche chapel, which has an obnoxious billboard out front. The place is a dump. A floor fan is blowing a rancid air inside the carpeted chapel, and the mildew cascading down the walls has to violate every health and safety code. I don't want to touch anything and cling to Nash as a Fake Elvis greets us.

"Are you two the future Mr. and Mrs. Sanders?" The man inquires in a fake deep voice. His cheap sunglasses are faded around the rims, and his costume reeks of smoke.

"We sure are," Nash says proudly, raising our clasped hands.

"I guess we're ready to rock 'n' roll then!"

He leads us into another small room, and we are engulfed by cheap perfume and vomit. "Sorry, our last couple had a bit of an accident," Fake Elvis tells us. "That's what you get after boozy brunch, right?" He laughs, and I force a smile.

Nash hands him our marriage license, which he folds up and sticks in his back pocket before leaving the room again.

"You are stunning," Nash tells me.

"This place is gross."

He laughs. "It looked different on the website. It'll be over before we know it. And then we'll leave."

"Are you sure we're doing the right thing?"

"Come on, babe, lighten up. Of course, this is right. I promise. Trust me, okay?"

"There has to be a better place than this, Nash. I don't want to get married here."

"Babe, it's just a building. What's important is that we're going to walk out of here, husband and wife. Me and you, Leah. Forever."

"But look at this place."

"I know. It is gross, but this place doesn't make our marriage. We do. The two of us together, that's what today is for, not some Vegas chapel, not a fancy church, or even a beautiful beach. It's just us, two people committing the rest of their lives to each other. That's what we're doing. And I'll tell you what. When we get back, I'll give you the best reception wherever you want. We can have it at Sugar Creek with your family. It'll be perfect—everything you want. Don't overthink this, Leah. Let's just have fun with it and then go celebrate."

The chapel is awful, and I wonder for a second if Taylor had suggested it. But we are finally here. Moments away from being married, and I want more than anything to start our lives together. Even the most beautiful weddings have their flaws. So, does it matter what the venue looks like as long as we are married at the end?

"You promise we can do the reception?"

"Babe, I promise."

"Anything I want?"

"Anything."

"I guess it will make for a good story in twenty years," I say as Fake Elvis returns. The ceremony lasts ten minutes, and as Nash handles some paperwork with Fake Elvis, I wait in the car.

Looking down at my ring, my mood is weird. I thought marrying Nash would instantly change me. Like the minute we said "I do," I'd be a different person, but I'm not. I'm not unhappy—at all—I just can't understand why I'm not floating or blushing or any of that other stuff brides are supposed to do. But I'm sure the dingy chapel has something to do with it.

However, the evening does improve. After a gondola ride, Nash and I dine at a famous Vegas restaurant, stuffing our faces with lamb chops made by a world-renowned chef, followed by an all-nighter of making love. Nash's insatiable sexual appetite is astonishing, and his performance on our wedding night is beyond impressive. Exhausted, we both roll out of bed at 5:30AM to prepare for our hot air balloon ride. As I'm brushing my teeth, I reach into Nash's toiletry bag to grab some nail clippers when I notice a small prescription bottle. I glance toward the bed to see Nash putting on his clothes and pull the bottle out. His name is printed on the label, and under that is the name for his *readiness* problem. As he walks into another room to find his shoes, I open the bottle to see the little blue pills.

"Babe, you almost ready?" Nash calls from the other room.

I place the pills back in his bag and spit my toothpaste out. It makes sense. Nash's arousal has not been a problem at all in Vegas, and it has to be due to his pills. I think about confronting him, but Nash is so sensitive. When I brought it up in the past, he went crazy, and as long as it's improving our sex life, he can take as many of them as he wants.

As we rise high above the city, Nash and I admire the breathtaking view. He puts his arm around me as the yellow-orange colors start to shine on the horizon. I reach out my hand just beyond the basket and snap a picture of my ring with the city below us. Nash smiles and kisses me, pulling me into him once more. As we watch the sunrise, the wind blowing our hair, I realize that relationships aren't linear, and happy endings differ for every couple. The way Nash and I arrived at our marriage wasn't the same path for everyone, but it was still a path. It might have been filled with mud, rocks, and pits, but it was also filled with beauty, new beginnings, and a fresh start—and that path is always worth fighting for.

After the hot air balloon ride, we head back to the hotel, loading our plates with buffet breakfast. At the table, I post my ring picture on Facebook. "Did something big in Vegas!"

I caption the photo as likes, loves, and comments start to light up my phone.

The weekend is over before I even realize it and, on the plane, Nash and I talk about how fun the it all was and ask each other what our favorite parts were.

"You go first," I say.

"Ladies first," Nash says in his most gentlemanly voice.

I roll my eyes. "Easy. Marrying you. Now your turn."

"Watching you walk out of that elevator. I've never seen a more stunning woman in my life," he says, smiling and kissing my hand. I lay my head on his shoulder, listening to the hum of the plane engine.

"Hey, when we get back, I need you to go with me to the courthouse to do some paperwork," Nash says.

"What paperwork?"

"Marriage stuff. No biggie, just some legal stuff we need to do in front of a notary, so we are official." I nod my head, and I'm fast asleep ringing in the New Year as Mrs. Leah Sanders.

## 18

I CALL my grandparents the next day and explain Nash's strange departure. Nana laughs, but Grandpa doesn't have much to say. I try to push for a reaction, even making a joke or two on the phone, but he is unmoved. He mentions Nash's inconsideration in not asking his blessing—a sign of respect he said was needed—and I assure him Nash will apologize, and the two of them will have a chance to talk soon. As we hang up, I make a mental note to tell Nash, but the heaviness of Grandpa's mood makes me uneasy.

With a few days left before the holiday break ends, Nash and I are at the courthouse filling out property documents and creating a joint bank account—the first time in three years either of us combined our finances. It's all surreal, and by the following Monday, I am still high from matrimony bliss as I walk into work. Showing off my ring to a few office secretaries, I catch Julia's gaze as she motions me into her office.

"Are we still friends?" I ask, sitting down in front of her.

"Depends," she replies.

"Depends on what?"

"Did you bring them?"

I pull the two small boxes from my purse and hand them to her. "Two dozen macaroons from the world-famous Las Vegas bakery."

Julia grabs the boxes and smiles. "I've never seen a girl who loves pastries as much as you."

"I don't judge you on your marriage choices, so you don't need to judge me on my pastries. Let's draw the line somewhere, Leah."

I laugh and give Julia a watered-down, two-minute version of my Vegas nuptials but highlight the hot-air balloon as my ultimate favorite—which it was.

"Well, it was someone else's favorite, too," she says.

"What do you mean?"

"Baby daddy commented on your picture."

"What?" I stammer.

"Yep."

"Also, don't call him that, and he doesn't have an account."

"He does now, and considering his comment on your post, he is absolutely in love with you."

"What did he say?"

"Check for yourself. He posted it this morning."

I open the app and go to my profile. Several people have said nice things, including those who weren't my friends. I'd made the ring picture a public post figuring the more support for Nash and me, the better. Nana and Grandpa commented, using the wrong emoji to show their happiness. I've told them the smiley-face-tongue-to-the-side emoji does not represent happiness like they think, but they refuse to listen. There's also polite comments from Allison and Kate, who texted me after the post and invited me to Dallas. I accepted the invitation, but we haven't followed up, which is typical. Thad has commented something less sentimental, as expected, but still sweet. I scroll down until I see the last comment from Ethan, posted at 3AM. *"A beautiful ring on an even more beautiful hand."* Stunned, I reread his words. A 3AM post only means a couple of things. I click on his name, and his empty profile suggests that his account is new. He doesn't even have a profile picture and just a handful of friends. The timing is suspicious, and I can't stop staring at his comment.

"Um, excuse me," Julia says. "I don't mean to interrupt whatever fantasy world you're living in right now, but we have a school to run."

"Stop. I'm not in any fantasy world."

Closing the app, I pretend I don't care—but, I have questions. It's suspect, and his words are sweet. Too sweet, and 3AM is an unusual social media posting time—unless he meant to do it on purpose. I fidget in my seat, and remind myself I'm happily married—hot balloon ride happily married—no matter what Ethan's 3AM texts says.

"Make sure you wipe that newlywed grin off your face before tomorrow," she quips.

"I'll try my best."

The following afternoon, Julia and I make time to go over the first semester data before the school board meeting.

"I'll meet you in the conference room," I say, finishing up an email.

As I type another sentence, a notification appears on my phone—someone else has liked my ring picture, and the reminder triggers me. I scroll to my settings and shut off the notifications, but the curiosity around Ethan's comment is killing me. We haven't spoken in almost two months, and even though I meant every word I said to him that night on the bench, I want to know why he said what he did. So I search for his blocked number, uncheck the option and type out a message. His response comes immediately.

*Ethan: You unblocked me*

*Me: You didn't answer my question. Why did you comment on my post?*

*Ethan: I need to talk to you*

Just as I'm about to send him another message, Julia walks in.

"It's gone," she says, panicked.

"What do you mean?"

"I can't find them."

"Can't find what?"

"The reports. They're gone. I left them in the conference room yesterday after I had them copied and they're gone."

I follow her to the conference room, and we nearly tear the room apart as we search. Not finding them there, we make our way back to the office and alert the secretaries. Everyone scurries around, searching every place we can. But in the middle of our search, Mrs. Olivares brings in a student for smoking. It's Estreya. Her eyes are full of worry, and I'm shocked to see her in the office, especially for smoking.

"Estreya, I'll be with you in a minute," I tell her as she slumps in the chair and stares out the window. I walk behind a long counter, pulling out drawers as Julia searches under a cabinet. A few more minutes pass, but we aren't finding anything.

"Miss McKinney, y'all looking for something?" Estreya asks.

"Yeah, Estreya, we lost some papers this morning, and we're trying to find them," I tell her.

Julia goes back to searching as I start to pull Estreya into my office.

"I saw Miss Kay throwing a bunch of stuff away in the dumpster earlier when I was—" she stops.

"Smoking?" Julia asks. "Estreya, you saw Miss Kay throwing stuff in the dumpster when you were smoking?"

"Yes, ma'am. Please don't call my mom."

Julia freezes. I glance at her as she's squatting in front of the cabinet where we keep the coffee. Her hand is gripping the handle of the cabinet so hard I can see the whites of her knuckles.

I spend exactly two minutes with Estreya in my office, telling her that smoking on school property is not allowed and that she will struggle the rest of her life finding a boyfriend with yellow teeth. I explain to her how expensive teeth whitening services are, and even though she's an honor student with a decent career ahead of her, those services will still be costly. As I finish my lecture, Julia is pacing outside my office with her arms crossed.

"Estreya, don't smoke at school anymore. Actually, don't smoke, period. It's terrible for you. If you need a way to decompress, try exercising or meditating, okay?" I conclude.

"Yes, Miss McKinney. Am I getting suspended?"

"No, but you are getting three days of detention, and if it happens again, you will be suspended. You're better than this. Make choices that reflect that, and know that we're here to help you."

Estreya picks up her backpack and leaves as I follow Julia into her office.

"I swear on everything; if those presentations are in the dumpster, I will personally kill her with my bare hands."

"Let me find her and ask," I say.

It takes me another hour before Miss Kay confirms that she has thrown some large stacks of paper in the dumpster earlier that morning.

"Did you bother to look at them, Miss Kay?"

"Oh, heavens, no. They were with some bags and other trash in the conference room, so I tossed them," she explains, crunching something on the other end of the phone. "Is that all you need, sweetheart? I need to finish my lunch."

"Okay, but I need to talk to you tomorrow. It's important."

"Mmhmm, sounds good."

I hang up and throw my head back in agony as Julia leans against the office wall.

"We have to go get them," I tell her.

At the green dumpster, the smell of sour milk seeps out from under the black lids. The dumpster is full of trash bags with spoiled school lunches, but the milk smell is the most putrid. Julia gags and sets a record for the number of cuss words used in a single sentence. It's almost 4PM, and with two hours to go before we have to be at the school board meeting, our choices are limited. Julia sighs and pulls two gloves out of her pocket.

"Julia, what are those?"

"Gloves."

"I know they're gloves. Where the hell did you get them?"

"From the drawer."

"From the drawer in my office," I correct.

"Maybe."

"Julia, those are my Hermés gloves! You are not using them to dig through this trash!"

"I know, Leah! I never said I was digging through anything. I need them so I can help you."

"Here," she says, lifting the black lid. "There's no way I'm touching that gross lid with my bare hands."

I glance down at my sparkly diamond.

"Julia, my ring."

"I just got a manicure," she responds, holding up her hands.

"Julia, my ring is more important than your stupid manicure."

"Maybe, but as the head of the school safety commission, it's in the best interest of the students and faculty that only one person dumpster dive at a time. It's in the handbook. Also, I'm wearing heels, so clearly I can't."

We argue a few more minutes about who will crawl in the dumpster before I give in and hand Julia my ring. We have to get the presentation materials, and fighting about it takes more time than we have.

Julia gives me a boost, and I am atop the dumpster, my feet resting on large, thin, clear trash bags. The sour milk smell rises from each bag, and the wet cheese from the half-eaten slices of pizzas (that were served the day before) is gooey as I move bags. The smell stews at the top of the dumpster, and I almost vomit. I assume the folders will be on top since Miss Kay disposed of them earlier in the morning, but I don't see them. I begin moving bags around, cautious that paper can slip down cracks. As I pull one bag away from another, it rips, spilling a potent mixture all over me. The chocolate milk mixed with pizza sauce emits a toxic smell on my pants so terrible that I am sure I'll have to burn them. I gag a few times before getting myself together and moving the bag to the side.

"I think I found something," I tell Julia. Pulling the completely intact presentation from between two trash bags, I hand it to her.

Julia checks the contents. "Everything looks okay, but we're still missing seven presentations," she reports.

"I know."

I start digging faster, hoping that I can find the seven presentations without going all in. Finally, after ten minutes of nothing, we are desperate.

"You're going to have to get in there," Julia states.

I glare at her but know she is right. With my legs reeking of garbage, I've been careful not to jump in all the way, but time is ticking away.

"Julia, how old do you think those bags are at the bottom?"

"Probably a day or two old."

"Is that true?"

"No, they're at least a week old, if not older. Also, you know those apartments across the street throw their trash in here, too, sometimes and—"

"Stop. Just stop. You're not helping."

"You got this, girl."

"I hate you so much."

Twenty minutes later, I find the seven remaining presentations at the bottom of the dumpster. They are wrinkled and stinky, but thankfully, there are no smears or tears. It's a minor success given the fact that I now smell and look like the dumpster they were rescued from.

"We're going to have to hurry," Julia says as we shut the dumpster lid and run back inside.

"I have to take a shower."

"Leah, we don't have time. I have some clothes. We'll make it work," Julia says.

We spend the remaining hour trying to flatten out the documents and cover the smell spewing from them. Julia sprays some of her Coco Chanel perfume, but the sweet scent of rose mixed with spoiled milk only makes the paper smell worse. With a few minutes before we have to leave, I walk to the bathroom to change. Julia has left some clothes for me on the counter, but it isn't until I strip down that I realize what she has picked out.

"Julia!" I shout from the bathroom. "You gave me leather pants!"

There's silence. Not a word. I wait, but nothing.

"Leah, we have to be there in fifteen minutes. You don't have time to be picky."

I contemplate putting my spoiled milk pants back on and toughing it out, but the smell is disgusting, and the stains are worse. I don't have a choice.

Dressed in Julia's black leather designer pants and a Hazelwood High School Eagles hoodie, we walk in silence to the administration building for the school board meeting.

"I'm not sure I'll ever forgive you for this."

"Well, at least you don't smell like spoiled milk."

"I'm wearing leather pants, Julia. To a school board meeting. With our bosses!"

"Those are designer vegan pants, and they were not cheap. So, you're welcome. If anything, you look like you have school spirit and taste."

The pants do feel good, but I'll never tell her that. They are a great date night outfit but not great for a meeting.

Julia and I enter the room and greet each board member. As we shake a few hands and try to keep our distance, I notice the stares. Wide eyes, whispers, and a few smirks as members gawk at my shiny, leather pants. Julia passes out the documents to the school board members, and a few of them pick through the disheveled papers. We have done the best we can in getting the wrinkles and odors out, but by the sideways glances and chatter of the board members, something tells me our attempt is futile.

I give the best presentation I can about our school data

and assessment scores in my leather pants. I highlight our thirteen percent increase in reading and writing from the previous year and take pride in the teaching strategies that our faculty are using in their respective classrooms.

"If you turn to page seventeen, you'll see a chart that shows the effectiveness of literature circles," I explain, hearing shuffling over to the side.

I glance up from my notes to see Julia whispering to one of the board members and taking something off her paper.

"Is everything okay?"

"Yes, I just thought for a second that there might be a maggot on my paper, but there isn't. Just a piece of what appears to be dried rice," Melissa Stoggar comments.

"I have a small piece of lettuce on mine," Jared Blakely, the assistant superintendent, chimes in. "Looks like someone may have had Chinese for lunch today, huh, Miss McKinney?"

"That doesn't explain the milk smell," Abby Timmons, the board's vice president, says as her nose wrinkles.

A few more muffled voices fill the room, as well as a few laughs, and my face is growing hot. I try to end the presentation upbeat about our school's growth, hoping Dr. Bradley will see my value as a principal, but the focus is on the putrid smells, and weird foods found in the presentation Julia and I have tried to save. As the meeting ends, though, Dr. Bradley says, "Leah, it does seem like Hazelwood High School has improved, and great things are happening there under your direction." It isn't the best comment, but I'll take it.

As we walk outside, the fresh air calms my nerves after the stressful presentation.

"Was that really dried rice on Melissa's paper?"

"I'm pretty sure it was a maggot."

"That was brutal," I say.

"I know."

"Do you wanna get a drink?"

"Yes."

Julia and I drive a few blocks to a small Irish bar famous for its local pints and cheap appetizers. We nurse two red ale's and dissect the board meeting.

"It could've been worse," I tell Julia.

"Right. Those maggots could've been alive."

"I'm not going to get this job."

"Our school has improved, Leah. That's the main thing. If they don't hire you, that's on them, but the data shows improvement, and what we are doing for our kids is making them better."

"Thanks for saying that, Jules."

"I'm going to Missouri next weekend."

"What? Why? Oh, my—"

"Stop it. Damien asked if I wanted to see him, and I am."

"You like him, don't you?"

"Well, I wouldn't be flying to that hillbilly town if I didn't, now, would I?"

I smile. "I'm happy for you, Julia. He's a great guy."

"Well, we'll see. He does make damn good donuts."

"Have you two—"

"Some things just aren't your business, Leah."

"So, you have. I think you might love him, Jules."

"I love his donuts because I love pastries."

"Like—his donuts *donuts*?"

She rolls her eyes. "Love is funny. Just when you swear it off for good, it sneaks around the corner and reminds you it's still there. Buried deep under layers of doubt and broken hearts. I mean, I'm sure that's how you feel about Nash. Not that I agree with you for marrying him, because I still hate him and think he's an asshole, but I do understand how love can make you delusional—or in my case, can make you love donuts."

"You think I'm delusional?"

"I mean, yes. You might be the most delusional person I know, but it takes all kinds," she laughs. "I'm just saying that love is weird and we all have a different story. Like maybe Damien and I are destined to be a classic Ralph Waldo Emerson tale of two self-reliant pioneers searching for the depths love can take them on."

"And what are Nash and I?"

"I think your story is a Shakespearian play."

"Like *Romeo and Juliet*," I smile.

"More like Proteus and Julia. Like when he promises to be faithful and then tries to get in Silvia's pants—but then Julia winds up with his broke ass anyway."

"Thanks, Julia."

"I'm hilarious and you know it."

As I drive home, my phone vibrates with a text, and as I pull into the apartment, I see Ethan's name on my screen. With the dumpster dive, I had forgotten to text him back earlier in the day. I hesitate to open it, afraid his words will trigger emotions I don't want to deal with, but the temptation is too great.

*Ethan: Piper and I are separating*

## 19

ETHAN'S REVELATION comes as a shock. I spend several days writing a response and deleting it. Then, I write it again and delete it once more. Happily, married women are not supposed to text their former lovers and offer condolences on their failed unions. And I shouldn't care anyway. The last time Ethan and I spoke, he was reminiscing about the stars and do-overs and giving half-assed apologies that were meaningless—as far as I'm concerned, he deserves whatever is happening between him and Piper. Life always has a way of giving back, and Ethan should've thought about that before leaving me in a parking lot. Yet, there's a heaviness in my chest that I can't explain.

By early February, Julia has made two trips to Missouri to see Damien, and the subtle changes in her behavior are noticeable. She smiles more and has cut her criticism of my relationship with Nash to one or two times a week. But the most obvious difference is her appearance. Her black outfits have been replaced with pops of color catching the eyes of the office secretaries.

"What are they talking about out there?" She asks as I walk into her office.

"You're wearing a green sweater."

"So?"

"You always wear black."

"Green is basically black. It's also trending for early spring, not that you would be aware of that, but it is. They're acting ridiculous like I have some disease."

"The 'I've fallen in love' disease," I wink.

"This is not about him," she snaps.

"Isn't Damien's favorite color green? Did you FaceTime him this morning and show him?"

"Okay, unless you have something important to tell me, you can go."

"I'm kidding," I laugh. "How is Damien?"

"He's good."

"And Missouri? How do you like Newton?"

"It's growing on me."

"Growing on you?" I repeat.

"I mean, I'm not moving there, Leah. I'm not an idiot, but it's a charming place. It's cute. Like the kind of town you raise a family in and go to the local market and check on neighbors and stuff."

"The quiet life," I remark.

"Too quiet. I'm a city girl."

"I never would've guessed that you, of all people, would be in love with a small-town boy who owns a donut shop."

Julia rolls her eyes and types something out on her computer. "Damien's friend works at Sugar Creek. I didn't know that."

"Who?" I ask.

"Some guy named Tanner."

"Oh! I didn't realize he and Damien were friends. Uncle Jack hired several seasonal employees before—" I stop.

"I know. I'm sorry, girl. I didn't mean to bring it up."

"It's okay. I just miss him. The holidays were hard, but Nash has been so great and understanding, and he's helped so much. Uncle Jack hired the best staff to manage Sugar Creek, but Nash had stepped in when they needed him. Grandpa was even impressed."

"Has he spoken to your grandpa about the whole marriage thing yet?"

"No, but he will. He promised me he would."

"Like he promised about the wedding reception? It's been a month."

"We haven't had time, Julia," I insist.

"I'm just saying."

"I know. It'll happen."

"I really wish you didn't sign his name to the deed. Marriage is one thing, Leah, but assets are non-negotiable especially considering the value of that place now. And the fact you haven't told your grandparents tells me you know they'd be upset."

"He's my husband, Julia. Leave it alone."

"I'm just saying, I wish you hadn't."

But Julia is wrong. The opposite is happening; if anything, Nash is helping with the management of Sugar Creek. The care and attention he's giving to our family property impresses me and having his support only makes our relationship stronger. We are building back trust, and Sugar Creek is a part of that trust.

But I understand Julia's point. Sugar Creek is valuable. At almost 13 million, it's a number I try not to think about. We'd had offers to sell in the past and turned them down because Sugar Creek was invaluable to Uncle

Jack and me. And Nash agrees. His commitment to helping Sugar Creek maintain its success brings a deeper love for him that I've never had before. And I think there's something deep inside me that always wanted a partner who loves the property as much as I do. Someone who can see the value and happiness Sugar Creek brings to everyone, which goes beyond a price tag. And Nash does.

"We start season six tonight," Nash grins as I comb through my wet hair.

"Will our favorite mafia family disappoint in the last season?"

"Why don't you jump in bed with me, and we'll find out."

I slip into a sexy teddy, a wedding gift from Nash, and snuggle under the covers. Since we'd been married, my collection of lingerie has doubled, and I don't mind. Nash's new appetite for my bedroom attire is a turn-on, and I have to admit, something about lingerie gives me sexual confidence. The purple teddy hugs my body, and the silky material makes Nash's touch feel erotic.

"You're leaving tomorrow, right?" I ask.

"Right. But I'll be back on Sunday. It's a short trip to Ohio, so don't watch any episodes until I get back."

"And if I do?"

"Well, then, Mrs. Sanders, you might be in some trouble," Nash whispers, pulling me close and kissing down my neck.

I giggle, squirming out of his grip. "I can't anyway. I'm going to see Allie and Kate on Friday. I've taken the day off. They're dying to see my rock."

"It's bigger than Allison's. Make sure you tell her that."

I roll my eyes. "Oh, she's already commented about it."

"I'm sure she has. Wait until she sees your Valentine's present."

"Nash, tell me what it is."

He zips his lips and smiles as he pushes play for episode one, but between my lingerie, Nash's touch, and my shaved legs, we only make it halfway through the episode before the purple teddy is on the floor. The mafia family will be on hold for another night, and I'm grateful for those little blue pills.

The next morning, Julia and I meet in her office to go over the checklist we've been working on all week, specifically the large number of teacher absences that are piling up in the third quarter.

The dreaded nine weeks after the holidays are always the worst. With very few breaks, each week seems to have more days than usual, and even February is sloth-crawling its way to the finish line. In addition, the students typically perform at an all-time low, forcing a fourth-quarter rally that every teacher hates. And the morale has taken a nosedive, so Julia and I decide we need something to get us back on track.

"Maybe we should plan a lunch? Have it catered in and show our appreciation?" I suggest.

"Do I look like a party planner to you, Leah?"

"Julia, I know, but these absences are ridiculous. We need to do something."

"Fire them."

"No. What if we do something fun for the next faculty meeting? Marion High School did that kiss-a-pig contest where they had each department raise money for a good cause, and then one of their principals had to kiss a pig."

"You want me to kiss a pig?"

"Yeah. It can be a contest between us."

"Right. Okay, well, I'm forewarning you that I will cheat to make sure all the money is on you. I am not above paying students and teachers off, so choose your fun faculty games wisely."

"You're on. This will be fun. We can tie it into Valentine's Day, and we'll add it to the faculty meeting agenda for tomorrow."

"Ugh, is that tomorrow?"

"Yes, Julia. It'll be short, and we have things we need to address."

"Whatever. I'll go add the kiss-the-pig to the agenda now and see if I can find any Valentine's Day pig stuff to go along with it."

"You're the best. Also, speaking of Valentine's, what are you and Damien doing?"

"He's coming to see me this weekend."

"Damn. I'll be out of town."

"We'll mourn your absence."

"I'm sure you will. By the way, nice yellow top. Looks amazing, Jules," I smirk as I stand in the doorway.

"Not everyone can pull off yellow, Leah."

I shake my head as I walk back to my office, coffee in hand, to plan our kiss-the-pig contest, knowing Julia is right, she will cheat to win, but I have a few ideas of my own.

That evening, I send a reminder of our faculty meeting the following day and wait for the excuses to pour in.

Everyone hates the meetings, and while attendance is mandatory, it never fails that a few teachers consistently miss the monthly conversations. The coaches always have practice, and the veteran teachers take turns pulling the seniority card, but the first-year teachers and the English department are always ten minutes early.

As I pack my bags, my phone vibrates with texts.

Checking the first two—they are from Coach Pike informing me of his after-school practice and how he might be a few minutes late. It's his excuse for every meeting, and he never shows up late—he just doesn't show up at all. It's frustrating, but then I remind myself that he has to deal with Trevor Miller, Trista's son, and that fact alone should excuse him from every faculty meeting.

I respond to a few more texts before washing my face and brushing my teeth. Then, as I crawl into bed and turn off the light, another text comes through. Reaching for my phone, I expect another excuse, but Ethan's name appears.

*Ethan:You up?*

Replying is wrong, and I realize that, but I give in.

*Me: Yeah. What's up?*

*Ethan: Do you remember the night we went to that bar and played Uno?*

*Me: Yeah*

*Ethan: I found the cards tonight. Made me think of you*

I could've left it there. I should've left it there, not responded, and continued packing, but I don't.

*Me: I'm flying to Dallas this weekend. Do you want to meet up?*

I instantly regret the offer but tell myself that it's friendly and Ethan is traumatized by his separation, and I'm happily married. The story sounds real in my head, and I even go as far as telling myself that seeing Ethan in shambles might do me good. It's a terrible way to think, and I know this, but I have to convince myself that I'm cold and heartless after inviting my ex-boyfriend to a meet-up.

*Ethan: What about Saturday?*

*Me: I'm having brunch with Kate and Allison, but I can meet you after.*

*Ethan: Sounds good, and Leah...*

*Me: Yeah?*

*Ethan: How many times did I beat you at Uno?*

A smile spreads across my face. I'd never seen a worse Uno player before, and he knows it.

*Me: Zero Ethan. Not one time*

I fall asleep dreaming about Barry's goulash and playing Uno with Ethan; his laughter fills the room as I beat him twice. There is obvious guilt, but everyone has had a dream about their ex. It's not something I'm proud of, but it happens—except it goes further than it should've. The Uno segues into Ethan and me at Sugar Creek, his hands all over my purple teddy—the one my husband bought me. The rubbing and touching advances to making out, and before I can stop it, I'm having a sex dream about Ethan. I wake up in a sweat and wish I had taken Julia's advice about buying another vibrator.

"Hey, we're keeping this short today," Julia says, holding her laptop in one hand and a macaroon in the other.

"I know. We have to go over the test prep stuff and make sure everyone signs off on the proctoring document."

"I made a Google form, so it should be easy. In and out, Leah. I'm serious."

"Hot date?"

"No, but if Ann Hayes starts with her bullshit questions, I'm shutting the whole thing down."

I laugh. Mrs. Hayes had held up more faculty meetings in her twenty-year career than was humanly possible. In the four years I'd taught at Hazelwood, every meeting had been extended by fifteen or twenty minutes because she questioned everything. Protocols, testing, district-wide initiatives; she had five to ten prepared questions for every meeting.

"I know, but if she has questions, we're going to listen."

"Principal problem. I'll be on my way home, and so will everyone else."

In the meeting, Julia presents the format for the upcoming ACT schedule, room assignments, proctors, and training videos that have to be watched, signed, and accounted for. "I've created an easy Google form for y'all to go over and sign once you've completed the training, and I also attached a spreadsheet for everyone to check their assignments on that day. We'll do demographics one day, and then the test is scheduled for the next week. Most of y'all have done this before, so it should be easy."

Heads nod in agreement, and then Ann Hayes raises her hand. Julia glances at me and waits. It takes all I have not to burst into laughter.

"Ann?"

"What about snacks?"

"We'll have stations set up in the hall."

"But that's not listed in the email Ms. De Loughrey sent."

I raise an eyebrow at Julia as she forces a fake smile.

"Ann, I'll send that out this evening. Thanks for asking."

"And what about after the test is over? Can the students go home? That's not listed here either."

As teachers shift in their seats, a few start zipping their bags while others jingle car keys indicating they are seconds from leaving.

"I'll send that, too. If you have other questions, just email me. I'm happy to respond to them by email, and I don't want to hold everyone else up," Julia snaps.

"Okay, but just one more," Ann says. The restlessness increases as a few muffled voices can be heard from the back of the room, and I know Ann's time is running out. "Today, there was a massive spill in the cafeteria, and it took almost thirty minutes before anyone from maintenance showed up to deal with it. I mean, there wasn't a single coach on duty either. We can't have that. It's a safety issue not only for the kids but for us, too. Can we make sure we're doing a better job of being present and alert when kids are at lunch?"

Some impatient teachers sneak out the side door as Ann vents a few more seconds about the spill, shaking their heads as Julia almost explodes in anger. "Thank you for bringing that to our attention, Ann. We'll make sure it doesn't happen again."

"All right, thanks for staying, y'all. Everyone, have a great night, and we appreciate the job you do every day. Let us know if you need anything."

The dismissal is thunderous as teachers hustle to their cars, groaning about the meeting. Julia and I walk back to the office, and I make a note to point out that she has failed to leave off important stuff on her fancy presentation.

"Who's dropping the ball now?" I laugh.

"Shut up. Are we seriously concerned about the snack station?"

"The kids need snacks, Julia, and the teachers need to be informed where those stations will be. Looks like someone is off her game."

"I'll paint her a map and have the cheer team line the halls showing her where the stations are. I mean, who cares about the snack stations anyway."

"Ann does, and I guarantee you she'll send emails every day until you give her those details. Seems like an assistant principal problem to me."

"Shut up, Leah."

I smile and try to put my hand around Julia's shoulder, but she moves to the side.

"I had a sex dream about Ethan last night."

"And?"

"It's wrong, right? Like there's something wrong with me?"

"It happens. Just don't picture him when you're having sex with Nash. That's when you have a problem. Or maybe you should. Gross, now I'm thinking about you having sex with Nash."

"Picturing someone else when you're having sex with your husband is like the first step to divorce, right?"

"Are you asking or telling me that you've done this?"

"I'm just saying."

"So, you've done it. I mean, everyone has. After a while, their face becomes boring, and you have to improvise."

"I haven't done that, Julia."

"Listen, I don't blame you. I would have to picture someone else, too, to get through sex with Nash. Maybe like Johnny Depp. Did you picture Johnny Depp? Or Leo?"

"I didn't picture anyone."

"Sure you didn't," she winks.

As I arrive in Dallas the following morning, Allison and I meet Kate for brunch at one of their favorite restaurants in Plano. The waitress takes our drink order as Allison shoves my ring in Kate's face.

"Look at that!"

"Damn, Leah. Four carats?" Kate asks.

"Yeah."

"Did you buy it yourself, or did Nash actually do it?"

"Allie, come on. That's such a shitty thing to ask me."

"I'm just kidding. I didn't realize he had such good taste, that's all."

"A friend of his helped, but he bought it himself."

"That friend has good taste," she quips. "Who knew he had it in him?"

I roll my eyes, not taking Allison's bait, but giddy that

her jealousy of Nash's ring purchase is making her question the shabby two and a half-carat ring Thad bought. As we dine on overpriced club sandwiches, Allison and Kate give me four minutes to summarize our Vegas nuptials before Allison takes over the conversation to talk about her wedding. With just four weeks left, Allison has trimmed the guest list to 350, and most of the items on her registry have been purchased, something she's more excited about than actually marrying Thad. As she rambles about new bedding that has been marked off the list and a piece of expensive artwork, I'm grateful for our simple ceremony in Vegas. Even if the chapel from hell was a disaster, a detail I purposely leave out at lunch, it's still better than whatever Allison has planned. As we finish eating, Allison and I take a left out of the parking lot going in the opposite direction of her house.

"What are we doing?"

"I need to run this tuxedo over to our ring bearer's family. I was picking up my dress yesterday and told them I'd drop his tuxedo off."

"Oh," I mumble. Consumed with the wedding and work, I haven't talked to Clive since our last visit, and I'm not emotionally prepared to see the place my son lives.

"It shouldn't take very long. I think it's a really nice thing that they agreed for him to do it. I mean, we literally don't have any friends who have young enough kids to walk down the aisle, and Thad and I talked about not having one, but it just worked out. Plus, it's not like the ring bearer has a big job anyway, and Britney said we could photoshop him out of the pictures if we wanted. It's just customary to have one."

An unexpected fire rises in my chest hearing her say she'd photoshop Spencer out of the pictures—not because

I'm shocked Allison would do that—but rather she believes he is that insignificant.

"I don't think you should photoshop him out. That seems weird, and he is carrying your rings."

"I know. We'll see how the pictures look and then decide. I mean, it's not like he's family, so who cares."

If she only knew. As Allison pulls into the Stewarts' driveway, I'm unsure of what I will see beyond the door.

"Oh, honey. Thank you so much for dropping this off. Do y'all have a few minutes? I just made some tea. Why don't you come in for a second?" Susana insists.

We take a seat in her great room as Susana sits opposite us on an oversized gray couch.

"Mrs. Stewart," Allison starts.

"Oh, honey. Call me Susana."

"Miss Susana, this is my cousin, Leah McKinney. I don't know if y'all met at Kate and Greg's."

I stand up and lean over to shake her hand. "It's nice to meet you, Mrs. Stewart."

"You too, sweetheart," she says, smiling warmly.

"Allison, are you so excited about the wedding? Tell me all about it. We're just thrilled that Spencer gets to be a part."

Allison beams as she fills Susana in with small details about the chapel and the country club.

"Oh yes, Clive loves that place. He's a member. He's tried to get Spencer to play, but that boy loves baseball."

"Is he here?" I ask. The question is awkward—and the moment it comes out, I wish I'd kept my mouth shut.

"He's not," a woman's voice echos behind me. I turn around as Piper walks out of the bathroom.

## 20

"OH, ladies. I'm so sorry. This is Piper. She's—"

"We've met," Piper replies, coldly taking a seat next to Susana.

"Allison, it's good to see you again. And Leah, right?" She asks, but her tone is icy.

"Hey, girl. We were just dropping off Spencer's tux. It's good to see you, too," Allison says.

I shift uncomfortably, crossing one leg over the other and then uncrossing only to cross the opposite leg over, knowing my body language is firing every red flag about my anxious energy. As we sip tea, Susana begins asking us questions.

"Now, we just love Kate and Greg and baby Caroline. They've been attending St. Vincent's with us, and they are the sweetest family. Y'all grew up in Missouri, is that right?"

"We did. Kate and I moved to Kansas City in middle school."

"And Leah? Did you live in Kansas City, too?" Susana asks.

"No, I lived south of Kansas City in a little town called Newton."

"Where did you go to college?" Piper inquires, taking a sip of her tea. The question startles me as I stare at her naked ring finger.

"I went to Baylor, and Leah went to Arkansas," Allison answers.

"Oh, that's funny. My son lived in Arkansas right after grad school. He loved it."

My cheeks flush, and my sweaty palms are losing their grips on my knees.

"Really?" Piper taunts. "I didn't know that. How fascinating."

I uncross my legs for the fourteenth time and take another sip of tea, wishing there were ice cubes in it to cool my face. Sweat droplets cover my nose and drip down the backs of my knees as I pray for the interrogation to end. *Had Ethan told Piper about us, and that's why they were separating? Is that why he texted? Or were they even separated?* Maybe I'm overreacting because of my own guilt. From the first moment I met Piper, her energy was cold and bitter. She isn't acting any differently now. Maybe my insecurities about my relationship with Ethan are playing into her questions.

"College, right? Seems like forever ago," Allison chuckles. "Where did you go to college, Piper?"

"Texas. That's where I met Ethan. He was in law school, and I rented him a house."

"Oh, so you're in real estate?" Allison asks.

"Dabbled. I'm an interior designer," she snaps, shrugging her bony shoulders. There's a cockiness about her that I find disgusting. But what she fails to add is that her father owns a nationwide trucking company, and she is a product of daddy's money. It was one of the things Ethan had shared at dinner.

Piper doesn't work and her interior designing is a side hobby she does with her millionaire friends. It's not a job and as I sit across from her I want to explain to her the difference between an actual career—where people make differences in the world, and whatever the hell she does with her daddy's money. We aren't the same and we never will be—all the more reason to wonder how Ethan fell for someone so shallow and empty. She's completely wrong for him.

"Oh, I'd love to get your info. Thad and I are looking for some inspiration in our new home, and with the wedding, I just haven't had time. Maybe you could stop by and give us a quote."

"Of course," she responds, turning her attention back to Susana. "It's just interesting, though, because Ethan never mentioned he lived in Arkansas."

"Oh, honey, I'm sure he did," Susana quietly insists. The moment is awkward, and Susana does her best to counter Piper without it coming across rudely. She smiles at me over her teacup, and there's something behind her eyes—which are identical to Ethan's and Spencer's—that I can't make out. It's not fear, but something only a mother would know.

"Girls, thank you for dropping the tux off, and I'm so glad we were able to chat. Allison, I can't wait for your wedding, and I know Spencer is very excited."

"I'm excited, too. I can't wait to see him, and thank you again for allowing him to be our ring bearer."

"Thank you for the tea, Mrs. Stewart," I say, too eager to leave.

"Piper, it was nice to see you again. And I'll get with you about stopping by soon," Allison adds.

I force a half-smile, unable to make eye contact with her. "Likewise," Piper muses. She is stone-faced as we leave, scrolling through her phone, and I'm sure her next move is calling the FBI to figure out why her husband has lied to her. We stand in the entryway as Susana thanks us again, her sincerity rich and meaningful. Just behind her, hanging on the wall, is a portrait I missed on the way in. Her family, all smiling, Spencer, Clive, and Susana on the beach in their white outfits. Spencer's fair skin is bright red against his icy blue eyes, the remnants of a sunburn I know too well. But his smile is wide as he stands hugging his parents in the pink sand—a moment I am proud he's had and selfishly heartbroken I wasn't a part of.

Allison and I ride in silence for almost a minute before she says, "Was that weird?"

"You thought that, too?"

"Did she have a total attitude, or am I dreaming?"

"No, I thought she was acting strange."

"Something was up."

"I thought it was just me," I say.

"No. Like I feel sorry for Mrs. Stewart. Piper was just so—"

"Bitchy."

"Yeah. I mean, maybe it's a bad day, or she doesn't feel well, but still. Thad should be so lucky I'm not like that to his mom."

"It was awkward."

"Totally."

But somewhere underneath Piper's callous behavior, I wonder if she has learned something.

Almost thirty minutes later, Ethan texts the address to where we are meeting, and before I can type the words fast enough, he mentions the visit with Piper and his mom.

*Me: Does she know about us?*
*Ethan: No*
*Me: Are you sure? It was weird*
*Ethan: That's how she is*
*Me: No, Ethan...this was different*
*Ethan: Leah, it's fine. I promise*
*Me: What about your mom?*
*Ethan: What about her?*
*Me: Does she know about us? Did you ever tell her?*
*Ethan: We'll talk about it later*

The question hangs in the air as I pull into the small cafe and join Ethan in a booth later that afternoon. He's already ordered us both waters and his wrinkled shirt and bags under his eyes tell me he might need something stronger.

"You look like hell," I say.

"Thanks, Leah."

"I'm sorry. Are you okay?"

"It's been rough. Things are terrible."

"Why was she at your mom's house?"

"They have a relationship, and my mom doesn't know how bad it really is. She thinks our marriage is worth saving."

"Is it?"

"No."

"Does she know about us, Ethan?"

"No. That night at dinner, her friend that saw us told her I was with another woman. She's suspicious, and she's pissed because I won't tell her details."

"Well, that's understandable."

"But Leah. It's been bad for years. This is just a chance for her to accuse me of shit. We're going to counseling, but she doesn't want to save our marriage."

"Does your mom know?"

"She knows that something happened in Arkansas when I was there, but we never talked about it."

"Why?"

"Because I didn't want her to know that I was a total piece of shit."

"In my head, I agree with you, but because you look so awful right now, I'm not going to say it."

"That's so nice of you, Leah."

"I'm kidding—kind of. So, you're working things out with her?"

"No. We both know it's over. It's just a matter of time."

"I'm sorry."

"It's fine. Or it will be."

"So, you didn't tell her about Arkansas?"

"No."

"Why?"

But before Ethan can answer, my phone starts ringing. Julia's name flashes across the screen, and I send it to voicemail, apologizing to Ethan for the interruption. Seconds later, a text comes through from her.

*Julia: CALL ME ASAP!*

"Ethan, I'm sorry. I need to take this."

"It's fine."

I step outside and call Julia.

"Leah."

"What's wrong?"

"It's Nash."

"What do you mean? Is he okay?"

"That asshole. Where is he supposed to be right now?"

"Cincinnati. Why, Julia?"

"Damien ran into him. He was meeting with some guy."

"What do you mean? When?"

"Two days ago in Newton. Leah, you've got to get back here. Damien overheard him talking about—"

"Talking about what, Julia?"

"They were looking at maps of Sugar Creek."

"Okay. Hold on. I'm sure there's a reason. Let me call him, and I'll call you back."

Julia and I hang up, my heart pounding in my ears as I call Nash.

"Hello?"

"Hey, babe," my voice cracks.

"Hey, gorgeous."

"You're still in Ohio, right?"

"Yep. I actually have a meeting in fifteen minutes. Why? What's up?"

"Nothing. Well—I know you're super busy, but I was just wondering if you were planning on going to Sugar Creek anytime soon. Grandpa was asking, and I don't know what to tell him."

"Is there something I need to go there for?"

"No, we just haven't been back there since before Christmas, and I think he wants to see us. But, it's no biggie."

"Yeah, babe. I mean, we probably should go back soon. It's been too long. We can make a trip maybe in a month once I finally land this client."

"Okay. It's fine. I'll let Grandpa know. Good luck at your meeting."

"Thanks, babe. I can't wait to see you. I love you."

I try to slow my breathing and force myself not to get lost in Nash's old habits. But there's something about his tone that's too familiar. Something my gut won't let me forget, but instead of accusing him of lying, I play it safe.

"I can't wait to see you, too, and I love you."

I hang up and call Julia back.

"It's me."

"What did he say?" she asks.

"He said he's in Cincinnati."

"Leah, he is lying to you."

"If he is, Julia, I need something more."

"Why? The fact that he's lying to you about where he's at should be enough."

"Maybe so, but with Nash, it's tricky. I'm going to need more. I'm coming home, and we can figure this out."

"Call me when you get back to Louisville."

"I will."

Lost in the chaos unfolding, I forget about Ethan sitting in the restaurant.

"Hey, I'm sorry, but I gotta go."

"Is everything okay?"

"I don't know. But I have to get back to Louisville. I'm sorry we didn't get a chance to talk."

"It's okay. Maybe another time."

"Listen, Ethan. I don't know what to tell you about Piper, but I think she knows something. If she sniffs too much, she'll find out the truth. So maybe you should be honest with her," I say, fearing Piper's detective skills might lead somewhere I don't want Ethan to know about.

"It'll be fine, Leah. I promise. Are you sure you're okay?"

"No, I'm not sure, but I'm going to find out."

## 21

I HUG Ethan before hurrying off to the airport. The last flight is leaving at 7PM, and luckily there are two open seats. It's not my ideal travel arrangement, but I'm desperate. I sit in the middle seat, the worst one on a plane, and try to get comfortable.

The middle seat is unforgiving and traps every passenger between two humans who either have weird smells or the ultimate disaster—the mom with a crying infant. Luckily for me, I have the lesser of the two evils—but at least the smells are perfume-y and not body odor. However, the window seat passenger has taken my armrest hostage, and the aisle seat passenger is heavy breathing— the dragon breath is potent—but at least it's not the crying baby. It's a small win. I slump down and jam my knees against the folded tray table, unable to move. But with uncertainty looming, it's hard to care about the horrible plane ride.

As we take off, I hope Nash's lie is harmless. *Maybe he's surprising me with something. He did mention the Valentine's gift would be significant*, I think, but it doesn't make sense that he would be at Sugar Creek. We land shortly after 11PM, and I rush to the parking garage. Pulling onto the interstate, I send Julia a text.

Me: *Just landed. Heading home*
*Julia: Let me know if you need anything*
*Me: I will*

The apartment is dark except for the small lamp on our countertop, giving just enough light for me to shuffle through the cabinet to find a wine glass. I'm grateful I don't have to confront Nash and have time to think about what I'm going to say.

Pouring a generous amount of Moscato, I walk toward the couch, but something catches my eye. At the end of the hallway, a faint light is coming from our bedroom. I tighten my grip on my wine glass, and I'm frozen, thinking of all the murder shows that began with a mysterious voice saying, *"the young girl thought no one was home, but she was wrong,"* and then they flash to the crime scene of her dismembered body lying in the bedroom. Taking a long sip of the sweet wine, I take a few cautious steps toward the light and stop when I hear talking. It's soft, and it disappears almost instantly as my heartbeat takes over, drowning any sound coming from our room. *Calm down, Leah,* I tell myself, trying to listen again for the voices.

*"Where are you going?"*
*"Fixing what you didn't fix, brother."*
*"It doesn't have to be like this."*
*"No, it has to be exactly like this."*

The mafia crime family; Nash is home. I decide that I'll take a cautious approach instead of screaming at him for lying. I'll ask questions and listen before accusing him of anything—also, I don't have evidence other than the lie of him being in Ohio—so I'll listen and be hopeful. But as my feet keep moving down the hallway, I stop in horror at our bedroom door.

The floor bottoms out underneath my feet as Mika is wrapped in Nash's arms. Both are asleep as the light from the TV illuminates their naked bodies—the room caves in. My eyes jump from Nash's bare chest to her yoga mat lying against our wall, to his arm around her body, to her black thong and purple teddy—the same one I have—lying in two different spots on our floor, to the peaceful look on his face, to her overnight bag sitting on my ottoman, and finally back to the TV—*our* show we watched together countless times. My heart is in my throat, blocking every ounce of breath I am trying to take. In a daze, I walk closer to the edge of our bed. Her brown hair is messy across the pillow—my pillow —and her legs are entangled with his. I have never been a violent person, but I know where the knives are, and the rage coursing through my body convinces me that I won't serve jail time with the right attorney. But before I can make that determination, Mika sits up, making eye contact with me standing at the edge of the bed.

"Nash!" Mika shouts.

Nash shoots up like someone has electrocuted him as his eyes meet mine. I don't feel my body, but I know I'm walking to Mika's bag and yoga mat. I pick them up and turn the light on. There are beer bottles on the nightstand as they both scramble to hide their nakedness. They're sitting paralyzed, waiting for me to react.

"Babe," Nash begins.

That's all it takes—one word.

With Mika's stuff in my hands, I go to our balcony and throw it over the side. Her keys and phone land somewhere in the pond surrounding our complex, and her clothes and yoga mat scatter on the ground.

"Get out," I demand. My voice is more controlled than I expect and not shaking like the rest of my body. There's silence as she glances at Nash for help. "Mika, get the fuck out of my apartment," I repeat.

Nash hasn't moved.

"You took my clothes, you psycho!" Mika shouts, wrapped up naked in my sheets.

"I'm not going to ask again."

"Nash," Mika pleads.

"Leah, she doesn't—" he starts.

I can't take it any longer.

"I don't give a shit!" I scream. The shrill sound of my voice rings through my ears and the control I had been impressed with before is gone. And the longer she sits in my sheets, the more irrational my murderous thoughts are becoming.

"Mika, get out! Now!"

Nash nods at Mika to go and she stands up taking a few steps toward the hallway.

"Where's my phone? And my keys?" She yells.

"Outside," I fume, following her down the hallway to the door. The familiar smell of lavender—the same lavender I noticed the night Nash proposed—passes between Mika and me.

"This isn't the first time, Leah!" She hisses.

"Oh, I know, Mika. Why do you think you're almost fifty and still single? No one wants to marry a whore, and with that face and your age, it's no wonder Nash has to take his little blue pills. You're so disgusting he can't even get it up without help."

Nash stumbles into the living room, and glares at me.

"You thought I didn't know, didn't you? But, I get it now. I'd have to be drunk or on medication to fuck her, too."

"Ask him who he was screwing the night he put that ring on your finger? Or maybe ask our friend Taylor, she can tell you. He's into things you'll never do. That's why he wants a woman instead of you."

"Mika!" Nash roars.

"You're not a woman, and you never will be, Mika." Pushing her into the hallway, I grab my sheet and jerk it from her body.

In the living room, Nash puts on a shirt, but there's something uneasy about his eyes. It's something I've never seen before—like hate or evil—and as much as my gut is screaming to be careful, I can't control myself.

"You piece of shit," I say, glaring at him, noticing for the first time the empty wine glasses in the sink. I pull my ring off and throw it at Nash, hitting him in the chest. "I want you out of my life for good. Permanently. Do you hear me?" I ask. "Tonight. Pack your shit and get out!"

Nash's glassy eyes are hollow and empty, and in his intoxicated state, nothing I say will matter, but I can't stop.

"Why did you even marry me, Nash? You don't love me."

He shrugs. "I guess we all make mistakes."

"Fuck you."

"You're right, Leah. You're right. No, really. You're right. Fuck me. You're right," he stammers, walking in front of me.

"Get the hell out, Nash!"

I head for the bedroom, but he yanks my arm, and for a moment, I lose my footing and fall into him. Pulling away, I side-step to the kitchen and he grabs me again, pinning me against the refrigerator. "Leah, I'm not going anywhere, and you'll see that soon enough. This marriage isn't just about you. And you have no idea how much hell I can cause. So, you're right—fuck me—but just wait and see what happens."

"Nash, stop! Let me go!" I yell, trying to push him off me. But, instead, his grip tightens on my wrist, and he twists my arm behind my back.

"You think I wanted to marry someone like you? You're nothing, Leah, and you never will be. But you do have something that's mine now—at least you're good for that."

"Get off, you asshole! You're drunk! Let go!" I push him away with my body, giving me just enough space to try to squeeze out of his grip, but it fails. He jams my wrist behind my back again, puts his hand around my neck, and as I wrestle to get free, I'm struggling to breathe.

"You're so pathetic and weak. You'll never make it without me," he growls, pushing me harder against the fridge. My back winces in pain as the handle presses into my shoulder. Tears well in my eyes as Nash's drunkenness has gone too far, and for the first time, I'm terrified of him.

"Let her go." I hear Julia's voice cut through.

With his grip still firmly around my forearm and neck, Nash spins around to see Julia standing in our doorway; her Glock 43 points directly at his chest, and her Louis is hanging over her shoulder.

"I'm not going to tell you again. Let her go, Nash," Julia says, cocking the gun back.

Nash stares at Julia for several long moments before finally letting go of my arm, his grip leaving red marks.

"You're nothing but a bunch of bitches," Nash says as he walks past Julia and out the door.

"Leah, let's go."

We waste no time inside my apartment. I grab just the necessities and throw them into a bag—the adrenaline soaring through me. As we pull out of the parking lot, I catch sight of Mika's white car parked by Nash's SUV on the side of our building, hiding like the pathetic people they both are.

We blaze down the interstate, the faint hum of music coming through Julia's Audi car speakers.

"Here," she says, handing me a cigarette.

"I'm good."

"Take it," she insists.

Inhaling the tobacco and rolling the window down, I'm too numb to do anything but stare at the passing street lamps.

Twenty minutes later, Julia and I pull up to her custom-built farmhouse just outside the city. With dried tears on my cheeks, Julia leads me upstairs to a spare bedroom. The teal and navy bed sheets crumble as I throw my bag down on the bed.

"Wash your face and come outside," she instructs. In a haze, her words sound distant, but I shuffle inside and do as I'm told, letting the hot washcloth sit on my face breathing in the blue oil she's soaked it in. The minty smell opens my senses, and all of a sudden, I can feel everything. I drop to my knees—it's the worst pain I've had since they took Spencer out of the hospital room. My body is shaking on the floor and my chest feels like it's going to explode. I think I'm having a heart attack and it scares me, so I take slow, deep breaths and wait for the pain to stop.

Somehow, I struggle to my feet and make it downstairs joining Julia outside as we sit in rocking chairs on the wrap-around porch.

"Here," she says, handing me a cup of hot tea and another cigarette.

I take a sip, tasting the licorice root and peppermint as it coats my dry throat. "No alcohol?" I ask.

"Not tonight. Drink the tea, and then I'm giving you

some sleeping pills. It'll be a rough couple of days, and you'll need rest."

We sit in silence, listening to the crickets and night bugs sing songs back and forth until finally, I ask, "How did you know?"

"Gut feeling," she replies.

"Were you going to shoot him?"

"A girl only aims her gun for one reason."

Seconds later, I'm sobbing uncontrollably, replaying the images of Nash's hollow eyes and the fear of being pinned against the fridge, trying to rationalize that he wasn't going to hurt me; he was just drunk and got caught.

"Julia, there was nothing behind his eyes. Empty. He was staring at me like I wasn't even a person."

"That should tell you something."

"He was drunk. Like, blackout drunk."

"Leah, a man who puts his hands on you like that is capable of anything. Drunk or not, there's no excuse. None."

We finish our cigarettes and take our tea inside. Falling onto Julia's couch in a heap, I'm hoping the sleeping pills will start to do their job.

"You were carrying your Louis."

"And?" Julia responds.

"And you were pointing a gun with a $3000 bag on your shoulder."

"I always carry my gun in my Louis," she says.

"To work?"

Julia smiles. "No comment. Drink your tea."

"Did you see Mika when you came up?"

"Yes," Julia responds.

"And?" I ask.

"Don't worry about it."

"Julia, what did you do?"

"I helped her get an Uber and gave her a jacket. The girl was naked."

"I hate her."

"I know."

"I threw her stuff off our balcony."

"I know."

"Like her keys and phone and everything."

"As you should've."

"How do you think she'll get into her house?"

"It doesn't matter. And here's what you should know. Women like Mika Templeton are everywhere. Desperate girls like her pry their way into the lives of unavailable men and cause chaos. Eventually, she'll age out of being a whore. She'll wind up alone and used and miserable. She's garbage and always will be garbage—a total waste of your time. Nash, on the other hand," Julia looks at me. "We will discuss all of this. Not tonight, but Leah, it's serious, and you will listen to me."

I take another sip of tea and nod in agreement, knowing Julia deserves more than just a conversation after what happened.

"Is this the steamer trunk?" I ask, inspecting the vintage ensemble I have propped my feet on.

"Yes."

"It's beautiful."

"I know. That's why I bought it, so you could put your dirty feet on it," she grins as I pull my feet off.

"Sorry."

"I'm kidding—kind of. Those pills should be working soon. You really need to rest."

But I can't relax; I start crying again, but this time over the realization that I made the ultimate mistake with Nash.

"Julia, what about Sugar Creek? He's going to—" but I can't finish the words.

"Leah, one thing at a time. We'll figure it out."

"I can't do that to my grandparents, Julia. Uncle Jack trusted me. I promised him I wouldn't let anything happen to Sugar Creek."

The tears are rolling down my face, and my mind is racing to every worst-case scenario it can find. Every red flag I ignored is now flashing like police lights, and for a second —I wish Julia would've shot him.

"It will get better, right? This pain?" I sob.

"Yes, it will. But not before it gets worse."

## 22

THEY SAY the third day of anything is the worst. A sprained ankle—the third day will be the worst pain. A new job—the third day everything will fall apart. A broken heart—the third day will be debilitating. The third day after I catch Nash in bed with Mika is Valentine's. Life is a karmic bitch like that.

*Stay off social media*; Julia's text comes through my phone.

Other than using the bathroom, I haven't moved in three days. The blackout curtains in Julia's guest bedroom shield any acknowledgment of time, but thanks to the calendar reminder on my phone, the morning notification alerts me that it's Valentine's Day, and I'm alone.

The holiday is stupid. As a society, we reserve one day out of the year to be romantic and post all over social media how beautiful our relationships are. It's bullshit, but as critical as I am of the day, I did plan to post something sweet about the first Valentine's Day as Nash's wife.

Instead, I'm in bed—barely alive—fighting chest pains and eating sleeping pills like candy. I curl into the smallest fetal position and sob. It's not even sobbing—at this point— it's convulsions. The shake crying that only third-day sadness brings. It also brings suffocating thoughts about life —that it will never be the same, that depression will be an unwanted friend I'll have forever, and worse—do I even want to live at all. But that's what day three does. It's the evilest, debilitating day of pain. If it's a character on *Game of Thrones*, day three is Ramsey Bolton—and I am not going to be eaten alive, so I get out of bed on day four.

Showering for the first time in almost a week, the water soothes the broken cracks in my heart and the visible ones on my skin. Tears roll down my face as I rub shampoo through my hair, and I wonder how it's even possible to have any tears left, but they don't last as long. Whether it's the healing qualities of a shower or the realization that I am still alive, a feeling starts to take shape—something a little like peace.

In an oversized black sweater, dark sunglasses, and leggings, Julia and I go for a walk.

"See? Isn't this nice?" She asks as we walk along a small trail on her property. I don't respond. "It's not freezing or bitter. The trees are still standing after the winter destroyed them. It's transformative, Leah. Exactly like you." I stare at her and raise an eyebrow, feeling for the first time how loose my bra is around my body. I haven't even thought about food.

"Did you cancel the kiss-a-pig contest?" I ask.

"No."

"Why?"

"Because you're going to kiss that pig, and I really need to see that happen."

I crack a smile.

"There she is."

"It kind of hurts my face."

"Listen, I know you don't want to hear this, but you need to call an attorney—like today. And I need to take pictures."

"Pictures? Of what?"

Julia stops walking and lowers her gold-framed Ray Ban's. I look down at my feet, the shame and embarrassment engulfing me. The two bruises on my neck where Nash's hand had been, the large ugly one on my back where he shoved me against the fridge, and the three on my wrist along with what I think is maybe a fracture.

"Shit, Julia. Look at me. When did I turn into this girl?"

"The girl who told her dirtbag husband to get out? That kickass girl?"

I give a half-smile.

"You've always been that girl."

"Yeah, but how did I let this happen?"

"You didn't let anything happen. Nash is sick, Leah. Sociopathic, narcissistic sick. The man doesn't feel anything. No empathy, no emotion. He's an empty vessel, and that's the scariest type because he doesn't see anything wrong with his behavior. It's pure evil. The depths he'll go to destroy someone is infinite, and you saw that in his eyes that night. Hollow, dead. You're not a person to him, but property. This wasn't your fault, but it's your responsibility to leave and never look back."

When we get back to Julia's, I call her attorney to schedule a meeting for the next day. The initial conversation is less painful than I imagine, and we agree to talk in the upcoming days once he has a chance to review my case. To avoid Nash, Julia goes over to gather the rest of my clothes and belongings after I'd attempted to do it myself, only to break down in the parking lot. Some things will take more time.

Over the next couple of weeks, Julia stuffs unknown amounts of kiss-the-pig money into my bucket, even stooping low enough to switch our names when she finds out several science teachers are plotting against her. But I don't mind her cheating strategy. It's a welcomed distraction. During an assembly the following week, I apply a bright red lipstick and pucker up to Charlie, the pig. Through roars and cheers, and too many cellphone videos, I laugh hard for the first time since Nash cheated. A moment I swore a month before would never happen again, but it does. Bruises heal, hearts mend, and somehow time reminds us that there's life again through kissing a pig's snout.

"I think Charlie liked you."

"I think they bathed him. He smelled like dish soap."

"It was good to see my friend laugh again. I kinda missed her."

"Jules."

"I said kinda, let's not get carried away."

I smile as we walk into the office.

"Allison's wedding is next week."

The idea of attending the wedding solo hasn't crossed my mind with everything else going on.

"I know, and then spring break. I'll be in Cabo, so you'll have the house to yourself."

"Damien will love it."

Julia smiles. "He's never been. So, it should be fun."

"When are you leaving?"

"Monday."

"Julia—" I raise my voice an octave, hoping what I'm about to ask her will make her feel sorry for me.

"Shit. I know that look. What do you want?"

"Would you go with me to Allison's wedding?"

She doesn't respond. Her eyes narrow on mine, and her mouth twists to one side.

"Is that a no?"

"I'll go on one condition."

"What?"

"I want you to tell the truth. I want you to come clean to Clive and Ethan about the past. It's time, Leah, and I'll be there with you, but it's time to let this go."

After the past month, I'm not sure I can handle more heartbreak and revelations of the truth. I'm still healing myself, still moving through the ruins of my relationship with Nash, but she's right. Ethan deserves to know the truth. Everyone does. But Allison's wedding is not the right place to deliver that kind of news. If I can get Ethan alone and tell him, maybe, but the odds of me actually confessing are slim. I explain this to Julia, but she isn't listening.

"No, you have to, Leah. It's insane that you do this to yourself. You've carried this with you your whole life, and it's destroyed you. Pretending everything was fine, pretending that it doesn't matter. But it's not, at all. Instead, you're your own villain. It's affected every part of your life, and you need to stop holding it in. And here's maybe the biggest thing—I know you can do it, and you do too. I watched you walk away from Nash and fight to put yourself back together. That takes courage, and this does, too. And it will hurt like hell, but I'll be there, and more than that, you'll be free. Do this for you."

Julia ends her rant, and we're both in shock. Other than the occasional student shouting in the hallway, there is silence in her office.

"I just said some profound wisdom—like an Oscar-worthy speech. We just had a Nobel Peace Prize moment in here, and you're the only one that heard it. Damn," she says.

I start to smile, but tears fill my eyes. Lying about my past has become part of who I am. It's the one thing I've had control over since that day in the clinic parking lot, but that control has ruined me inside.

The shame of giving up Spencer destroyed my self-worth even though I know I did the right thing. It hurts that I wasn't good enough to care for my child, so I've punished myself in various ways.

And lying to Ethan has kept me emotionally connected to a man I wasn't ready to lose—and to someone I believed owed me more than running away from an obligation he helped create.

But the other side of the truth is a fear that I'm not sure I can face. *Who am I without this secret? What will I lose if I let it all go?* Or, more importantly—who will I lose?

"You're right," I tell Julia. "I need to tell them."

"No, you *will* tell them," she corrects.

"Fine, I will tell them."

"For yourself. Not for me or anyone else. Do it because you deserve to have peace and freedom from this. Please," she says, giving me a rare hug but pulling away almost instantly.

"Sorry. Ew, god, how do people do that all the time?"

"Miss McKinney, you have something you need to sign for," Miss Kay says, standing in Julia's doorway. I walk through the office where a young man is standing. He hands me a thick envelope and asks, "Leah McKinney?"

"Yes," I answer.

"You've been served."

Retreating to my office, the secretaries are all whispering and wide-eyed. As I try to open the envelope, Julia grabs it. Combing through the divorce documents, she suddenly stops, examining one of them.

"Shit."

"What?"

"Sugar Creek is listed under joint assets. That selfish asshole."

"He's not getting it, Julia. He can't. I'll do whatever it takes," I say, wiping a tear off my cheek.

"That's exactly right. Call your attorney, and don't forget we have evidence of what that dickhead did to you."

I make the phone call and schedule a meeting for the following week, but my attorney isn't as optimistic as we are. With the property deed in both our names, the case will be a fight and one Nash can drag out if he wants. The unsettling news is not what I want to hear, and as Julia and I board the flight to Dallas, the weight of my life choices have never been so crippling.

## 23

---

"ARE you getting a spray tan so that yellow doesn't make you look like a Russian gymnast who never sees the sunlight?" Julia inquires as we take our seats in first-class, an upgrade she insists on for the short trip.

I sigh. "No. Spray tans make me look like a Cheeto and stain my fingers. I'm just going to suffer the consequence of my lack of melanin."

"Allison is going to be pissed."

"I don't care. She's already mad that I'm missing rehearsal tonight."

Julia crosses herself and says, "God, help all those flash mode pictures you're in."

"Shut up, Julia."

As the plane takes off, we discuss strategies of ways to tell Ethan and Clive the truth. Julia suggests I take the mic during the wedding and blurt it out to Allison's 350 guests.

"And, then you'll drop the mic, I'll cue the sound guy and we'll do the electric slide down the aisle together. It's genius and it'll shatter Allison's dream wedding. I'm fucking brilliant."

"First of all, you've never done the electric slide in your life, and secondly, I'm not announcing this publicly. It needs to be done in private. I just need to get Ethan and Clive alone."

"I like my plan better, but whatever," Julia says, dryly rolling her eyes. We agree it will be best to do it after the wedding.

On Saturday morning, I slip into my dreaded yellow dress and zip the side, but something is wrong. The color is worse than I recall, but it's Julia's dropped jaw that has me nervous.

"Oh, my—"

"I lost weight," I say, thinking how my happiness has started to come back, but my appetite hasn't.

"How much? What the hell?"

"Ten pounds. It's noticeable, right? Like Allie's gonna be able to tell?" I ask, pulling at the excess fabric around my hips and breasts.

"You didn't think to try this on before we left?"

I glance down at the bunched-up fabric around my waist.

"Of course, you didn't. I swear, Leah," she mumbles, walking over to her suitcase and grabbing her travel sewing kit. Twenty minutes later, Julia has altered just enough that the dress doesn't fit like a square of fabric hanging on my body, but it's left a small train in the back.

"Do you think Allison will notice?"

"I'm sure she will, and if she says anything, tell her they altered it that way at the boutique."

"I didn't know you could sew."

"Leah, I can do anything. I'm a genius."

"You can't camp," I joke.

"Because it's stupid and archaic. There's a reason why cavemen are extinct. Let's go."

At the country club, wedding preparations are underway. A few bridesmaids take filtered pictures of Allison getting ready and comment all over social media about how she is the *most* beautiful bride. As they hashtag the crap out of #WorthingtonTheWait, they keep updating Allison every five seconds about who likes what picture and how many comments each is getting. The obsession is frightening, but Allison has bigger problems. Vanessa has disobeyed Allison's hair guidelines opting for an elaborate updo complete with baby's breath. Allison has to be removed from the room as Kate instructs Vanessa to redo her hair in a simple half-up, half-down style. As I join her outside, she's cussing about Vanessa's inconsideration for her feelings.

"And what happened to you?" She asks, inhaling a cigarette.

"You really shouldn't be smoking in your dress, Allie."

"Don't judge me, Leah. Answer the question."

"What do you mean?"

"I mean, this isn't the dress I picked out. The back of it is all messed up. I will never use that damn boutique again, and you better believe that I will be calling them and complaining as soon as this is over. The whole fucking day is ruined!"

"Allie, it's not ruined. Vanessa is redoing her hair, and everyone will be focused on you today. They won't notice hair or dresses or any of it. All they care about is seeing you and Thad get married. And you should know this, too. Your wedding will be perfect, but the love you and Thad have is more important than whether your bridesmaids have the best hair or dresses. Those things will not matter in the end.

The strength you and Thad have together—that's what counts."

"I am really strong, aren't I, Leah? I mean, Vanessa isn't even my friend, and I'm still letting her be a part of my day. And, I'm only going to tell *you* this, and if you tell anyone I said it, I'll deny it, but I hired a cheaper videographer than the one I originally was going to use," she says, puffing the last of the cigarette. "So, it's probably going to look like shit."

I laugh too hard, not because Allison and I are having a moment, but more because this is Allison's 'Nash moment.' Bridesmaid updos and altered dresses. This is her *day three*, and it's probably as bad as it'll ever get for Allison—if we could all be as lucky.

With the hair disaster squashed and Allison breathing on her own again, we line up waiting for the music to start. I feel a tap on my arm and turn around to see Spencer smiling wide.

"Hey, Spencer."

"Hi. You look pretty."

"Aw, thanks. You look handsome. Are you nervous?"

"Naw, I just have to carry this to the front," he explains, jerking the ring pillow up and down like he was shaking a toy from a dog's mouth. I smile, thinking how angry Allison will be if her ring comes untied. Spencer would be photo-shopped for sure. As Vanessa takes her place to walk next, I glance at Spencer one more time; his icy blue eyes and nose freckles warm my heart.

Halfway through the wedding, I spot Ethan sandwiched between Susana and Piper. He catches my suspicious glance and forces a smile before I see Julia sitting a row behind him. She holds a fake microphone up and pretends to let go and then nods her head toward the center aisle. I almost lose it and quickly turn my attention back to Pastor Jon, who is droning on about what "God has joined, let no man separate." I imagine those words are coming at that exact moment through some divine wisdom as a reminder for me to keep my eyes off Ethan. The message is received, but I still wonder what the status is between Ethan and Piper. *Why is she at the wedding?* We'd left things unclear the last time I saw him, and Ethan had gone silent since my encounter with Nash. As the final moments of the wedding conclude, and Pastor Jon announces Allison and Thad as husband and wife, the chapel erupts in applause. *Oohing* and *ahhing* at the happy couple's first kiss as Mr. and Mrs. Thad Worthington. Spencer wrinkles his nose at the kiss, the moment tattooing itself on my heart. As the guests file out, Julia finds her way to the front.

"This reception is an open bar, right?"

"Yes."

"Cool. When you're done taking pictures with the other Skittles, come find me."

"It's ridiculous, isn't it?"

"I made memes. I'll show you later."

"Julia."

"I'm sorry, Leah. I can't hear you over the wine."

"Do not get drunk without me."

"I make no promises. But you, on the other hand—"

"I know," I say, realizing I have to get Ethan alone.

The pictures are quicker than I anticipate and as we make our way to the country club, Grandpa and Nana stop me to say they are going back to the hotel.

"Cricket, we're pretty tired, and Nana needs to put her feet up."

"Okay. Do you need anything?"

"No, we're fine. I think we may just order room service. Our flight leaves early in the morning."

"You look beautiful, sweetheart," Nana says, kissing me on the cheek.

"Thank you, Nana. I'll call in a bit. Love you."

"We love you, too."

The ballroom is packed, but Julia has texted where our table is, and as I squeeze through the crowd, I find my way to the front. Allison has worked meticulously on seating arrangements, ensuring the wedding party and guests are all situated far enough away from exes and drama and spotting Julia at a front table; I am thankful it's empty.

"Hey," I say, taking my seat.

"Hey, yourself."

"You look like you're having fun," I comment, eyeing her empty glass of wine.

"Not as much as you're about to have."

"What do you mean?"

"This is us," Ethan says, standing across the table.

"See," Julia beams.

I give a polite smile watching Ethan and Piper take their seats. He looks at me and then gives a puzzled glance toward Julia, but Julia is taking the lead before I can say anything.

"I'm Julia," she says, reaching her hand toward Piper first and then Ethan.

A few moments later, Lily and Peter join us just as the ballroom lights lower. Pastor Jon walks to the middle of the room. He's removed his suit jacket and tie, sporting a more casual appearance for the reception, but his wireless mic is fastened securely to the side of his cheek. Pastor Jon tells a few corny jokes about marriage, church, and buffet food as he waits for guests to take their seats.

"This guy is a douche," Julia whispers.

"I know."

"He's everything I hate about church. Pretentious,

trendy, and fake. I bet he preaches about tithing and goes home to his four-million-dollar mansion. Gross."

"But his wireless mic."

Julia rolls her eyes as Pastor Jon stands in the spotlight.

"Y'all, I am just so honored to be a part of this special day, and if you're looking for a church home, our services start at 10AM tomorrow, even with your hangover," he laughs. But the room doesn't react, and his standup routine is starting to fail.

He clears his throat. "Okay, the moment we've all been waiting for. Ladies and gentlemen, please welcome for the first time, Mr. and Mrs. Thad Worthington!"

The room explodes with clapping and yelling as the intro music blasts through the speakers—Allison and Thad wave and smile as they walk to the head table.

"God, aren't weddings the best?" Julia quips.

Everyone smiles and nods, agreeing with her as I give her a suspicious side-eye.

"I mean, it's like the last time you'll ever be that happy —" she says, pointing to Allison, "ever again in your whole life. Starting tomorrow, it will be one continuous shitty day, with the same person—over and over—until you die. But today," she picks up her wine glass, "today is the best day you'll ever have again. Cheers to the happy couple!"

She raises her glass, and Ethan nearly chokes on his water. My mouth falls open as Julia taps my wine glass with hers, and right on cue, music starts playing as the whole table sits in shock. I know Julia's toast is more about pointing to Allison's flaws as a human and less about how she really feels about marriage, but she's not doing me any favors.

The uncomfortable moment lingers for a few minutes as guests start making their way to the buffet. Julia excuses herself to the bathroom, Ethan and Piper get in line, and I'm alone with Lily and Peter.

"Girl, your friend!"

"She has a mind of her own."

"Completely," she says, horrified. "Okay, is it just me, or is there something funky between Piper and Ethan?"

"What do you mean?"

"You don't know? Oh, my gosh, of course, you wouldn't," Lily says, answering her own question. "Rumor is he's cheating, and Piper knows."

I listen as Lily explains that the Dallas gossip is swirling with talk about Ethan's mystery woman a few months ago, and Piper exploded one night, kicked Ethan out, and changed the locks on the doors.

"I mean, I totally get it. Can you even imagine?" A sharp pain shoots through my knotted stomach. I can imagine.

Through dinner, we all listen to Lily's stories about her VIP access to Dallas' best entertainment, and I'm eyeing Julia waiting for her to say something else dramatic, but she controls herself as Lily name-drops famous bands and celebrities she's promoted.

"I mean, if people really knew what goes on backstage, they'd be shocked. It's just a perk of working with celebrities, though. You get to know all their secrets."

"Your job sounds *so* amazing," Julia laughs. "I mean, how do you even do it?"

"Oh, girl, it's a struggle sometimes. They can be very demanding and ugly."

Julia cocks her head to the side and puts her hand over her chest. "Bless your heart."

The cattiness of two queen bees is comical, but Julia's timing is impeccable, and Lily retreats in defeat to a side conversation with Peter. With dinner finishing and guests filling up the dance floor, I'm struggling to find a moment alone with Ethan, so I send Julia a text.

*Me: I'm going to text Ethan to meet me outside. Distract Piper so she's not suspicious*

Julia sends back, *"Good luck,"* and a gif of a burning building. I glare at her, and she laughs as she takes a long sip of wine.

"I'm going to go talk to Kate. I'll be back," I say to Julia, but loud enough for the table to hear me. As I exit the ballroom, there are too many people outside, so I slip into the country club's closed dining room, trying to figure out a place for us to meet. The room is dark, but I notice the outdoor terrace and walk over to one of the doors. It's open.

Outside, the cool night air sends chills down my bare arms. The full moon is glowing brightly against the night sky, illuminating the smooth green of the golf course. I hate to ruin such a peaceful moment, but I have to tell Ethan the truth about Spencer. It's time. I open my clutch and type out a quick text to him.

*Me: Meet me on the terrace*

*Ethan: Ok*

Ten minutes later, Ethan is standing in front of me.

"It feels nice out here," Ethan says.

"I know. Listen, Ethan, I need to talk to you about something."

"You're not wearing your ring, and your husband is missing. What's going on, Leah?"

"No, it's not about that, but I could ask you the same thing. Why is Piper here? I thought you were separated?"

"It's complicated, Leah. We are done. I am done, but it's more difficult than that." He pauses. "He hurt you, didn't he?"

I drop my head and stare at my hands, picking at the

French manicure Allison made us all get. Ethan puts his hand on my shoulder and rubs down my arm, soothing me. "What happened? You can tell me."

"He cheated and filed for divorce. But Ethan, that's not why I need to talk to you."

"That piece of shit. God, Leah, I'm so sorry. A guy like that," he shakes his head, "he deserves to have his ass kicked."

"It's fine."

"Is it? Are you fine?"

"I'm better, but Ethan—"

He turns to face me. "You look beautiful. You are beautiful, Leah, and he's a jackass for cheating on you."

Ethan's words hang in front of me, clouding the conversation I am supposed to be having with him. Nash's affair had hurt my self-esteem, and hearing Ethan say I'm beautiful breathed life back into my confidence that is struggling to stay on her feet. He rubs the back of his hand against my cheek. "I mean, look at you."

The fact that Ethan finds me gorgeous in this smock of a dress is shocking.

"I look like a school bus."

"I'd ride it."

"Ethan!"

"You walked right into it, Leah," he laughs.

I smile, but it fades fast, knowing what's coming next.

"Ethan, I need to tell you something important."

"Stop. Listen to me," he starts. "I told myself if I ever got the chance to talk to you again, I wanted you to hear this."

"Ethan, wait. I need to tell you this first."

"No, Leah. Just listen."

"But you don't understand."

"Leah, I love you."

## 24

"I'M in love with you, and I always have been. I made the biggest mistake of my life leaving you. I'd never been loved like that before, and it scared the hell out of me, so I ran. I wasn't ready for us—I wasn't ready for you. I couldn't be the man you needed me to be, and I got scared. I'm sorry for hurting you and for walking away when you needed me the most. I'm sorry for not getting the chance to love you the way you deserved to be loved. You were the best thing that ever happened to me, Leah," he says, grabbing my hand. My confession about Spencer echos in my head, but telling Ethan the truth will only ruin whatever he's going to say next. So instead, I keep quiet.

"While I did marry Piper—it wasn't love. Not what we had. She's not you. She'll never be you."

We stare at each other for a few seconds before it gives way to the undeniable connection Ethan and I always had. The second his lips touch mine, I'm lost in his apology, and I can't fight the love I've always had for him. I've drifted off with him on a rooftop in Fayetteville, and I don't want the moment to end. But as quickly as I'm swept away, visions of the positive pregnancy test, me standing alone in an empty parking lot, and the looming truth about our son takes over. "I can't do this," I stammer. "We can't."

I run through the dining room and back to the reception, sitting at the table as Julia is in mid-conversation with Piper about breeds of horses. I down the rest of my wine as she explains that Piper used to take riding lessons, but I can't react because seconds ago I was kissing her husband.

A minute later, Ethan joins us.

"That took a long time," Piper says.

"I smoked a cigar," Ethan responds.

Piper rolls her eyes but runs her hand down his back, caressing him. The territorial mark is sickening, and the anger seeps through my flushing face. She leans over and kisses his cheek, but it's strange. Her movements are stiff and unnatural on his body, almost mechanical; I recognize the act, and I'm not impressed.

"Leah!" Kate shouts, walking up to our table. "I tried to get your attention earlier, but you were talking to him," she bellows, pointing at Ethan and spilling drops of wine from her glass.

The table falls silent as all eyes stare from Ethan to me.

"Well, this is awkward," Julia says.

Piper drops her hand from Ethan's back. "Where was this, Kate?"

"Outside, but it doesn't matter. Listen, we are having brunch at our house tomorrow—" she begins as Greg walks up.

"Hey, y'all. My wife has over-indulged on the wine tonight, but what she's trying to say is we'd like y'all to come for brunch in the morning. Who's in?"

"Leah, you have to come 'cause you're family. It's required," Kate insists.

"We'll be there, too. Thanks, Greg," Piper snaps.

"Great! I'm going to get this one to bed. We'll see y'all in the morning," Greg says, grabbing Kate's hand and leading her away.

"Julia, it was nice chatting with you. Ethan and I are leaving," Piper announces, grabbing her purse and walking away. Ethan fakes a smile and nods at us, "Have a good night, you two," he says, following Piper out.

Julia turns to face me.

"Did you tell him?"

"No."

"What the hell, Leah?"

"He kissed me."

Julia grabs a bottle of wine and fills our glasses. "Again, what the hell?"

Another bottle of wine later, we are both hammered. I explain to Julia what Ethan has told me and the part where I omitted telling him about Spencer, and her anger escalates with each glass she drinks. Finally, hours later, we both fall into bed and pass out.

Rushing around the next morning, I can't get Julia out of bed.

"Go without me," she groans. "Leave me here to die in peace." I'm not any better, but I have managed to stand upright, which is more than I can say for Julia, whose eye mask is crooked on her face.

Speeding through Kate's neighborhood, I have already taken two Tylenol but pop two more in, hoping the extra will speed up the process. My head is pounding, and my eyes are puffy—in fact, my whole body feels bloated and stiff, and for a minute, I think about leaving. But I've already made the trip, and somewhere inside—I want to see Ethan again.

In the dining room, tiny morning buns, fruit tarts, and Sangria lemonade sit on fancy plates. But, while my hangover is screaming for water, my anxiety grabs the Sangria and downs it too quickly.

"I don't know how you're drinking still," Kate mumbles. She's wearing a matching pink pajama set, and her hair is tied into a messy top knot.

"Someone had a fun night."

"Funny, Leah. My head feels like it's going to fall off my body. I'm going upstairs. If I don't come back down, bury me in that pink dress. Allie knows which one," she informs, grabbing a morning bun and disappearing. Twenty minutes later, she's downstairs—sans pajamas—as Lily, Vanessa, and Andrea sit down in the dining room. All three look like the rest of us. Oversized t-shirts, leggings, and sandals with messy hair and bare faces—we resemble college girls after a night of bar hopping. As I get up to use the bathroom, Kate is at the door talking to someone. I peek around her to see Clive and Susana.

"He forgot to bring this last night," Susana says, holding a wedding gift. "We were on our way to eat, so we thought we'd swing by. Can you make sure your sister gets this?"

"Of course, but I'd love for y'all to stay. We're just doing a little brunch."

The southern hospitality of an invitation is not one a person rejects without good reason. It's rude and considered bad manners. The rule is ingrained in our upbringing from an early age, and the automatic response is to accept. Susana looks at Clive, who gives a slight nod, and they walk in as I close the door to the bathroom.

We load our plates with enough carbs to last a week, and everyone is chatting about Thad and Allison's wedding, emphasizing how fun the DJ was and, more importantly, how delicious the six-tiered cake had been.

"I swear, I've never tasted something so good in my life," Lily proclaims.

"I know," Vanessa agrees. "The blueberry cake was my favorite. It reminded me of my grandma's."

Heads nod, and the room grows silent as the food cures our hangovers.

"I have something interesting to share," Piper says, never taking her eyes off me.

"What's that, dear?" Susana asks as an uneasiness takes over. There's a smug look on Piper's face—she knows something. She's confident—cocky almost—and I grip the chair, bracing for the worst.

"I've done some digging," she begins. "Well, that's not true. I hired an investigator to do some digging."

My heart is racing as I glance at Ethan, who has dropped his fork and sits back in his chair.

"Ethan, you had to know this was coming. Especially after running into Kristen," she says, condescendingly lowering her voice like she is disciplining him. "I mean, what did you expect?"

Ethan crosses his arms as Piper continues.

"Leah and Ethan went to college together. In Arkansas. They were there at the same time. Isn't that funny? And, get this—this is hilarious; Ethan was her teacher."

There are a few gasps in the room, and Ethan's face has turned white. Clive takes off his glasses and rubs his temples while Susana's eyes are locked on Ethan.

"But that's not all," Piper laughs, taking a dramatic pause and pulling out a sonogram picture.

"You're pregnant?" Susana asks.

"No, not me," Piper smiles as she turns the picture over and starts reading.

*"Ethan, I know we didn't plan this, but we made something incredible. We can get through anything as long as we have each other. I love you so much, Leah."*

The words I had written to him the night I found out I was pregnant hang in the air as all eyes in the room dart to me. My eyes are filling with tears just as Julia walks around the corner. She pops a piece of pineapple in her mouth, not noticing the seriousness of the moment.

"Hey," she murmurs, giving a small wave as she chews. But no one makes a move. Then, finally, she catches sight of Piper and the sonogram picture, and as her eyes meet mine, she realizes what's happening.

"The investigator found this letter and sonogram picture in Ethan's storage unit. The picture is from ten years ago and the hospital listed was in Little Rock, Arkansas. So, he investigated a timeline of births at that hospital and—"

"Piper, stop!" I yell.

"Leah, what the hell is going on?" Kate demands.

"Yes, Leah, please do tell everyone what the hell is actually going on. And don't forget to tell everyone about the abortion clinic," Piper hisses. "We found those records, too."

"Leah!" Kate shouts.

My body is shaking as I rise to my feet.

"I'm so sorry. This is not how I wanted to do this," I begin as tears fall down my cheeks. Julia hands me a tissue and takes her place on the other side of me as I wipe my face and start again.

"I did know Ethan in college, and he was my teacher. We fell in love, and then I got pregnant, but Ethan—" I glance at him as the tears roll down my face, "I couldn't go through with the abortion. It was never my choice. It was always something you wanted, and I couldn't go through with it."

"Wait. Ethan?" Clive asks, confused.

"Clive, Ethan's the biological dad," I say, squeezing the words out.

Clive looks at Ethan. "Is this true?"

"I thought she got an abortion," is all Ethan can say.

"Honey, why are you talking to her like that?" Susana asks.

"Because I helped her. I was her doctor. I'm sorry I never shared that part of my life with you, but I helped women who needed a choice about their lives. Leah was one of those women."

"At an abortion clinic?" Susana asks.

"Yes."

Susana drops her head and I can see her labored breath.

"But, Susana, Clive saved my life and the lives of countless other women. Not everyone will agree, but when I didn't have anywhere else to turn, he was there."

"So, you had Ethan's baby?" Susana clarifies.

"Yes."

"And you delivered her baby?" she asks, staring at Clive.

He drops his head, knowing the last part still isn't finished.

"Susana, we agreed to do a closed adoption, and on May 11th, I delivered a boy."

"Honey, I didn't know," Clive says, exhaling sharply.

Susana pauses. "May 11th."

"No," Ethan whispers.

"That's Spencer's—" Susana starts.

"Birthday. I had Spencer on May 11th. It wasn't until a few months ago, when I ran into him here, that I realized Clive had adopted him."

Piper laughs and rips up the sonogram picture, the pieces falling all over Kate's wood floors.

"You people are disgusting."

"All right, that's enough, Piper. You know what's really disgusting?" Julia roars. "That an insecure old bitch like yourself enjoys destroying people. That's disgusting. Look around this room. Look at their faces and the hurt they are feeling. Have some fucking sympathy and respect for other people. You could've handled this privately, but you wanted an audience. You're sick—like you probably should use all of your dad's money to invest in a decent therapist because there's something seriously wrong with you. You get off on exposing people and playing the victim, but you're worse than all of them. And here's the funniest part. Ethan never loved you, and you know that, which is why you spend all your time trying to make others miserable— because that's how you are. You're a miserable person, and you wanna know the best part of all this? Tomorrow, Leah will wake up free from a past she believed would break her, and you'll wake up the same trash human that you've always been—and somewhere deep down, Piper, that pisses you off because you know you'll never feel that kind of happiness in your fucking life. You enjoy starting shit too much."

"I think everyone needs to leave," Kate says suddenly.

"I agree," Greg adds, standing up and ushering people to the door.

I take one more glance at Susana, whose eyes are fixated on the wall, before ducking out a side door in the kitchen. Julia joins me a minute later.

"Julia, I need to tell Susana I'm sorry."

"No, you don't. She knows, and she doesn't want to hear it right now. Let's go."

My legs feel weak with each step I take but quickly give way as I drop to my knees.

"Breathe," Julia instructs. "You did it, and you didn't die, but we need to go. This might soon turn into a war zone, and I did not wear the right shoes for battle. Also, I think I'm still too hungover, but that pineapple was delicious, and I grabbed the whole bowl," she says, opening her Louis. "We can eat some in the car."

She pulls me up, and as we start to walk again, Ethan stops us.

"Leah!"

Julia and I turn around. "Ethan, I'm sorry. I can't."

"Don't walk away. You owe me more that!" He shouts.

"She doesn't owe you a damn thing. Leave, Ethan. It's something you're pretty good at anyway."

"It's true? What she said about Spencer? Is it true?"

"Every word."

"I need to talk to her."

"That's not going to happen."

A few minutes later, Julia gets in the car. "Is he okay?"

"He's fine."

We ride in silence, the tears falling fast, but it isn't from pain. As much as I hate the way it all came out, for the first time in my life—I'm free.

"Here," Julia says, handing me an envelope.

Inside is the letter Piper's private investigator found in Ethan's storage unit.

"As much as I think he's an asshole, I'm still a good friend, but don't read it now. I can't handle any more of your crying."

"Thanks, Jules."

"All the things, Leah."

## 25

OCTOBER *10TH*

DEAR LEAH,

I can always tell what the night will look like around 6:30. How bright the stars will be and how the moon will shine. I could tell today that the sky would be beautiful tonight, and I wasn't wrong. It's one of the most beautiful night skies I've ever seen...and it reminds me of you.

A year ago tonight, we were sitting by a fire, at Sugar Creek, and you were telling me about your day. It's one of the things I miss the most. It's been almost a year since I've seen you. There was a time I couldn't imagine you not in my life, and now I've been without you for an entire year. How can that be possible? I don't know if you'll ever read this, but somewhere in my heart—I hope you will.

Leah, I have never known someone like you. Someone who has always seen me—for me. I used to read about soulmates and think how stupid it was. I didn't believe in things like soulmates. But then I met you and, I knew I was meant to love you for the *rest of my life. My soul had found peace in yours. I don't know if that's a soulmate, but I do know—in you—I had found every-thing my heart had always been searching for. And then I fucked it all up.*

*Leah, I never intended to hurt you and I never should've put you in the position I did. I wish I had a do-over. I wish I could've been better to you. To take care of you and to make things right. I'd give anything to go back to that day on the parking lot. To tell you how you deserved more than what I gave you. I should've been there for you and loved you like I promised. I'm so sorry I gave up on you and more than that—I'm sorry I gave up on us—all three of us. I wrote this the night you told me you were pregnant.*

*You are loved. I don't know what happens, but you are loved. I'm certain about a few things. I love your mom more than anything in this world. She is amazing, and you will adore her. She is kind, and funny, and beautiful. She's a protector, a lover, and the most amazing person I know. And she's real...what she tells you will always be her word and promise to you. She's a fighter and we will both be lucky to have someone like her in our corner. And when you mess up...and know that you will, she's the most forgiving person you'll ever meet and we'll love you no matter what. We'll protect you, and I love you both so much.*

*It's not fair of me to tell you that, but I want you to know that I think about our child every day, and I'm so sorry, Leah. I'm sorry I let you down.*

*I miss you so much. I miss waking up in the morning with your arms around me. I miss your smell. The way you laugh. I miss running my hands through your hair and rubbing your back. I miss our conversations...especially the ones in bed at 2AM when we first met, and I miss every single night we ever shared. And sitting out here under this starry night—all I want is you by my side again. You're always there in everything I do. I look for you every day. I hear your voice when I fall asleep, and it washes over me like a song I've listened to a million times. It's comforting. It's everything. You're everything.*

*If this letter ever makes it to you, just know that I wish I could've been better for you. I'm sorry I wasn't. And if I could do it all over, I would. I would make you mine forever and the three of us would've found a way. I wish I could go back.*

*My heart is yours...if you find your way back to me, I'll be waiting to give it to you. You're my best friend, and I love you more than anything, Leah.*

ETHAN

---

## 26

"You sure you'll be okay?" Julia asks as the plane taxis into the small Arkansas airport.

"Yeah, I'll be fine. I just need time to process this and to talk to my grandparents."

"I'm here if you need anything."

"Have fun in Cabo," I say, joining the line of passengers deplaning. Julia gives me a wave and remains with the others continuing to Louisville.

That night, after downing Nana's famous hot tea, I take two of Julia's sleeping pills I'd found in my bag and melt into the mattress. Listening to the crickets, I recall Uncle Jack's hysterical laughter after frying one up and convincing me it was a pork rind. I threw up the whole night and refused to speak to him for almost a week. He and Grandpa could never tell the story to completion without tears rolling down their faces, and as the sleeping pills work their magic, I drift off, missing the comfort Uncle Jack's laugh always gave me.

As the morning sun peeks through the cabin blinds, I get up and take a walk. Following a trail along the water until I get to a swimming hole known as *Sweet Water*. The solemn spot is my favorite. Visitors never venture down to this part of Sugar Creek because it isn't accessible by canoes, and it's on Uncle Jack's private property. But it's hallowed ground.

Twenty years ago, in waist-high water, on a warm Sunday night, I was baptized here. Brother Raymond, my grandparents, Uncle Jack, my mom, and a few church members witnessed the event, and the spot has always been a place of refuge and grounding. But it's also a place—where that same grace—turned dark.

After discovering I was pregnant and Ethan didn't want our baby, I showed up at the spot, crying out to God, begging for the right answer. And when I left the hospital without my son, I walked into the water, again—contemplating suicide. The days, weeks, and months after I had Spencer were some of the darkest of my life, and being alive hurt too much. But Uncle Jack kept careful watch, and if it hadn't been for his tent set up at *Sweet Water*, I think the outcome could've been different.

But once again, I am here, searching for something, after life has taken a wrong turn.

"I knew I'd find you here," Grandpa says, holding two fishing poles.

"You're a good guesser."

"Such a beautiful spot. Lots of memories here," he says.

"I know."

"Let's go."

A short walk later, we are casting our lines into the water, and if I understood one thing about Grandpa, fishing always led to a talk about life. We had our lines in the water for twenty minutes when it starts.

"Cricket."

"Nash and I are getting a divorce," I say.

He draws his line in and casts again. "I know."

"You do?"

"There was an appraiser here last month."

"Last month?" I gasp. "Why didn't you say anything?"

"I knew you'd tell us when you were ready."

"Grandpa, I'm so sorry. I never thought—" I choke back tears.

"What happened?" he asks.

I tell Grandpa about Nash and Mika and the way Nash put his hands on me. He doesn't say anything for several minutes, and just as I figured he is going to give me a lecture, he takes out his handkerchief and wipes a tear from his eye. I'd never seen him cry. Not once. It destroys me.

"Grandpa, I don't know what to say. I know sorry isn't enough. I ruined everything. I hate myself for what I've done to you, Nana, this place. It's all my fault. I let everyone down," I sob.

"No, you didn't."

"But you're crying. I'll never be able to forgive myself for what I've done."

"That's not why I'm upset. I could've talked to you a while ago about my suspicions about Nash, but I've lived a long time, honey, and sometimes you have to see it for yourself before you'll leave it. Some experiences have to damn-near kill you before you can walk away, but I never wanted you to get hurt. That's why I'm upset. I knew he was a bastard, and I didn't stop it."

"But, what about this place? What about Sugar Creek?"

"Come on. I want to show you something."

Grandpa and I walk back to the house and upstairs to his office.

"Sit."

I slump into a chair as he grabs a green file folder from a small cabinet and slides it to me.

"What's this?"

"Open it."

Inside there are a few items I'd never seen before. A business card for a grief counselor in Newton. Two brochures—one on postpartum depression and the other about depression after adoption.

I move the brochures to the side and pick up a stapled clump of papers. My hospital discharge papers. And underneath is a picture of a baby lying in a hospital nursery.

"Uncle Jack took it," Grandpa explains as I hold the picture in my hands.

"You knew?" I ask.

"Not until a few weeks after he was born. Your Uncle Jack was acting strange, and we hadn't seen you in months. He eventually told us what happened."

"I'm sorry I never told you."

"I'm sorry you did it alone."

"Did Kate call you?"

"She did."

"So you—" I stop.

"I knew something was wrong at the christening, but I didn't know what it was until the wedding. He reminds me of you at that age."

I look back down at the picture. "I've hurt so many people, Grandpa. Things I can never undo."

"I want you to listen to something, Leah. I was an alcoholic when I met your Nana. I was wild, good-looking," he says, giving me a wink, "and didn't have a care in the world. We married young, and she got pregnant right away."

He pauses and adjusts his worn-out Cardinal hat.

"I had a job at the lumber yard, and it didn't pay well. We struggled with money. It was stressful, and while your Nana stayed home with our kids, I went out and drank. I was scared that my income at the lumberyard wouldn't be enough. I was scared that your Nana would resent me for not being able to provide. And I was scared that I'd be a terrible father. So, I drank to numb the pain. And sometimes I wasn't so nice when I got home."

Grandpa continues about how he became violent and yelled at Nana on those drunken nights. How his behavior caused unnecessary pain for his family and caused things he couldn't undo. He became depressed, unsure how to repair the damage he'd caused.

"Nana couldn't help me, Cricket. No one could—except me. That's why I've always tried to warn you about the undertow because I know what it's like to be caught up in it and not be able to get out. I had to undo the damage on my own—when I was ready. One night, I was sitting at a bar drinking. I had just finished my first bottle, and the bartender asked if I wanted another. I opened my wallet, and something hit me. I realized if I ordered another beer, and then another and then another as I had for several years, that money was taking away from my family, and that was my rock-bottom. I was complaining every day about not having enough money for my family but drinking every cent we had away at night."

"So, did you order the beer?"

"Nope. I walked out of the bar that night, and I've never had a drink since. What I'm telling you is this. Everyone has a low point in life. We've all done things we wish we could undo, but forgiveness is a journey, Cricket. Some of us will get more practice with it than others, but it always starts with yourself. Nana could forgive me—and she did—but if I didn't forgive myself first, I'd still be in that bar or buried in the ground. The choices you made are things you must forgive in yourself before you can move forward. We are your family—and no matter what—we love you."

"What about Sugar Creek?"

"What about it?"

"What's going to happen?"

"I don't know, but I'll tell you this. Sugar Creek is not the reason we love this place. Everything here is replaceable; the canoes, the buildings, even the property. It all can disappear in a second. But what's not replaceable is our family. You aren't replaceable, Cricket. So, I don't care what happens to this place as long as we are together. That's all that matters."

"I'm so sorry, Grandpa."

"You have nothing to be sorry for."

That evening, I drive the Honda to the base of the bluff and hike to the top. As I take in the horizon, an unexpected calm takes shape.

Living in the shadows of my mistakes made me believe that the choices I'd made were life sentences that couldn't be undone. I had neglected to see the beauty in all of it. Grandpa is right, there is learning in the undertow, and it's only in those debilitating moments that we learn how to let go and breathe on our own. That life isn't meant to be lived at the bottom, tangled in our own messes, but no one will save us either. Not a relationship, not a job, and not family. The real change happens when we decide to save ourselves and live life by forgiving first, accepting where we fail, and letting go of the rest.

As the pieces slowly fall into place, I laugh at how

ridiculous it all sounds. *Let go, forgive, trust life*—it's like a motivational poster at Hazelwood—but it's all starting to make sense. I have carried more people downstream and rescued others from the undertow more times than I can remember—all along—forgetting the one person that needed it the most—myself.

## 27

OVER THE NEXT couple of days, Grandpa, Nana, and I decide to put Sugar Creek up for sale after consulting my attorney. The decision is gut-wrenching, but it's the only choice that will leave our family whole.

As I walk into work Monday morning, I'm grateful to be back doing what I love. Something about routine and being around students sends my mood soaring, but I receive an ominous email from Dr. Bradley just as the day starts. He requests a meeting, and as I head to Julia's office, reading it for the fourth time, I'm freaking out.

"Do you think I should be worried?"

"No. He meets with people. It's his job."

"I have a bad feeling, though."

"Don't. But also, don't wear something stupid like that tacky shirt you have on right now."

I glance down at my floral blouse. "What's wrong with this?"

"Florals went out with jumper dresses, Leah. We aren't educators from the eighties."

I roll my eyes and close my email.

"How was Cabo?"

"Perfect."

"That's it?"

"Yep, that's it."

"Are you in love with Damien?"

Julia pauses and takes a sip of her coffee. Her olive skin glows from the Mexican sun, but there's a different glow, too —something I've never seen from her.

"I am," she answers. "He's moving here this summer."

"What about the donuts?"

"He's going to keep it in Newton, but he wants to open one here."

"Julia, that's amazing!"

"I know. I can't believe I'm even saying that."

"I'm really happy for you."

"Thanks, Leah. How was Sugar Creek? Did you talk to your grandparents?"

"I did. I'm putting it up for sale. I talked to my attorney, and it's the best option. Nash isn't going to budge, and I'm not putting my family or myself through an ugly divorce."

"I'm sorry."

"I know."

"Have you talked to Ethan?"

"No, and neither Kate nor Allison will take my calls. Clive called a couple of times, but I haven't called him back."

"I'm a little disappointed."

"About what?"

"About Piper. I mean, I didn't even get a *thank you*."

I laugh. "I don't think anyone's ever talked to her like that. And thank you."

"I will say—she was smart about the PI."

"You're defending her? Really?"

"I'm not defending her, but if I were in her situation, I'd

do the same thing. She didn't want to look like an idiot, and she wanted to know the truth. I mean, she's a shit human being, but private investigators really are worth the money."

"Whatever," I say, walking out of the office.

"All the things, Leah."

"All the things," I groan, shaking my head.

That afternoon I respond to Dr. Bradley's email setting up our appointment, still feeling unsettled.

The week crawls by, and I know it's because all I can think about is what I've done or who I've pissed off that Dr. Bradley wants to meet. As I sit in the district parking lot, I check my makeup, hair, and teeth, ensuring I didn't have a leftover poppy seed stuck somewhere. Meetings with bosses are intimidating at all levels. In my short tenure as principal, I hadn't fired anyone yet. Still, as I sit in the car, my mind convinces me that if I were going to fire someone, I'd send an ominous email on Monday and make the employee wait until Friday because—you know—anxiety is fun. It's the last thought I have before I get out of the car, and I curse myself for playing the worst-case scenario minutes before my meeting.

"Miss McKinney?" Dr. Bradley says, entering the lobby.

Taking a seat in his office, I try to remain calm, but his stone face makes me uneasy.

"Thank you for coming this morning. Unfortunately, we are not going to be offering you the position at Hazelwood. I appreciate your service to this district and to the staff and students, but we've decided to go in a different direction."

Fired—the ultimate middle finger. My heart is in my throat. I've never been fired before, and the shock and disappointment are overwhelming. I can feel the tears start to form but push them back.

"Can I ask why?" I croak.

"There are concerns about your ability to handle the demands of the job, and we have determined this is the right move for all of us. We wish you the best."

Dr. Bradley shakes my hand as I walk out of his office—the whole meeting lasts less than ten minutes. As I shut my car door, I'm paralyzed with fear. I realize the year has been rough, but fired? It's harsh.

Speeding down the interstate toward the school, I'm engulfed with shame and frustrated by my lack of responsibility. I haven't given my best effort—and I can admit that—but it isn't termination quality. It was something less. Maybe a warning, but not fired.

I pull into my parking spot at Hazelwood and go straight to Julia's office.

"Did you hear?"

"Hear what?"

"It's over. Everything I've ever worked for is over," I sigh, dropping my head into my hands.

"He fired you?"

"He isn't offering me the position, so yeah, he fired me."

"What the hell? Why?"

"He said they had concerns."

"Oh, that's bullshit."

"It doesn't matter if it is or not. I'm done, Julia."

"Here. You're done here, but that doesn't mean you can't get another job. So, take a step back and realize it's going to be okay. You're a great principal, and you'll find something else."

"But I love it here."

"I know, girl. I'm so sorry."

As the semester rolls into fourth quarter, Julia and I spend nights eating sushi and hunting for jobs. She gives me pep talks when my mood slips into despair and reminds me that I can work at the donut shop with Damien if all else fails. Three weeks later, with my future unemployment still fresh, Trista Miller walks into the office. Her hot pink nails grip the side of her coffee cup as she paces back and forth in my office, livid at Dr. Bradley's decision.

"Leah, I will fight tooth and nail for you. Whatever I have to do, hon. This is ridiculous. Was it because of that sex situation? Or did he mention the wine?"

"You told him about the wine, Trista?"

"No, I told a friend. Well, a school board member friend in confidence. It wasn't a big deal. I'm sure she didn't tell him."

"Trista," I sigh.

"I'm sorry. I didn't think—"

"What sex situation?"

"Trevor said some kids got into a maintenance closet and were having sex. I guess someone had left it unlocked."

"I didn't know anything about that."

"There was a video. It was all over social media."

"Why didn't you tell me?"

"Oh, hon, I thought you knew."

"I didn't, Trista! That would've been nice to know."

"I'm sure that didn't have anything to do with his decision, Leah. It was a while ago anyway."

"It's fine. It's not your fault," I mutter, slumping back in my chair. "I should've been more aware of what was going on."

"Well, just so you know. Some parents have written letters to Dr. Bradley and the board members. They aren't happy with his decision, and I think it's important that they know how much we love you."

"I appreciate that, but it won't do any good."

"Oh, I just hate this, Leah."

"Me too."

A moment later, one of the office secretaries stands at my door.

"Miss McKinney, you have a phone call. I'm transferring it back."

"Okay, thank you. Trista, sorry, I need to take this."

As Trista leaves the office, I pick up the phone.

"Hello?"

"Leah, it's Ethan. I need you to come to Dallas. My parents and Spencer were in a car accident."

## 28

MY BODY GOES LIMP, and had it not been for my office chair, I would've collapsed on the floor. On my way to the airport, I call Ethan back.

"What about Spencer?" I ask, my voice shaking, listening for Ethan's response on the other end.

"He's okay. But he's in the ICU. It's precautionary," he says, putting my panic at rest. "They're taking my mom back to surgery. I gotta go. I'll call you later."

It takes me almost five hours to get to Dallas, and as the Uber drops me off in front of the hospital, I run inside.

"I'm here," I announce nervously.

Ethan wraps me in a hug. "Thank God," he says. "I haven't—I've wanted to—"

"It's okay," I tell him. "How's Spencer?"

"Bruised, and he has a small burn on his arm, but other than that, he's fine. They're keeping him here for observation. To make sure he doesn't have a concussion."

"And your parents?"

Ethan drops his head. "Clive didn't make it, and my mom's still in surgery. They are amputating her leg."

284 | KAREN DAUGHERTY

"I'm so sorry."

"Me too. I'm glad you're here, Leah."

We sit down as Ethan explains the awful accident. A box truck ran a red-light t-boning the Stewarts' SUV. Clive sustained most of the impact, but Susana's legs were crushed in the collision.

"Spencer was lucky. It could've been so much worse."

My stomach is in knots as a nurse rounds the corner.

"You can go see him," she says to Ethan. He glances at me and nods toward a small hallway, but I hesitate. Hospitals made me queasy in general, but ICUs are the worst. The hopeless section of the hospital, and now I have to see my son in whatever condition requires him to be in the ICU. I'm not prepared, and the fear in my eyes must've indicated that to Ethan. "Leah, he's just a little bruised. I promise." He reaches for my hand.

"Oh, Mr. Erickson, Spencer can only have one visitor at a time and only family members," she says as she smiles politely.

"She's family," he replies.

She's hesitant but finally agrees to let Ethan and me see Spencer together. Walking into his room, I expect tubes and wires and an unconscious little boy lying on the bed, but instead, Spencer is sitting up, a large, gauze bandage attached to his small forearm.

"Hey, bud," Ethan says.

Spencer looks at us, his eyes hazy. "Do you remember Leah? From the wedding?"

Spencer glances at me but doesn't say anything.

"Hi, Spencer. How are you feeling?" I ask, but he still doesn't respond.

"It's been a long day," Ethan says, but I understand what he means. I recall how strangers would come by the hours and days following my mom's death, offer their condolences, and check to see how I was doing. People I'd never met before, and it was weird.

"Come here," I mumble to Ethan.

"Spence, I'll be right back," he says, following me to the hallway.

"I'm going to go back to the waiting room. He needs time with people he's familiar with, so you stay here with him."

"Are you sure?"

"Yes. Thank you for letting me see him. He needs some rest."

"I'm sorry."

"Don't be. I'll be here if you need anything."

"You don't have to stay."

"I want to."

"I appreciate you, Leah. It means a lot that you're here."

"Of course," I say, giving him a hug that lasts too long.

Somewhere in the night, Susana has made it out of surgery, but with her age and severity of her injuries, she is in critical but stable condition. Ethan has come out of Spencer's room three times to update me on his sleeping habits and complaints about the noise, but overall, he is making a steady recovery.

"I think he's finally asleep," Ethan says, sitting down next to me.

"Good. He needs it."

"Piper filed for divorce."

"Ethan."

"A few days after the wedding. It's fine; we were never right for each other."

"I'm sorry."

"Really, Leah. It's okay. I've wanted to talk to you. I mean, we need to talk."

"Now?"

"I'm tired of putting things off."

"I read your letter. Why didn't you ever send it or come find me?"

"After what I did to you, I was sure you'd never speak to me again."

"Did you mean what you said?"

"Of course I did. And I'm not just saying that now because he's alive. When I looked at that sonogram picture —" he stops. Tears fill his eyes as his voice shakes. "It killed me. What I did to you was selfish. I don't deserve to tell you this now, but I always hoped you didn't go through with it. You were always a better person than I could ever be, and I hoped all this time he was alive."

"Is that why you kept the picture?"

"This one?" He asks, pulling the taped sonogram from his wallet. "Yes. It was the last thing I had of you and what you made."

I run my finger over the cracked edges of the picture, and recall hearing Spencer's heartbeat for the first time. "What we made, Ethan. Spencer is here because of us. Both of us."

As I lay my head on Ethan's shoulder, he wraps his arm around me, and it's weird to think of us as two parents waiting in a hospital for our son to get better. I don't feel like Spencer's mother—not the kind that's raised him—but somewhere deep in my heart, he's always been mine. He's always been the child I fought to keep and loved despite knowing him.

The following day, Ethan invites me back to Spencer's room to see his progress.

"Hey, Spencer," I say, watching him eat hospital applesauce. The color has returned to his face, and a few more scratches are visible on his arms.

"Hi," he says, his mood different from the night before.

"We're going to move him out of ICU. The doctor will be in to talk to you," the nurse informs Ethan.

"That's great news, bud!" Ethan says, squeezing Spencer's leg. "Spence, I'm going to send Leah to your house to pick up some things. Is there anything you want her to get for you?"

Spencer smiles wide and asks for his iPad, and as Ethan and I walk out, I sense the heaviness of what he's about to do.

"Are you okay?"

"Yes."

"Ethan, I'm sorry you have to tell him about Clive. I can stay if you want."

"No, it's fine. I can do this."

I hug him, and he kisses me on the cheek before pulling me back once more and squeezing hard. "I love you," he whispers.

At the Stewarts, I let myself in with the key Ethan has loaned me and locate Spencer's iPad on the kitchen counter. Next to it is a picture of Clive and Spencer at a baseball game. Spencer's sweaty face and missing front tooth are adorable as Clive's arm wraps around him. The loss of a parent is a loneliness unlike any other. A perpetual empty space that can never be filled, and knowing Spencer will carry that pain with him for the rest of his life shatters me. Therapy will help, but he'll always have days when even coping strategies won't be enough. Had Uncle Jack and my grandparents not stepped in when my mom died, I would've never made it and thinking about Spencer—he needs the same in his life.

When I get back to the hospital, they have moved Spencer out of ICU, and Ethan has texted his room number.

Me: *Did you tell him?*

But there's no response from Ethan. I sit in the waiting room for a few minutes before deciding to go back, but I overhear Spencer talking to Ethan about God at his door. I step to the side of the doorway, listening to the two of them talk.

"Is dad with God?" Spencer asks, sniffing with each word.

"He is," Ethan responds.

"Is God mad at me?"

"No, buddy. You didn't do anything wrong. God isn't mad at you. He loves you."

"But I'll never see him again. It isn't fair."

"It's not fair, Spencer. You're right, and you can be angry or sad or feel anything you want because all of it is fine. But listen to me, just because dad's not here doesn't mean we can't feel him. Remember how I told you my real dad died?"

"Yeah."

"Well, I feel him every day, and even though I can't touch him, I know he's here."

I can hear Spencer sniffle as Ethan adjusts on the squeaky bed. "And listen, Spence, we can talk about him anytime you want. Okay?"

"Okay."

"Come here," Ethan says as I wipe away tears outside the door.

It's a difficult place to be in. The love I have for both of them is unconditional—but my reach is limited. I want to run in and hug both of them, but my place has always been outside Spencer's door. From the moment he was born, I gave those rights to someone else to take care of, and I have to trust that my decision is, once again, being fulfilled.

"Ethan," Spencer says.

"Yeah, bud?"

"Does God love the Cubs, too?"

I know this answer. There's zero chance our sweet Lord loves that unspeakable team. Every Cardinal fan knows this, every baseball fan, too, but how does one tell a grieving, ten-year-old that his favorite team is doomed to hell? I lean in as far as I can without being seen to hear Ethan's answer.

"Yeah, bud, God loves them, too." I shake my head in disappointment, knowing it won't be the last lie he'll ever tell our son.

## 29

ETHAN CALLS a few nights after Susana has been discharged —it's been almost a month—and as I pick up the phone, I'm hopeful for a good report.

"Hey, Ethan."

"Leah, it's Susana."

I freeze. I have not spoken to Susana since Kate's, and her voice sends chills through me.

"Do you have a minute to talk?" She asks.

"Yes." There's a long pause, and her voice is weak.

I can't find the words to express how sorry I am. No apology in the world will be good enough anyway, and as my heart races, her frail voice cuts through again.

"Leah, are you there?"

"I'm here. Susana, I'm so sorry about Clive."

"Thank you, but that's not what I'm calling about. I need to talk to you about Spencer."

I listen as Susana explains she will likely have another surgery, and complications might arise.

"Leah, the choice you made for Spencer allowed me to love again. After Ethan's father died, I was broken. But when

I met Clive and Spencer, that boy brought life back into my world. And I have to know that if something happens to me, you'll help them both through this."

"Both?"

"Ethan loves you. And I know you love him, too. Do you remember when you came for tea?"

"Yes."

"When you told me you went to school in Arkansas, I knew you were the girl Ethan had met when he was there. A mother knows these things, and he was so distraught when he moved backed to Texas. I'd never seen him like that since his father died, and I knew something terrible had happened. And the minute you walked into our house— again, a mother knows. Whether my surgery goes well or not, I know you'll be in his life and Spencer's. They'll need strength, and I know you have that in you. Just promise me you'll love my boys if—" she pauses.

"Susana," I say, trying to push back tears. There are so many things I want to tell her. So many ways to thank her for raising Spencer as her own and loving him when I couldn't. Facing her own battles of recovery, I can't imagine the fear she has of what lies ahead or the strength it takes for her to call and ask me to help if something god-forbid happens to her. "I will. Of course, I will."

"Thank you, Leah. And if I may, I want to tell you something. Being a mother isn't always about who gives birth and who doesn't. Or who raises their child and who allows someone else to. It's so much more than that. Being a mother is about selfless love. It's about giving up what you might want for the sake of someone else. It's unlike any other form of love. If you carried a child in your arms or your womb, you're a mother. So, don't ever forget you may not have raised him, but you carried him, and you'll always be Spencer's mother."

As we hang up, something stirs in my heart. A responsibility that I have never had before—and instead of running from it, I decide to see what happens if I accept it instead.

Over the next few days, I take a bold step forward and do what every mother does—I shop. Not for shoes or clothes, but groceries. It seems like a natural step—but grocery shopping is literally my worst nightmare. In the cabinets Julia designed as mine, lies too many boxes of cereal and a shameful amount of gummy bears. But I place a grocery order for Ethan anyway and wait.

Later that night, Ethan calls to thank me but suggests the next delivery should include less fruity, high-sugar snacks and more protein. I think he's too sensitive, or maybe he's even joking; I mean, I did include eggs.

"Did you get the yogurt?"

"The ice cream?" He asks.

"Ethan, it's fro-yo and it has protein."

"It's cookie dough ice cream, Leah."

"Okay, I'll send more eggs next time."

He laughs as we talk about Susana and her recovery and he always ends the conversation by telling me he loves me. I haven't said it back and he doesn't pressure me, but I know I do—I'm just not sure what that means.

I do my best to include more protein as I continue sending deliveries—and by the eighth, to be exact—I have figured out that Spencer and I share a love for fruit roll-ups and Lunchables, and Ethan does not—which is unfortunate for him.

My last week at Hazelwood is bittersweet, and saying goodbye to a place that has given me a new beginning proves to be more challenging than I imagined.

"Come here. I want to show you something," Julia says.

As we walk into the hallway, students file out of their classrooms with teachers trailing behind them.

"What's going on?" I ask.

"Just wait."

Julia leads me outside to the front steps of the building as students, staff, and parents stand holding signs of support, calling out Dr. Bradley's decision.

"What's this?"

"Civil disobedience," Julia responds.

Chants erupt in my name from students and parents as my staff stands together, clapping in appreciation. Scanning the crowd, I stop on a familiar face. Trista Miller is standing with a group of moms, all wearing matching white shirts that read: *McKinney's Moms*.

"Trista made a group page a few weeks ago. Her crazy ass organized this," Julia explains.

Trista and I make eye contact, and she smiles wide, forming her fingers into a shape of a heart. I laugh and nod in appreciation, realizing that despite her flaws, we all have a little Trista in us. The protest only lasts an hour, but I am thankful that the job I've done has impacted those I was fighting for the most.

That evening, Julia and I go to a bar on Bardstown Road to celebrate the last day.

"I'm officially a divorced, unemployed, thirty-something. I thought I'd never see the day," I say, holding my wine glass in the air.

"You're not divorced yet, so technically you're only an unemployed thirty-something."

"It'll be final next month. Then, once the paperwork goes through for that buyer, it'll be done. It's just a matter of time."

"Well, it could be worse. You could have some secret love child stowed away somewhere. Can you even imagine that drama? I mean, what a shit show that would be."

I glare at her over my wine glass as she takes an unassuming sip of hers.

"Thanks, Jules."

"I'll be here all night."

As Julia and I reminisce over Hazelwood, a text from Ethan buzzes on my phone asking how my last day was.

The calls and texts from Ethan have slowed down, but it's a given considering his new role in Spencer's life. With a pending second surgery, Ethan moved in with Susana and Spencer. The new life has kept his messages brief, and I have moments of guilt thinking about him doing it alone. But he assures me he doesn't mind and that he has help. People from St. Vincent's are cooking meals (I'm still sending him grocery deliveries, too), Ashley is getting Spencer to practices and school on time, and Ethan is tucking him at night. The home care nurses are giving Susana the best possible care, and despite the tragic events, life is moving on.

As Julia and I sit at the bar, I reflect on the people stepping in to surround Ethan, Susana, and Spencer at a time when they all need it the most and how life tends to provide when we least expect it.

I smile at Julia.

"What?"

"I couldn't have done this with you—all of it; work, Spencer, Nash, Ethan. But, no matter what happens, I want you to know how much it's all meant to me. How much you've meant to me."

"You've come a long way, Leah—" she pauses. Then, in a

rare sight of emotion, Julia looks away and wipes a tear from her eye."

"Are you crying?"

"No, I'm not crying. I'm just wondering how this works now. I mean, you were such a trainwreck. Who's going to entertain me with their sad life? You think Cammie O'Neal is going to be as tragic as you were? She's already blowing up my phone with school events she wants me to help her plan. It's disgusting. I don't plan school events, Leah. That's not my job. I show up, I look perfect, and I occasionally talk to kids about making good choices. Everyone knows this."

"You'll be besties with Cammie."

"The hell I will. Have you seen her outfits? They're worse than yours on a bad day. Patchwork sweaters, embroidered cardigans, shoulder-padded dresses, Leah. The graveyard where educator outfits go to die. She's resurrected them, and you don't come back from that."

I laugh, knowing Julia and Cammie's personalities—fashionably speaking—are different, but running a school together—they are going to be great. As much as Julia likes my unorganized personality, she craves structure, and working alongside Cammie is going to be a dream for her, even if she doesn't want to admit it.

"I love you, Julia."

"All the things, Leah."

As the heat and humidity welcome the beginning of summer, I find myself back at Sugar Creek, helping Grandpa and Nana pack up forty years of life. With a potential buyer looming, they have opted to downsize and settle on an apartment, and boxing up their life is a task none of us are ready for. One evening over Nana's smoked brisket, we sit around the table sharing memories of our life on the creek.

"A toast," Grandpa announces, holding his Coke in the air. "To a family this old man never deserved. And to a new beginning waiting. May the love we shared here be felt long after we're gone."

Nana's eyes fill with tears, and I wipe a few of mine as well, praying for protection over the place that has given me the same. Sugar Creek will always be where our family learned invaluable lessons about life and love, and those things aren't for sale.

The next morning as Grandpa and I devour Damien's donuts, my phone rings, flashing the name of my attorney. I step into the living room to take his call. With our divorce close to finalizing, there are disturbing things he's found from Nash's text messages and phone calls, but nothing to suggest any hope of a different outcome.

"Are you sitting down?" Hank asks.

"Why?"

"The Vegas chapel just got shut down."

"What do you mean?"

"It's in the news, Leah. It's a huge scandal. The guy was a total fraud."

Hank explains that Fake Elvis—Adam Drury—lied about his credentials, and obtained them illegally on the dark web. As a result, he wasn't authorized to officiate weddings, and by law, the marriage licenses he'd signed are illegitimate.

"He's facing jail time, Leah. And more importantly, this may be the break we've needed."

"Hank, what does that mean?"

"It means your marriage to Nash was never legal, and we can use that in court. It might be a battle, but it's a battle we can win."

## 30

Using the evidence from the fraudulent documents, Hank makes our case bulletproof. A bonus is the discovery Hank makes from Nash's trashed emails. In his deleted folder, Nash had forced my name on bank documents and others related to Sugar Creek. With the revelation, Hank applies pressure to Nash's attorney and informs me if the court's decision isn't in my favor, the forgery charges will be enough for Nash to back away. It's sickening to know the lengths he'd gone to for the sake of money.

And Julia has done some investigating on her own. A private investigator finds substantial evidence of Nash exchanging texts with a buyer long before we were ever married. The resorts he'd looked up online turn over emails and texts to the PI showing Nash's interest in selling Sugar Creek to the highest bidder. His game is up, and, by the end of summer, the court sides with me and determines that Nash and I were never legally married and he has no stake in Sugar Creek.

After the ruling, I walk out to my car and sob for twenty minutes. The release of the past six months rolling down my face with each tear. The win is more than I deserve and a blessing I'll never jeopardize again. A few weeks later, I meet with Julia and Damien to celebrate.

"Tell me exactly what Nash's face looked like when the judge read his decision," Julia demands.

"It was a shock I've never seen before. I thought he was going to puke or come out of his seat and choke the guy."

"Dammit, I wish we hadn't been on vacation."

"Thank you for hiring the PI. Those texts were brutal to read, and they weren't all about business. He found stuff on Nash's social media that he was sending to other girls. It was disgusting."

"Like I always said, Nash doesn't have that many friends. When a man spends all his time glued to his phone, there's someone else he's talking to."

"I know. You were right."

"Leah, I'm really happy for you and your family. I can't imagine the relief y'all must feel," Damien adds.

"We do, but it's funny. They're still moving into the apartment."

"Your grandparents?" Julia asks.

"Yeah. Nana said it's time for them to transition to something smaller and more manageable, so they're moving."

"What are they doing with the house?"

"I'm going to live there."

"Alone?"

"Yes, Julia. Alone."

"Well, you never know with you. So, I thought I'd ask," she laughs.

Damien checks his watch and glances at Julia. "Babe, we gotta go. Leah, sorry, but we have an appointment."

"Wedding venues so soon?" I joke.

"Um, no. We're getting a dog," Julia mumbles, rolling her eyes.

"What?"

"I convinced her it's the next step in our relationship," Damien smiles.

"No, the next step is proper luggage or some nicer dishes, not a dog that poops everywhere."

"She's gonna love it," Damien mouths as they get up to leave.

"All right, you two have fun. Julia, I'll call you later to see how the dog situation is going."

"Can't wait," she says, hugging me tightly.

As they walk out of the cafe holding hands, I decide to order something before heading to the airport.

"Hi, we had a shift change. I'll be taking care of you. Are you ready to order?"

Her raspy voice cuts through, but I'd know it from anywhere. Her face is gaunt, and she is nearly half the size she used to be. The bags under her eyes show signs of sleepless nights I'd once known. As I meet her gaze, she freezes.

"Mika?"

"Leah," she gasps.

"Why are you working here?"

"I got fired. Well, Nash—" she starts, tears forming in her eyes. I know where the conversation is going. The puffy eyes, the dark circles, the unintended weight loss— hollowing out cheeks that used to be pink. The remnants of a life with Nash are horrifying to see up close.

"You don't need to explain."

"He cheated on me," she informs, choking back tears. "He said he loved me. He said he wanted to spend the rest of his life with me."

I stare at her, unmoved by her admission.

"I'll just have a turkey sandwich on wheat, please," I say, handing the menu back to her.

"Aren't you going to say anything, Leah? I'm sure this is what you wanted."

"Don't presume to know what I want. No one asks to be cheated on. Maybe you understand that now and maybe you don't; either way, I don't care."

"You know, he was right about you," she snaps. "You're one of those girls who thinks she's above women like me, but if you really knew the truth, you'd see it differently."

"I know my truth, Mika; ask yourself if you know yours."

I leave the cafe without my turkey sandwich, but I do leave enough tip money for Mika to buy a nice bottle of wine or at least a mediocre therapist—I'm not above charity.

By mid-October, Grandpa and Nana are settled into their new apartment. I've visited them several times, and even though Grandpa insists he misses mowing the yard, they love their low-maintenance lives.

"How are the renovations going, Cricket?"

"They're good, Grandpa. The screened-in porch is almost complete, and the new cabinets have all been installed."

"That porch will be nice this winter. Who knew they could make heated floors?"

"I know. I'll have you over to try it out," I say, giving him a wink.

The changing of the seasons always excites me, and as the air grows colder, I make my way to Fayetteville for the annual Oktoberfest. The weekend event brings the finest art, food, music, and local beers to residents across the area. As the new director of the youth shelter, I'm proud to have a booth represented for the first time, and I'm settling into the role with ease. Watching kids overcome obstacles has always been a beautiful thing to be a part of, and the kids at the youth shelter are all fighting battles I once knew myself. To help them find that beauty after weathering storms has breathed new life into my career.

A few of the case workers are standing at our booth talking to some teachers, handing them brochures about our services. I smile and recall my last conversation with Julia and her complaint about Cammie's new dress code policy banning leggings. The outrage was immediate, and I realize how different my priorities had been at Hazelwood compared to Cammie's. Maybe banning leggings correlates to an increased student achievement that I'm unaware of—but I have my doubts.

As I peruse the other tables and pick through a funnel cake, the crisp fall air sweeps across my face, and I inhale the beginning of a new season. Down from our booth, kids line up for face painting, and across the street, a local band plays cover songs under a pavilion. I venture off the downtown square, finding myself a few blocks away from the festivities but back in a familiar spot. The whitewashed, brick exterior of the bar is more weathered than I remember, but the inside is still the same. A few patrons sit on barstools watching the news on a tube TV. A young red-haired bartender fetches my drink as I sit down next to them and order a red ale.

"Here ya go," she says, setting the glass in front of me. Glancing around the bar, the memories flood back of nights spent with Ethan and Barry's horrible goulash. The thought reminds me of his call a few weeks ago, which I forgot to return. With no signs of a menu, I wonder if Barry is somewhere in the back cooking his horrible food or if enough people rejected it, he's stopped offering.

"Does Barry still own this place?"

"He actually sold it recently. We have a new owner."

"Who bought it?"

"I did," Ethan's voice booms behind me.

I turn around, seeing him for the first time in months. His hair is longer, and he's lost some weight, but as his icy blue eyes stare into mine, I've never been happier to see him.

"You didn't," I say.

"I did. How are you, Leah?" He takes a seat next to me. "Tammy, I'll have what she's having."

"What? How?" I stammer.

"Everything happened pretty fast."

Ethan explains that Susana had the surgery on her leg but suffered a stroke during the operation.

"Ethan, I'm so sorry."

"Me too. She lost her speech and her quality of life is pretty bad. It's been tough."

"When did it happen?"

"A few weeks ago."

"I wish I would've know. I'm really sorry."

"It's okay, Leah."

"So, you bought this place?"

"I was here a couple of months ago and ran into Barry. He said he was thinking about selling, and I saw an oppor-tunity—plus," he pauses and takes a sip of beer, "plus, this place is special, and there's a great view from the roof. Best in town."

My heart beats fast in my chest and I smile wide as Ethan winks at me.

"So, where's your mom and Spencer?"

"I looked for the best medical facility for her, and there's actually one here, so we moved last week. They had an opening, and I was lucky to get her in. And it worked out that Ashley is going to Arkansas, so I have someone to watch Spencer when I'm working. I tried calling, but you didn't answer."

"I know. I'm sorry. I should've called you back. Where are you living?"

"Spencer and I found a rental. But it's temporary. We'll find something soon."

"How is he?"

"He's okay. Honestly, he's the one who wanted to move. I think he needed a change. A fresh start, but he's good. He likes his new school."

"You didn't tell him, did you?"

"No. Maybe in time. He's gone through too much. We talked about what could happen to my mom before she had the surgery, but it's still been tough. We go almost every day to see her and some days he's fine and others he's not. But I'll tell you this—he's a pretty resilient kid. He's gentle with my mom and sensitive, but he's also tough. Kinda reminds me of someone else."

"Ethan."

"We did good, Leah. You'd be proud."

"You'll have to bring him to Sugar Creek. I think he'd have a great time. Will you do that?"

"I would, but someone banned me for life one time, so I'm not sure I can."

I shake my head, agreeing with Ethan's statement, and take a drink of my red ale. "Maybe I can pull some strings. I do know the owner. I'll see what I can do."

Ethan laughs and walks around behind the bar, squeezing by Tammy to grab something.

"You know, Leah, it's funny that you're here because I was just thinking how these were going to waste," he says holding up a deck of Uno cards. "I think I owe you a rematch."

"Ethan, you don't stand a chance. Honestly, I've never seen a worse player. It's actually kind of sad, and it'd be embarrassing for you to lose again in your *own* bar."

"All the more reason to show you I've changed. I'm better at this now."

"You think so?"

"I know so. Are you ready?"

"I guess we'll see. Deal the cards, Ethan."

## ALL THE THINGS

First and foremost, I'd like to thank every friend and family member I've ignored for the past decade of writing this book and offer my sincerest apologies for missed calls, unreturned texts, and failed dinner plans. Thank you for loving me anyway and riding this journey with me. I'm free now... let's hang out.

Sue Strecker and Amy Soto, thank you for making me a better writer and for pushing me outside my comfort zone. I am grateful for your talent and ability to take my vision to the next level.

To the NY pitch and my friends in Room 160, thank you for embracing a southern girl and her journey to become a writer. I didn't believe I could call myself an author until I attended that conference. Thank you for giving me the confidence to finish.

Kurt and Mariposa, thank you for showing me a different way to live life. I am forever grateful for you both and our time in Sedona. I will never forget the life-changing experience I found in your care. Abundant blessings to you both.

To my students and athletes, past and present, thank you for being a source of beautiful light in my life. Every laugh we've shared, tear we've cried, and accomplishments we've made have always been because of you and your willingness to go the extra mile when I've asked. Being your teacher and coach has meant the world to me and watching you grow into amazing humans is a gift I'll cherish for the rest of my life. Make good choices, follow your dreams, always show kindness and know that I'm always cheering you on.

To my coworkers, past and present, thank you for endless laughs, inside jokes, comfort to lean on, and friendships that have meant more than you'll ever know. And thank you for loving kids with me and showing every day how truly remarkable educators are.

To my parents and extended family, thank you for the love and support you've always given me. And for always being so gracious when I showed up late to family events. I love you.

Ryan, without your support I'm not sure where I'd be in life. Thank you for every conversation, for your patience, and your ability to walk me through life.

Mechelle, thank you for 30 years of the most amazing friendship. We've been through the greatest highs and the deepest lows and somehow always found our way out together. Thank you for always being there when I needed you. This story wouldn't have happened without you. I love you.

Heather and Cassie, our friendship has meant the world to me. Thank you for our Trader Joe's trips (even though I just get the PBJ snacks), our dinner nights, and keeping me entertained during the pandemic. Somewhere in our Marcos is another book waiting to be written. I am inspired every day by your roles as mothers and wives and I hope you know what a beautiful display it is to me. Our souls have always connected in the deepest of ways, and I love you both so much. Thank you for believing in me, for the endless laughs, and for always being by my side through everything.

Julie, the first pass of this was another chapter in the book. I felt like that was excessive, but so much of us has been another chapter. So, I'll say this, thank you for picking me up and putting me back together a little at a time. Thank you for every late-night text, for feeding me, for being brutally honest when I needed it most, and for giving me a space to write, cry, and laugh. From every porch confession to every car ride just to clear my head, your friendship has meant everything to me. Thank you for being a sounding board for this book. All the things, Jules. I love you.

Nathan, thank you for your love, support, and patience. You've always stood beside me and given me strength when I couldn't find it. Thank you for showing me a different side of life and how beautiful it can really be.

In loving memory of my grandparents, Raymond and Leona Daugherty. I'd give anything for one more porch conversation with you. Thank you for filling in when I needed it most. I miss you both so much. Hold those two babies tightly for me and give Tyler a hug.

Mom, thank you for always believing in this crazy dream with me and for letting me be exactly who I am. None of this would be possible if you hadn't bought my first journal and showed me that it was okay to write what I felt. Thank you for always giving me space to grow, create and sometimes mess up recipes. All those tough years when life seemed to knock us down, thank you for taking my hand

and showing me what it looked like to get up and try again. You're the strongest woman I've ever known, and your love is the most beautiful thing I've ever had. *"When the world wasn't there for us, we believed that we could touch the sky."* We made it...and I couldn't have done this without your love and support. I Love you, Sab!

# ABOUT THE AUTHOR

Karen Daugherty is a graduate from Indiana University Southeast where she was published for her research in Irish literature. She received her Masters from Missouri State University and currently teaches high school English in Springdale, Arkansas.

Please visit: www.karen-daugherty.com for more information

Made in the USA
Coppell, TX
03 September 2021